STAR TREK

VOLUME 4

STAR TREK®

VOLUME 4

Collection Cover by Tim Bradstreet, Colors by Grant Goleash
Collection Edits by Justin Eisinger and Alonzo Simon
Production by Shawn Lee

"Mirrored" based on the original teleplay of *Mirror, Mirror* by Jerome Bixby.

Star Trek created by Gene Roddenberry.
Special thanks to Risa Kessler and John Van Citters of CBS Consumer Products for their invaluable assistance.

IDW founded by Ted Adams, Alex Garner, Kris Oprisko, and Robbie Robbins

ISBN: 978-1-61377-590-5

16 15 14 13 1 2 3 4

IDW®

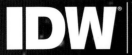

Ted Adams, CEO & Publisher
Greg Goldstein, President & COO
Robbie Robbins, EVP/Sr. Graphic Artist
Chris Ryall, Chief Creative Officer/Editor-in-Chief
Matthew Ruzicka, CPA, Chief Financial Officer
Alan Payne, VP of Sales
Dirk Wood, VP of Marketing
Lorelei Bunjes, VP of Digital Services

Become our fan on Facebook **facebook.com/idwpublishing**
Follow us on Twitter **@idwpublishing**
Check us out on YouTube **youtube.com/idwpublishing**
www.IDWPUBLISHING.com

Originally published as STAR TREK Issues #13–16.

Written by
MIKE JOHNSON

Art by
STEPHEN MOLNAR, and **ERFAN FAJAR,**
HENDRI PRASETYO,
and **MIRALTI FIRMANSYAH** of Stellar Labs

Colors by
JOHN RAUCH, and **Ifansyah Noor**
and **Sakti Tuwono** of Stellar Labs

Creative Consultant
ROBERTO ORCI

Letters by
NEIL UYETAKE

Series Edits by
SCOTT DUNBIER

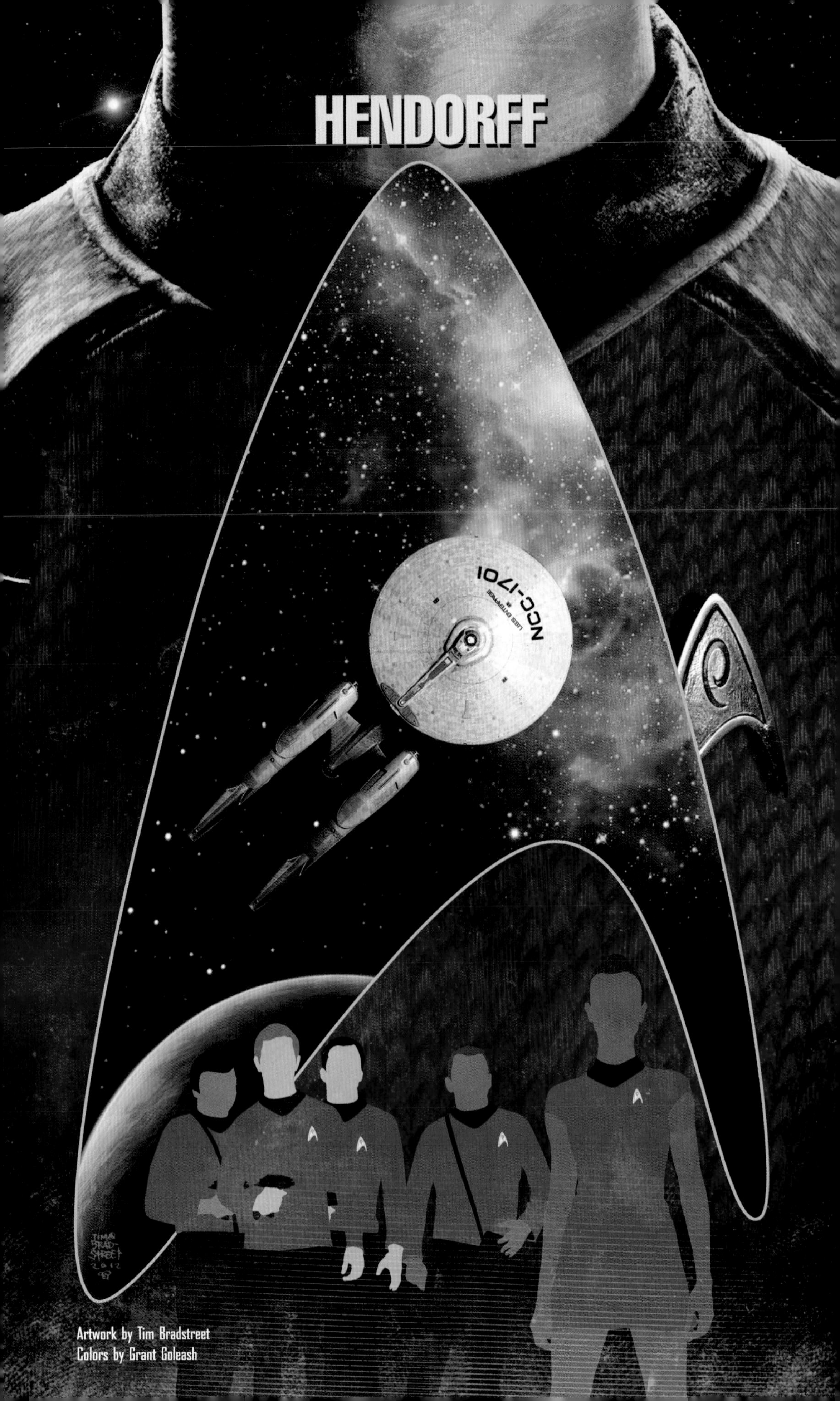
HENDORFF
NCC-1701
USS ENTERPRISE

Artwork by Tim Bradstreet
Colors by Grant Goleash

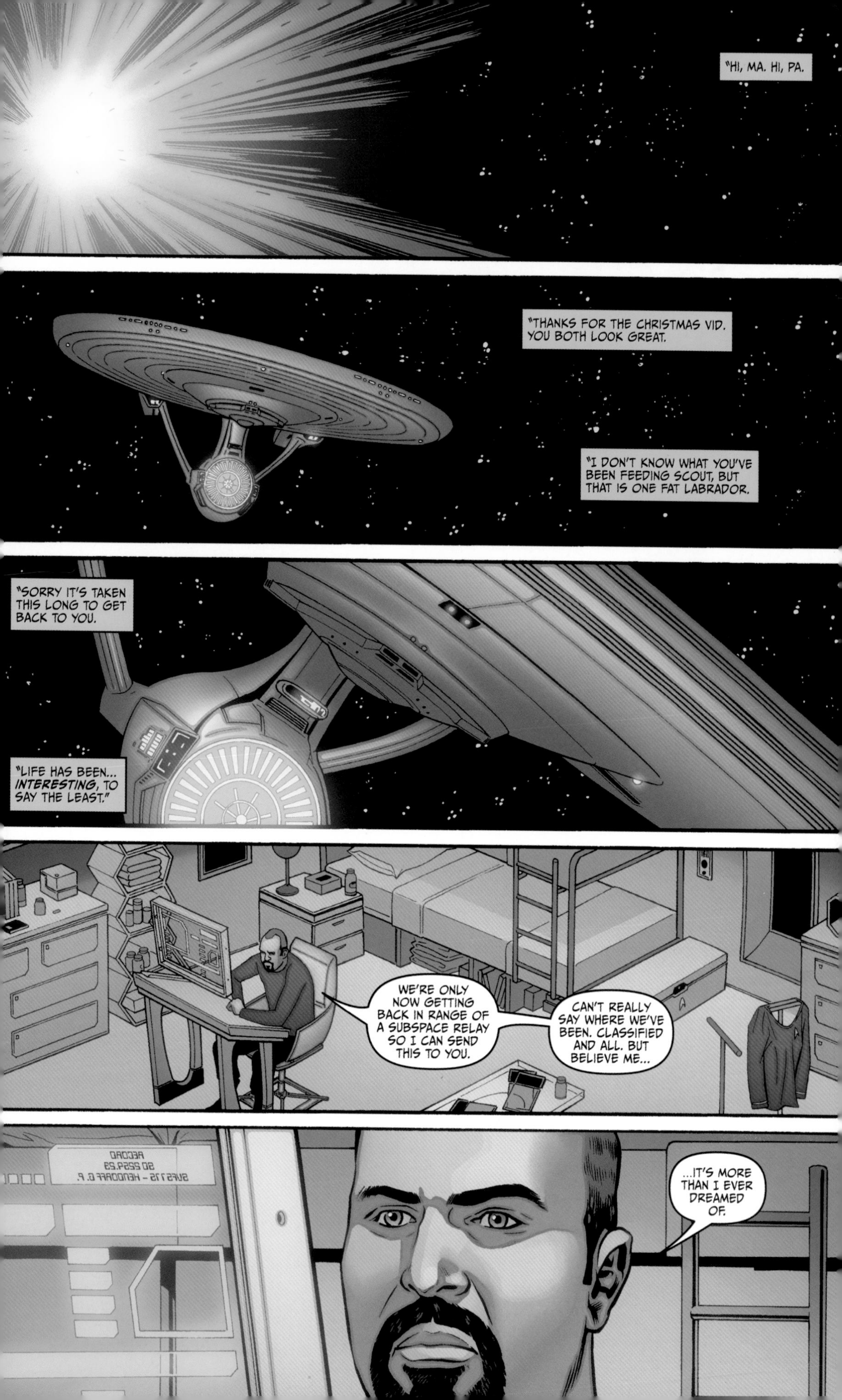

"HI, MA. HI, PA.
"THANKS FOR THE CHRISTMAS VID. YOU BOTH LOOK GREAT.
"I DON'T KNOW WHAT YOU'VE BEEN FEEDING SCOUT, BUT THAT IS ONE FAT LABRADOR.
"SORRY IT'S TAKEN THIS LONG TO GET BACK TO YOU.
"LIFE HAS BEEN... *INTERESTING*, TO SAY THE LEAST."
WE'RE ONLY NOW GETTING BACK IN RANGE OF A SUBSPACE RELAY SO I CAN SEND THIS TO YOU.
CAN'T REALLY SAY WHERE WE'VE BEEN. CLASSIFIED AND ALL. BUT BELIEVE ME...
...IT'S MORE THAN I EVER DREAMED OF.

OFFICIAL MEETING WITH THE CAPTAIN WAS A LITTLE...

"...AWKWARD."

WANTED TO SEE ME, SIR?

HENDORFF! YES, COME IN, HAVE A SEAT!

I WANTED TO, UH...

...CLEAR THE AIR.

SO TO SPEAK.

CLEAR THE AIR, SIR?

WELL, YEAH, I MEAN...

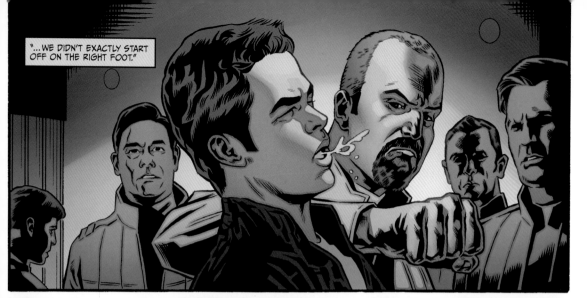

"...WE DIDN'T EXACTLY START OFF ON THE RIGHT FOOT."

ARE YOU REFERRING TO THE INCIDENT IN IOWA A COUPLE OF YEARS BACK, SIR?

THE "INCIDENT"? THAT "INCIDENT" RESET MY JAW.

SIR, IF YOU WANT ME TO APOLOGIZE, I—

NOT YOU, HENDORFF.

ME. I'M THE ONE APOLOGIZING. I WAS WAY OUT OF LINE THAT NIGHT. I DESERVED IT.

I SAW YOU A COUPLE OF TIMES AT THE ACADEMY LATER ON, WANTED TO SAY SOMETHING, BUT... DIDN'T KNOW WHAT.

"AND THEN THERE WAS THE SECOND TIME WE MET, WHEN I WAS AT THE WRONG END OF YOUR PHASER."

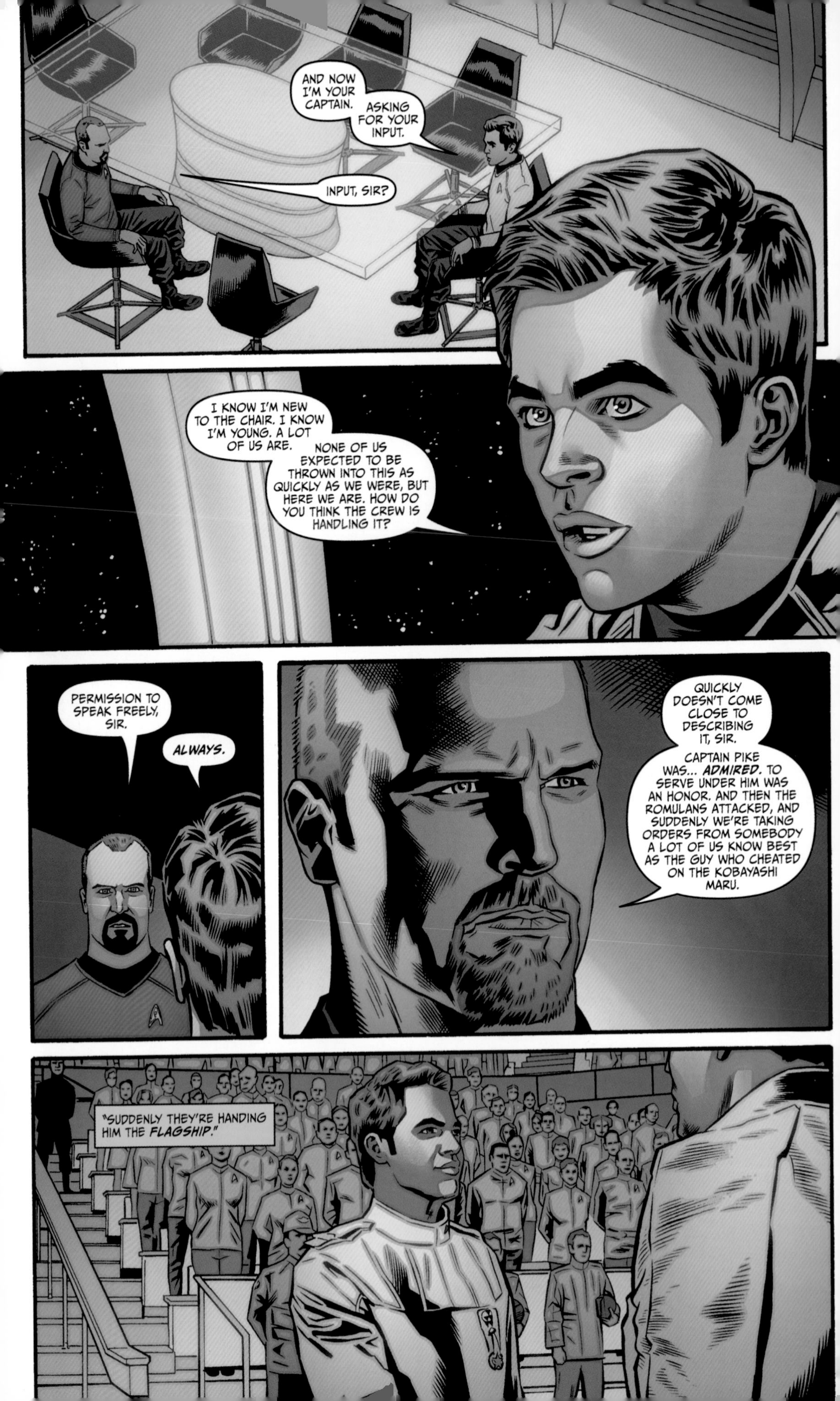
AND NOW I'M YOUR CAPTAIN.
ASKING FOR YOUR INPUT.
INPUT, SIR?
I KNOW I'M NEW TO THE CHAIR. I KNOW I'M YOUNG. A LOT OF US ARE.
NONE OF US EXPECTED TO BE THROWN INTO THIS AS QUICKLY AS WE WERE, BUT HERE WE ARE. HOW DO YOU THINK THE CREW IS HANDLING IT?
PERMISSION TO SPEAK FREELY, SIR.
ALWAYS.
QUICKLY DOESN'T COME CLOSE TO DESCRIBING IT, SIR.
CAPTAIN PIKE WAS... ADMIRED. TO SERVE UNDER HIM WAS AN HONOR. AND THEN THE ROMULANS ATTACKED, AND SUDDENLY WE'RE TAKING ORDERS FROM SOMEBODY A LOT OF US KNOW BEST AS THE GUY WHO CHEATED ON THE KOBAYASHI MARU.
"SUDDENLY THEY'RE HANDING HIM THE FLAGSHIP."

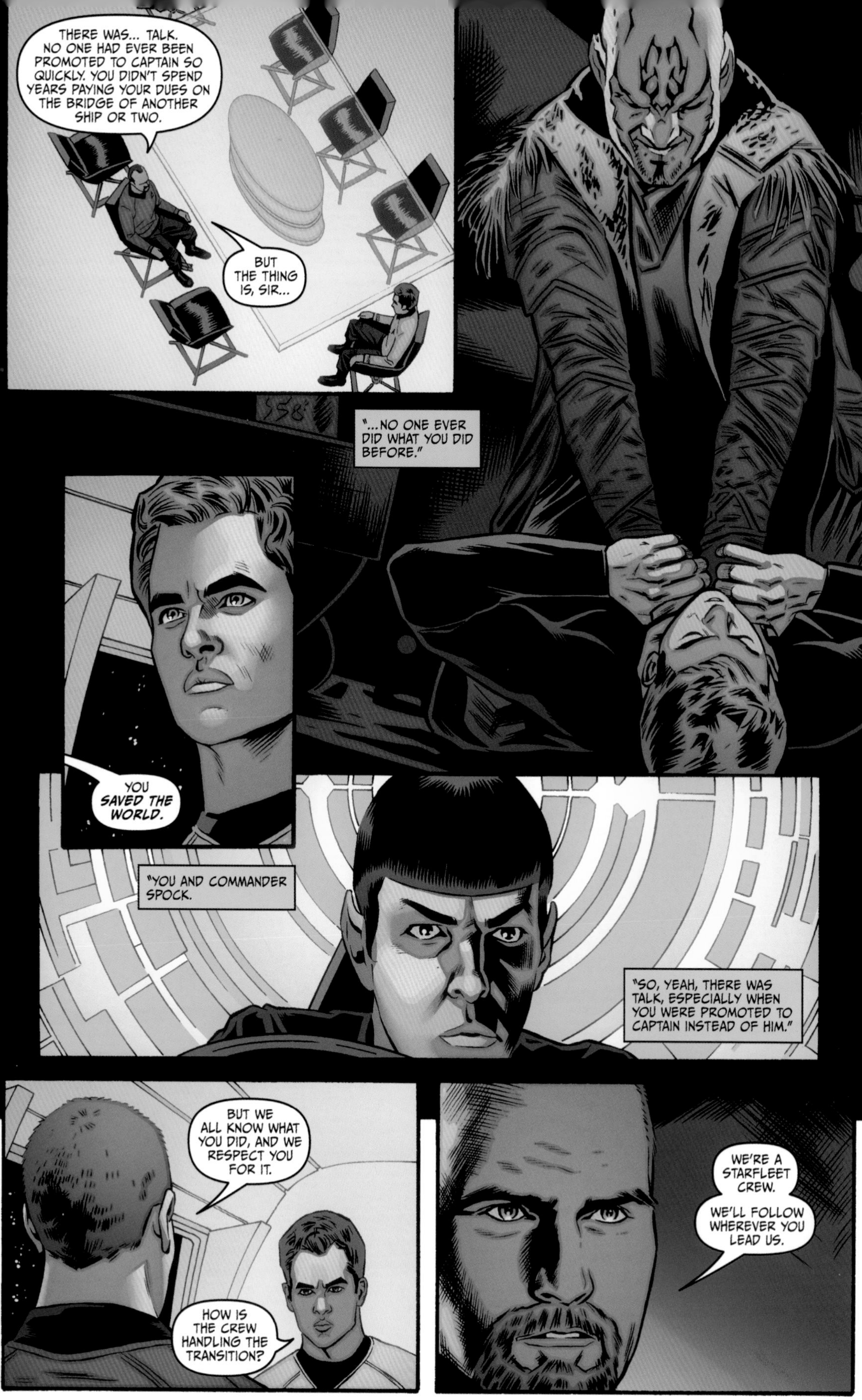
THERE WAS... TALK. NO ONE HAD EVER BEEN PROMOTED TO CAPTAIN SO QUICKLY. YOU DIDN'T SPEND YEARS PAYING YOUR DUES ON THE BRIDGE OF ANOTHER SHIP OR TWO.
BUT THE THING IS, SIR...
"...NO ONE EVER DID WHAT YOU DID BEFORE."
YOU SAVED THE WORLD.
"YOU AND COMMANDER SPOCK.
"SO, YEAH, THERE WAS TALK, ESPECIALLY WHEN YOU WERE PROMOTED TO CAPTAIN INSTEAD OF HIM."
HOW IS THE CREW HANDLING THE TRANSITION?
BUT WE ALL KNOW WHAT YOU DID, AND WE RESPECT YOU FOR IT.
WE'RE A STARFLEET CREW.
WE'LL FOLLOW WHEREVER YOU LEAD US.

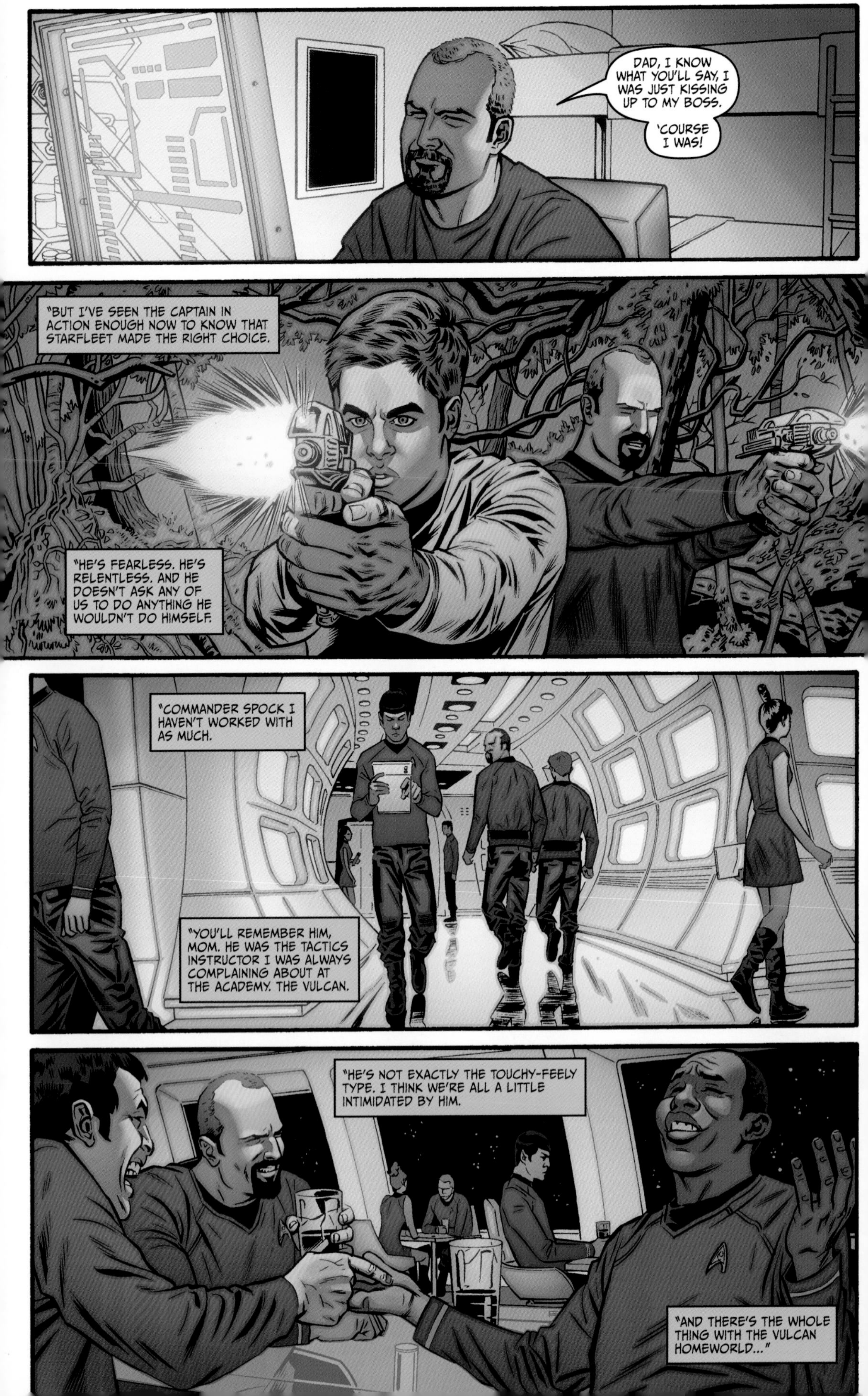
DAD, I KNOW WHAT YOU'LL SAY, I WAS JUST KISSING UP TO MY BOSS.
'COURSE I WAS!
"BUT I'VE SEEN THE CAPTAIN IN ACTION ENOUGH NOW TO KNOW THAT STARFLEET MADE THE RIGHT CHOICE.
"HE'S FEARLESS. HE'S RELENTLESS. AND HE DOESN'T ASK ANY OF US TO DO ANYTHING HE WOULDN'T DO HIMSELF.
"COMMANDER SPOCK I HAVEN'T WORKED WITH AS MUCH.
"YOU'LL REMEMBER HIM, MOM. HE WAS THE TACTICS INSTRUCTOR I WAS ALWAYS COMPLAINING ABOUT AT THE ACADEMY. THE VULCAN.
"HE'S NOT EXACTLY THE TOUCHY-FEELY TYPE. I THINK WE'RE ALL A LITTLE INTIMIDATED BY HIM.
"AND THERE'S THE WHOLE THING WITH THE VULCAN HOMEWORLD..."

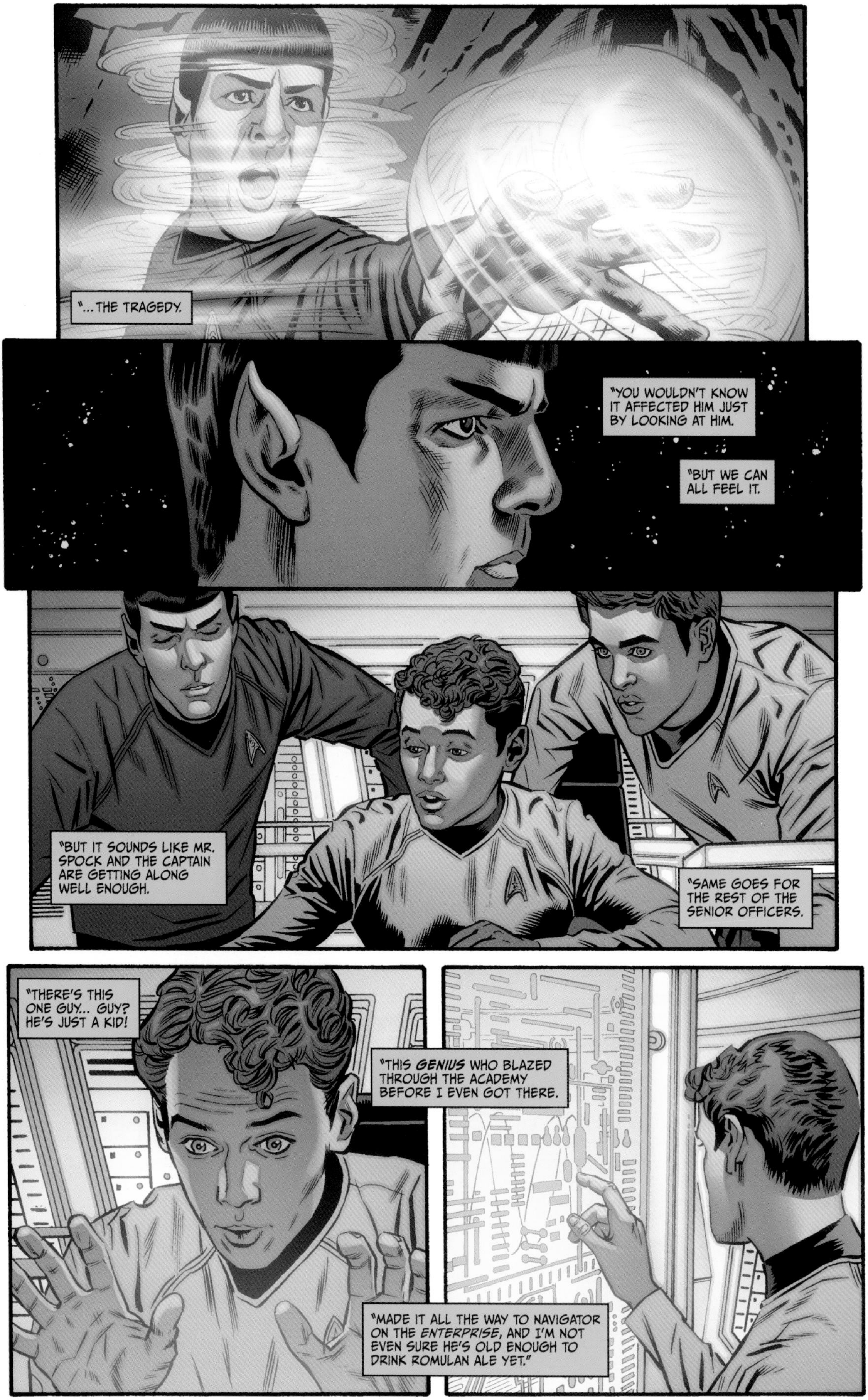
"...THE TRAGEDY.
"YOU WOULDN'T KNOW IT AFFECTED HIM JUST BY LOOKING AT HIM.
"BUT WE CAN ALL FEEL IT.
"BUT IT SOUNDS LIKE MR. SPOCK AND THE CAPTAIN ARE GETTING ALONG WELL ENOUGH.
"SAME GOES FOR THE REST OF THE SENIOR OFFICERS.
"THERE'S THIS ONE GUY... GUY? HE'S JUST A KID!
"THIS *GENIUS* WHO BLAZED THROUGH THE ACADEMY BEFORE I EVEN GOT THERE.
"MADE IT ALL THE WAY TO NAVIGATOR ON THE *ENTERPRISE*, AND I'M NOT EVEN SURE HE'S OLD ENOUGH TO DRINK ROMULAN ALE YET."

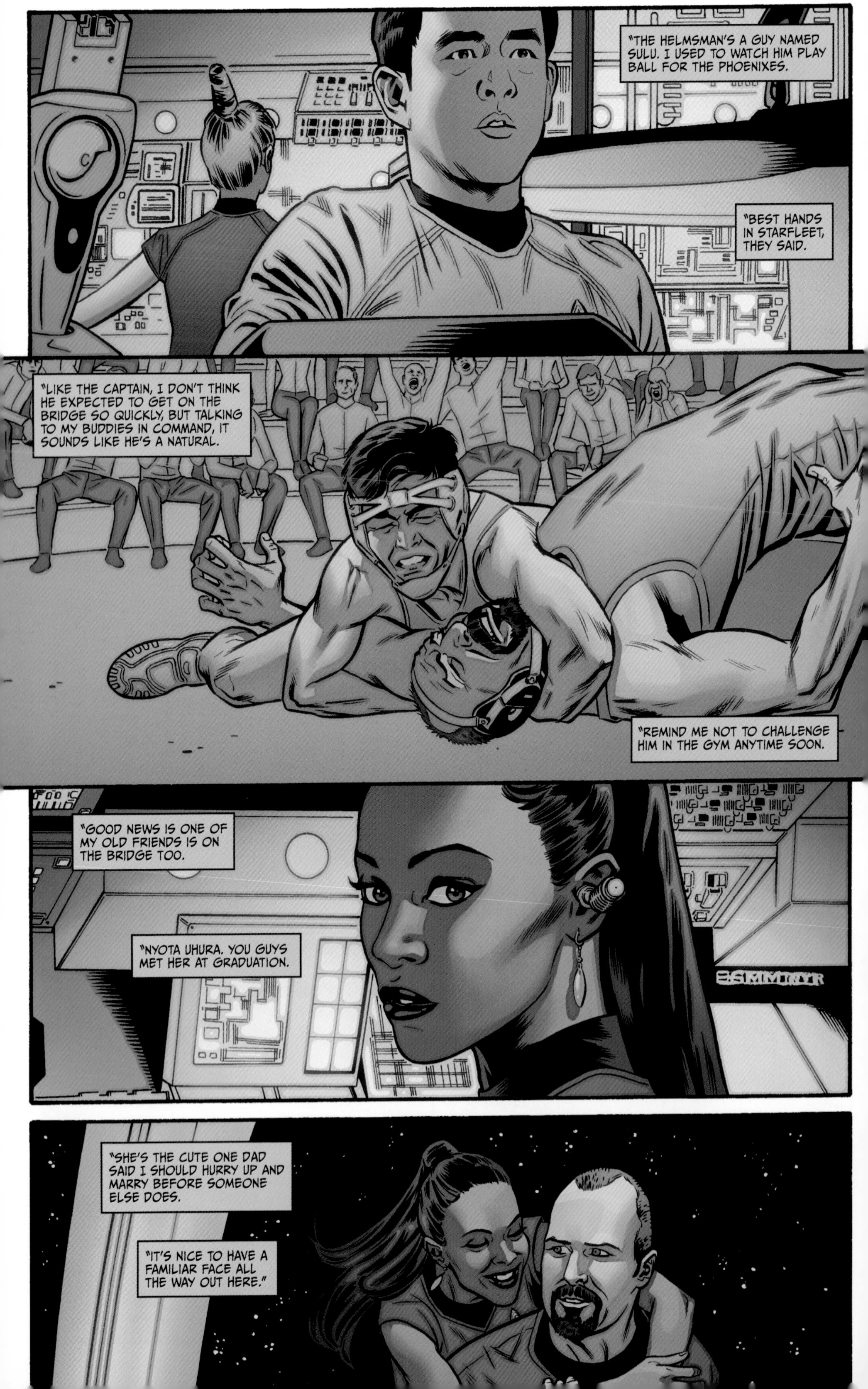
"THE HELMSMAN'S A GUY NAMED SULU. I USED TO WATCH HIM PLAY BALL FOR THE PHOENIXES.
"BEST HANDS IN STARFLEET, THEY SAID.
"LIKE THE CAPTAIN, I DON'T THINK HE EXPECTED TO GET ON THE BRIDGE SO QUICKLY, BUT TALKING TO MY BUDDIES IN COMMAND, IT SOUNDS LIKE HE'S A NATURAL.
"REMIND ME NOT TO CHALLENGE HIM IN THE GYM ANYTIME SOON.
"GOOD NEWS IS ONE OF MY OLD FRIENDS IS ON THE BRIDGE TOO.
"NYOTA UHURA. YOU GUYS MET HER AT GRADUATION.
"SHE'S THE CUTE ONE DAD SAID I SHOULD HURRY UP AND MARRY BEFORE SOMEONE ELSE DOES.
"IT'S NICE TO HAVE A FAMILIAR FACE ALL THE WAY OUT HERE."

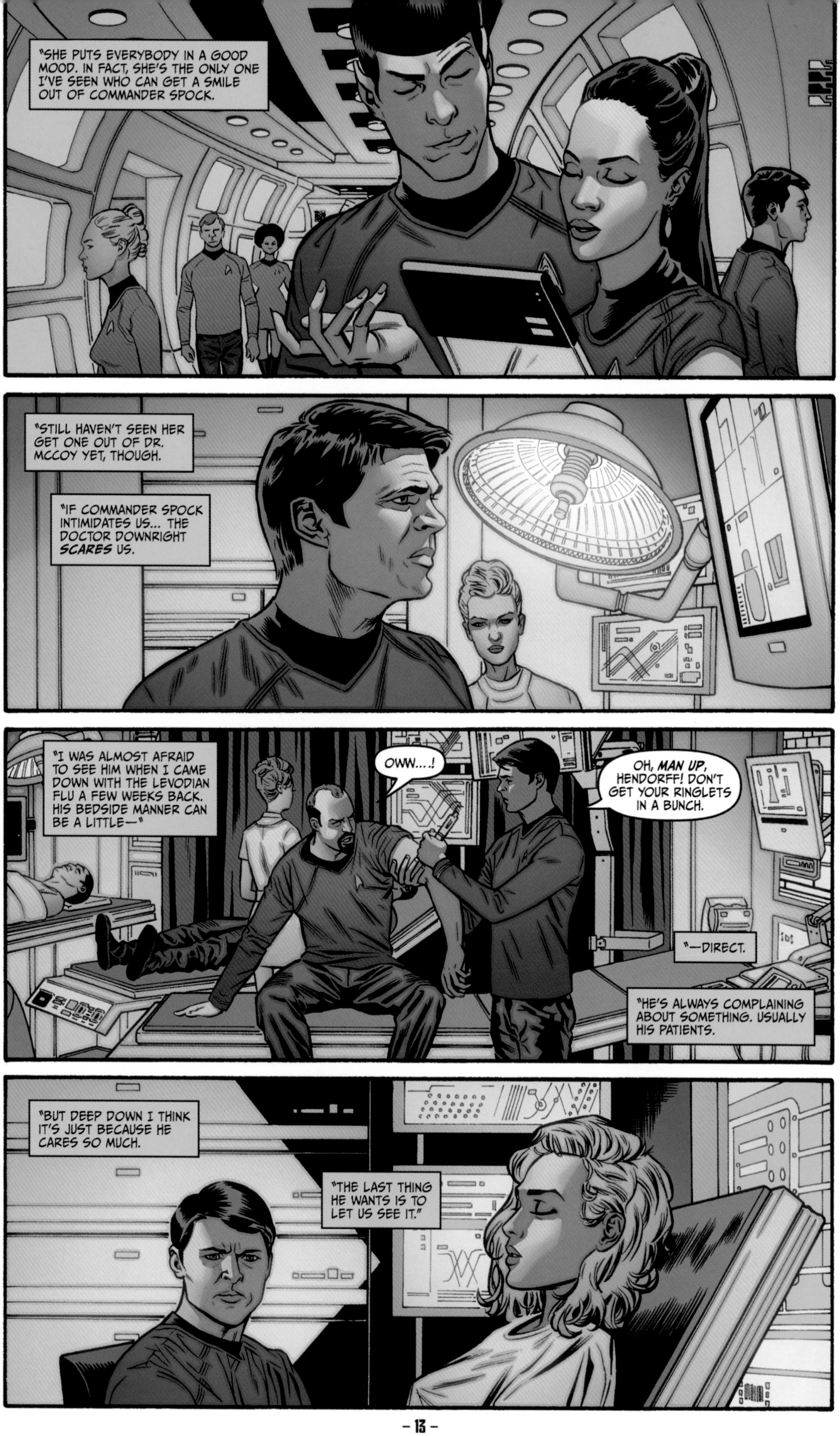
"SHE PUTS EVERYBODY IN A GOOD MOOD. IN FACT, SHE'S THE ONLY ONE I'VE SEEN WHO CAN GET A SMILE OUT OF COMMANDER SPOCK.
"STILL HAVEN'T SEEN HER GET ONE OUT OF DR. MCCOY YET, THOUGH.
"IF COMMANDER SPOCK INTIMIDATES US... THE DOCTOR DOWNRIGHT *SCARES* US.
"I WAS ALMOST AFRAID TO SEE HIM WHEN I CAME DOWN WITH THE LEVODIAN FLU A FEW WEEKS BACK. HIS BEDSIDE MANNER CAN BE A LITTLE—"
OWW....!
OH, *MAN UP*, HENDORFF! DON'T GET YOUR RINGLETS IN A BUNCH.
"—DIRECT.
"HE'S ALWAYS COMPLAINING ABOUT SOMETHING. USUALLY HIS PATIENTS.
"BUT DEEP DOWN I THINK IT'S JUST BECAUSE HE CARES SO MUCH.
"THE LAST THING HE WANTS IS TO LET US SEE IT."

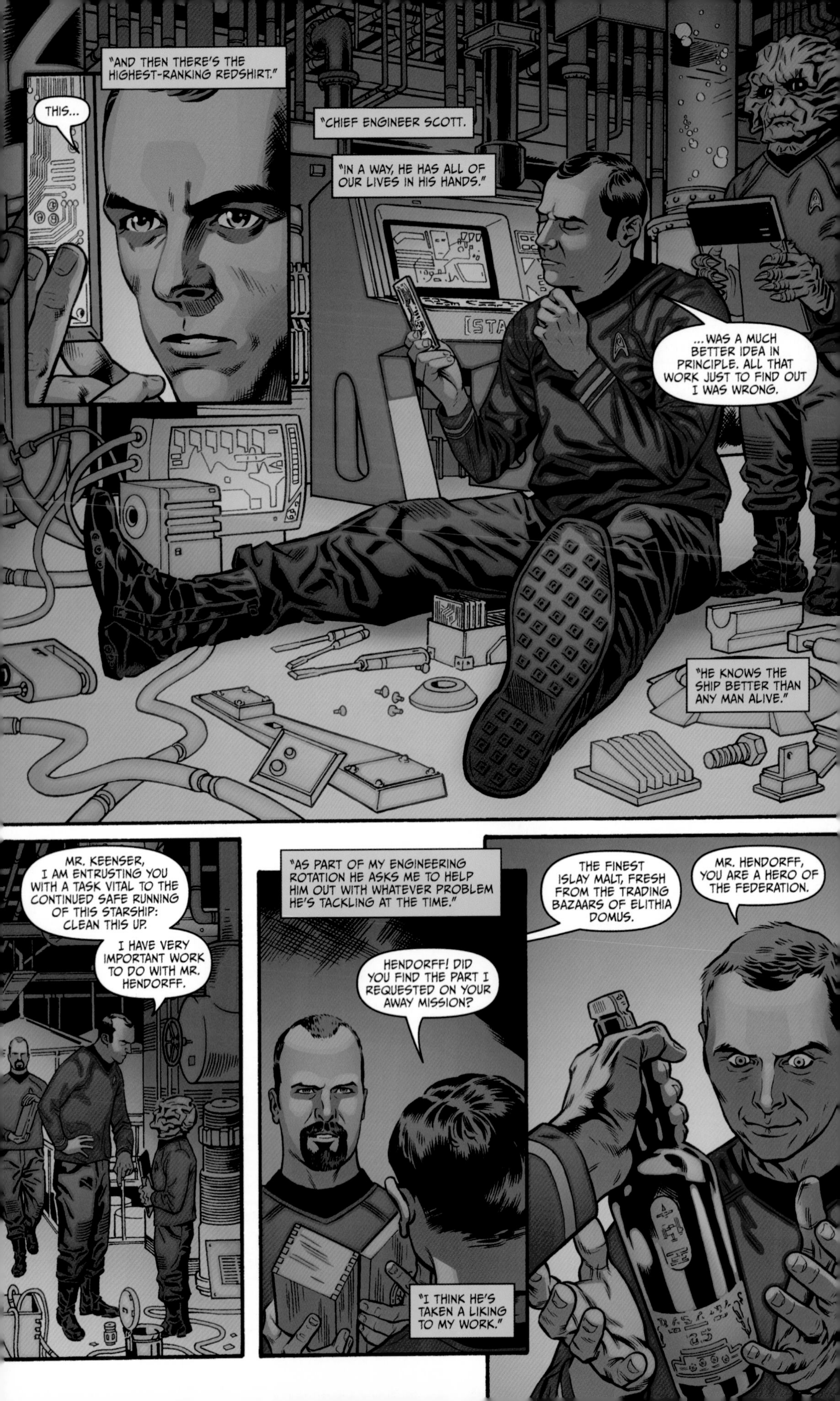
"AND THEN THERE'S THE HIGHEST-RANKING REDSHIRT."
THIS...
"CHIEF ENGINEER SCOTT.
"IN A WAY, HE HAS ALL OF OUR LIVES IN HIS HANDS."
...WAS A MUCH BETTER IDEA IN PRINCIPLE. ALL THAT WORK JUST TO FIND OUT I WAS WRONG.
"HE KNOWS THE SHIP BETTER THAN ANY MAN ALIVE."
MR. KEENSER, I AM ENTRUSTING YOU WITH A TASK VITAL TO THE CONTINUED SAFE RUNNING OF THIS STARSHIP: CLEAN THIS UP.
I HAVE VERY IMPORTANT WORK TO DO WITH MR. HENDORFF.
"AS PART OF MY ENGINEERING ROTATION HE ASKS ME TO HELP HIM OUT WITH WHATEVER PROBLEM HE'S TACKLING AT THE TIME."
HENDORFF! DID YOU FIND THE PART I REQUESTED ON YOUR AWAY MISSION?
"I THINK HE'S TAKEN A LIKING TO MY WORK."
THE FINEST ISLAY MALT, FRESH FROM THE TRADING BAZAARS OF ELITHIA DOMUS.
MR. HENDORFF, YOU ARE A HERO OF THE FEDERATION.

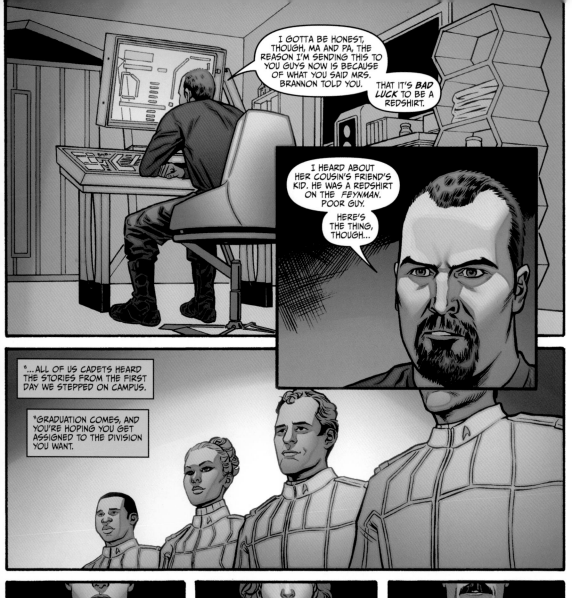

I GOTTA BE HONEST, THOUGH, MA AND PA, THE REASON I'M SENDING THIS TO YOU GUYS NOW IS BECAUSE OF WHAT YOU SAID MRS. BRANNON TOLD YOU.

THAT IT'S *BAD LUCK* TO BE A REDSHIRT.

I HEARD ABOUT HER COUSIN'S FRIEND'S KID. HE WAS A REDSHIRT ON THE *FEYNMAN*. POOR GUY.

HERE'S THE THING, THOUGH...

"...ALL OF US CADETS HEARD THE STORIES FROM THE FIRST DAY WE STEPPED ON CAMPUS.

"GRADUATION COMES, AND YOU'RE HOPING YOU GET ASSIGNED TO THE DIVISION YOU WANT.

"ALL THE HOT DOGS WANT COMMAND. GRAB THE GOLD. MAYBE YOU GET TO SIT IN THE BIG CHAIR ONE DAY.

"THE SMARTEST ONES HEAD TO SCIENCE. COOL BLUE. SOME OF 'EM SAY THEY'RE THE REASON STARFLEET EXISTS AT ALL.

"THEN THERE'S *US*. OPERATIONS. THE REDSHIRTS. ENGINEERS, COMPUTER TECHS, SECURITY. THE BLOOD THAT KEEPS THE HEART OF STARFLEET PUMPING.

"MOM, DAD, THE DAY I PUT ON *THE RED* FOR THE FIRST TIME...

"...IT WAS THE PROUDEST DAY OF MY LIFE."

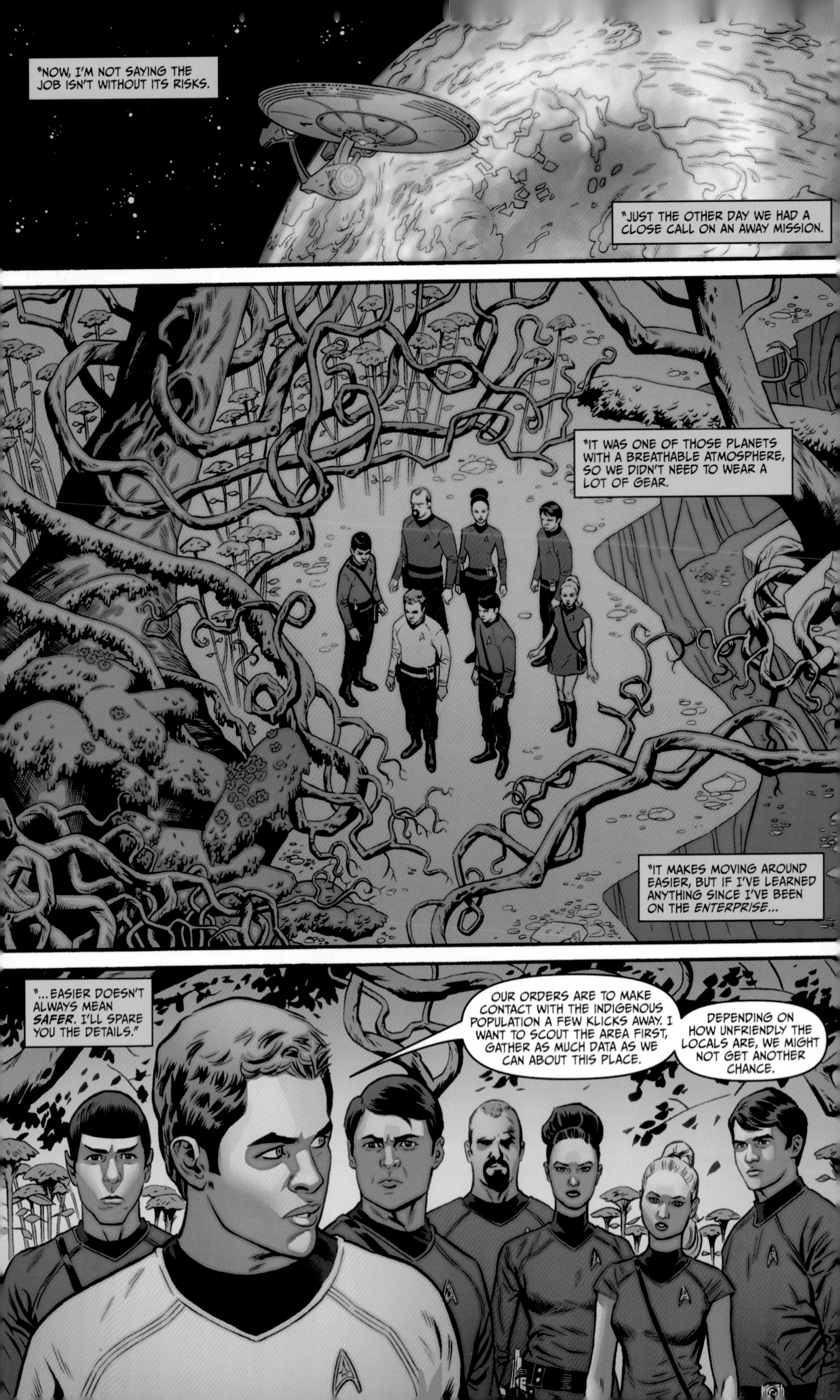
"NOW, I'M NOT SAYING THE JOB ISN'T WITHOUT ITS RISKS.
"JUST THE OTHER DAY WE HAD A CLOSE CALL ON AN AWAY MISSION.
"IT WAS ONE OF THOSE PLANETS WITH A BREATHABLE ATMOSPHERE, SO WE DIDN'T NEED TO WEAR A LOT OF GEAR.
"IT MAKES MOVING AROUND EASIER, BUT IF I'VE LEARNED ANYTHING SINCE I'VE BEEN ON THE *ENTERPRISE*...
"...EASIER DOESN'T ALWAYS MEAN *SAFER*. I'LL SPARE YOU THE DETAILS."
OUR ORDERS ARE TO MAKE CONTACT WITH THE INDIGENOUS POPULATION A FEW KLICKS AWAY. I WANT TO SCOUT THE AREA FIRST, GATHER AS MUCH DATA AS WE CAN ABOUT THIS PLACE.
DEPENDING ON HOW UNFRIENDLY THE LOCALS ARE, WE MIGHT NOT GET ANOTHER CHANCE.

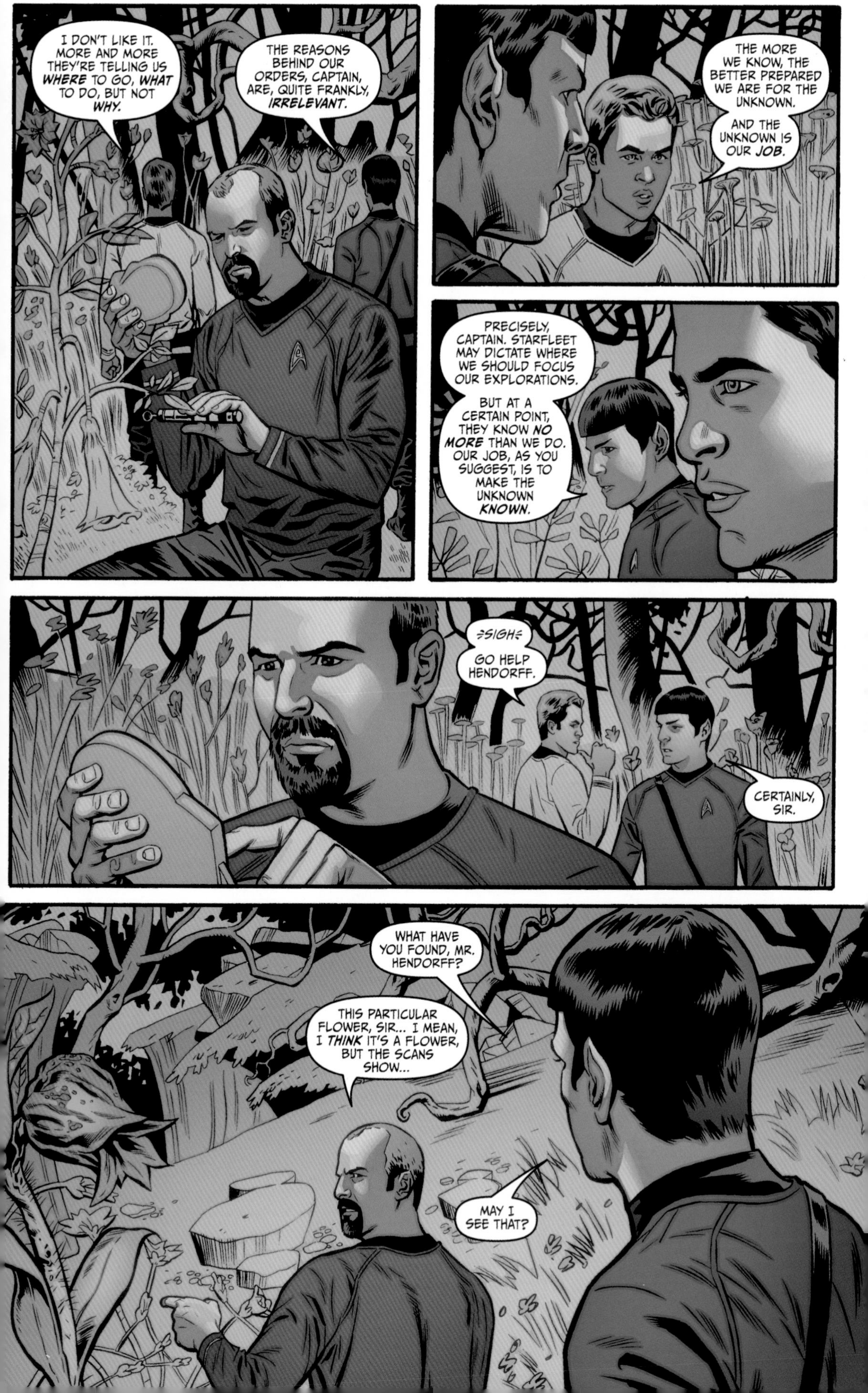
I DON'T LIKE IT. MORE AND MORE THEY'RE TELLING US *WHERE* TO GO, *WHAT* TO DO, BUT NOT *WHY.*
THE REASONS BEHIND OUR ORDERS, CAPTAIN, ARE, QUITE FRANKLY, *IRRELEVANT*.
THE MORE WE KNOW, THE BETTER PREPARED WE ARE FOR THE UNKNOWN.
AND THE UNKNOWN IS OUR *JOB*.
PRECISELY, CAPTAIN. STARFLEET MAY DICTATE WHERE WE SHOULD FOCUS OUR EXPLORATIONS.
BUT AT A CERTAIN POINT, THEY KNOW *NO MORE* THAN WE DO. OUR JOB, AS YOU SUGGEST, IS TO MAKE THE UNKNOWN *KNOWN*.
SIGH
GO HELP HENDORFF.
CERTAINLY, SIR.
WHAT HAVE YOU FOUND, MR. HENDORFF?
THIS PARTICULAR FLOWER, SIR... I MEAN, I *THINK* IT'S A FLOWER, BUT THE SCANS SHOW...
MAY I SEE THAT?

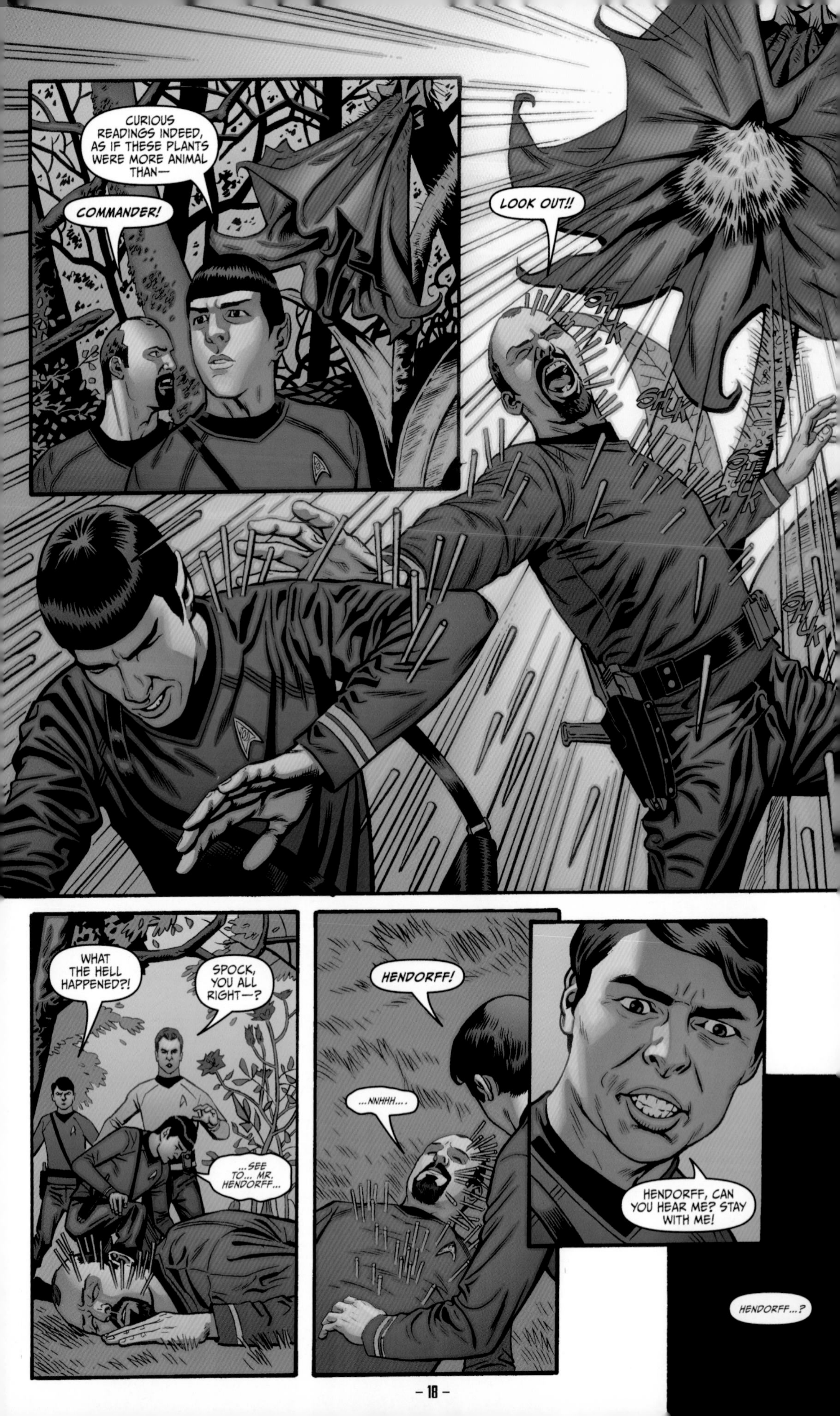
CURIOUS READINGS INDEED, AS IF THESE PLANTS WERE MORE ANIMAL THAN—
COMMANDER!
LOOK OUT!!
SHUK
SHUK
SHUK
SHUK
WHAT THE HELL HAPPENED?!
SPOCK, YOU ALL RIGHT—?
...SEE TO... MR. HENDORFF...
HENDORFF!
...NNHHH....
HENDORFF, CAN YOU HEAR ME? STAY WITH ME!
HENDORFF...?

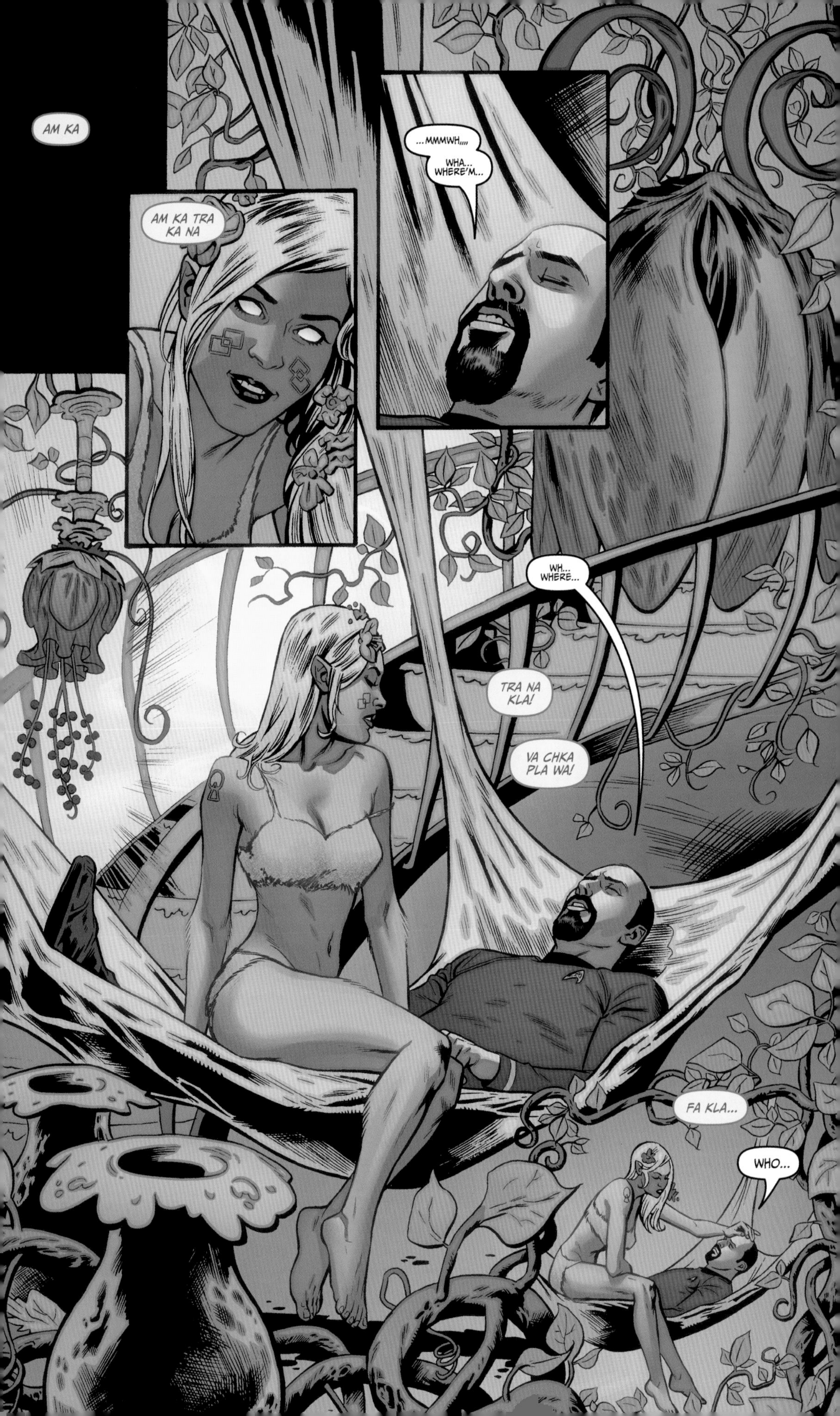
AM KA
AM KA TRA KA NA
...MMMWH,,,,
WHA... WHERE'M...
WH... WHERE...
TRA NA KLA!
VA CHKA PLA WA!
FA KLA...
WHO...

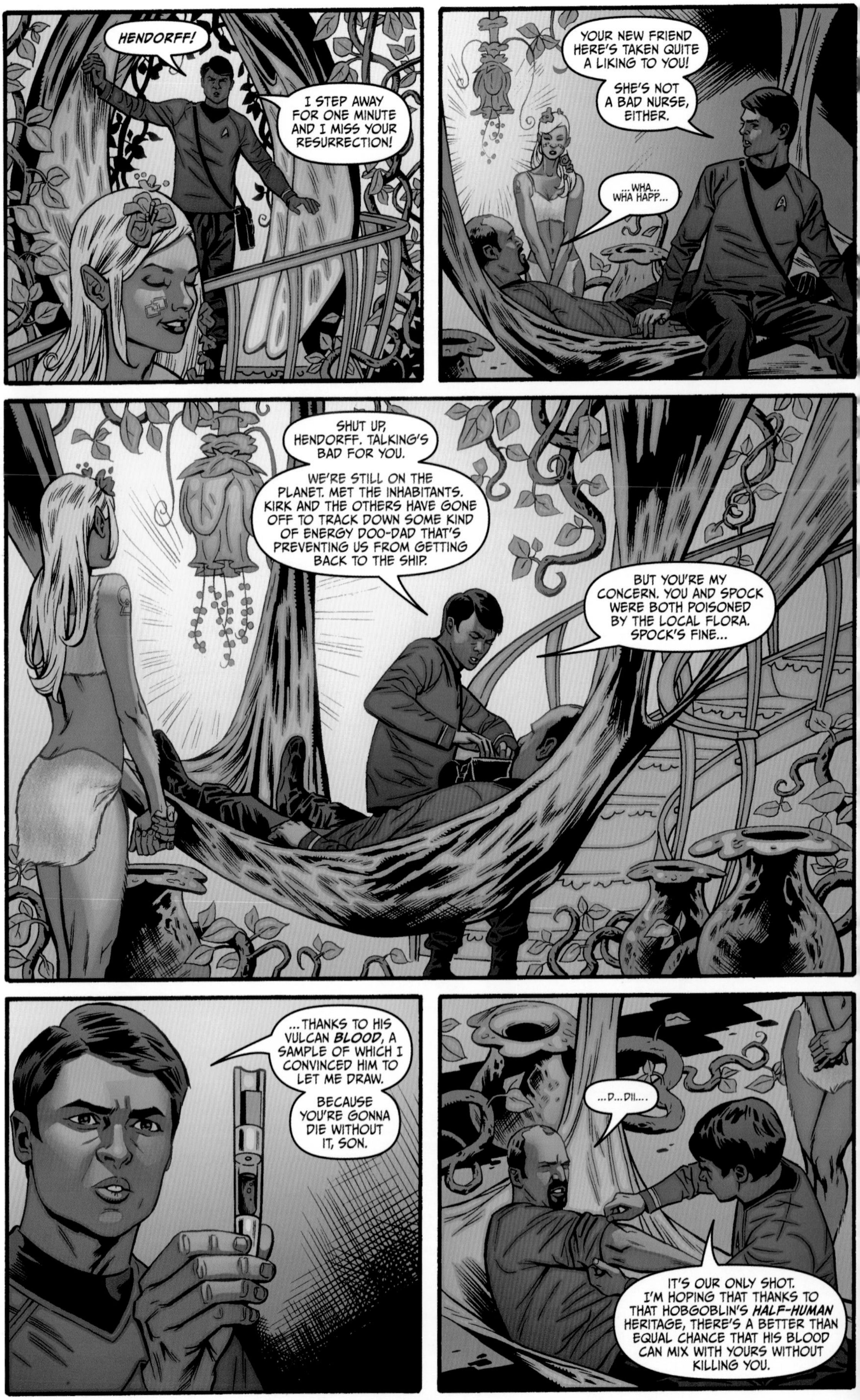
HENDORFF!
I STEP AWAY FOR ONE MINUTE AND I MISS YOUR RESURRECTION!
YOUR NEW FRIEND HERE'S TAKEN QUITE A LIKING TO YOU!
SHE'S NOT A BAD NURSE, EITHER.
...WHA... WHA HAPP...
SHUT UP, HENDORFF. TALKING'S BAD FOR YOU.
WE'RE STILL ON THE PLANET. MET THE INHABITANTS. KIRK AND THE OTHERS HAVE GONE OFF TO TRACK DOWN SOME KIND OF ENERGY DOO-DAD THAT'S PREVENTING US FROM GETTING BACK TO THE SHIP.
BUT YOU'RE MY CONCERN. YOU AND SPOCK WERE BOTH POISONED BY THE LOCAL FLORA. SPOCK'S FINE...
...THANKS TO HIS VULCAN **BLOOD**, A SAMPLE OF WHICH I CONVINCED HIM TO LET ME DRAW.
BECAUSE YOU'RE GONNA DIE WITHOUT IT, SON.
...D...DII....
IT'S OUR ONLY SHOT. I'M HOPING THAT THANKS TO THAT HOBGOBLIN'S ***HALF-HUMAN*** HERITAGE, THERE'S A BETTER THAN EQUAL CHANCE THAT HIS BLOOD CAN MIX WITH YOURS WITHOUT KILLING YOU.

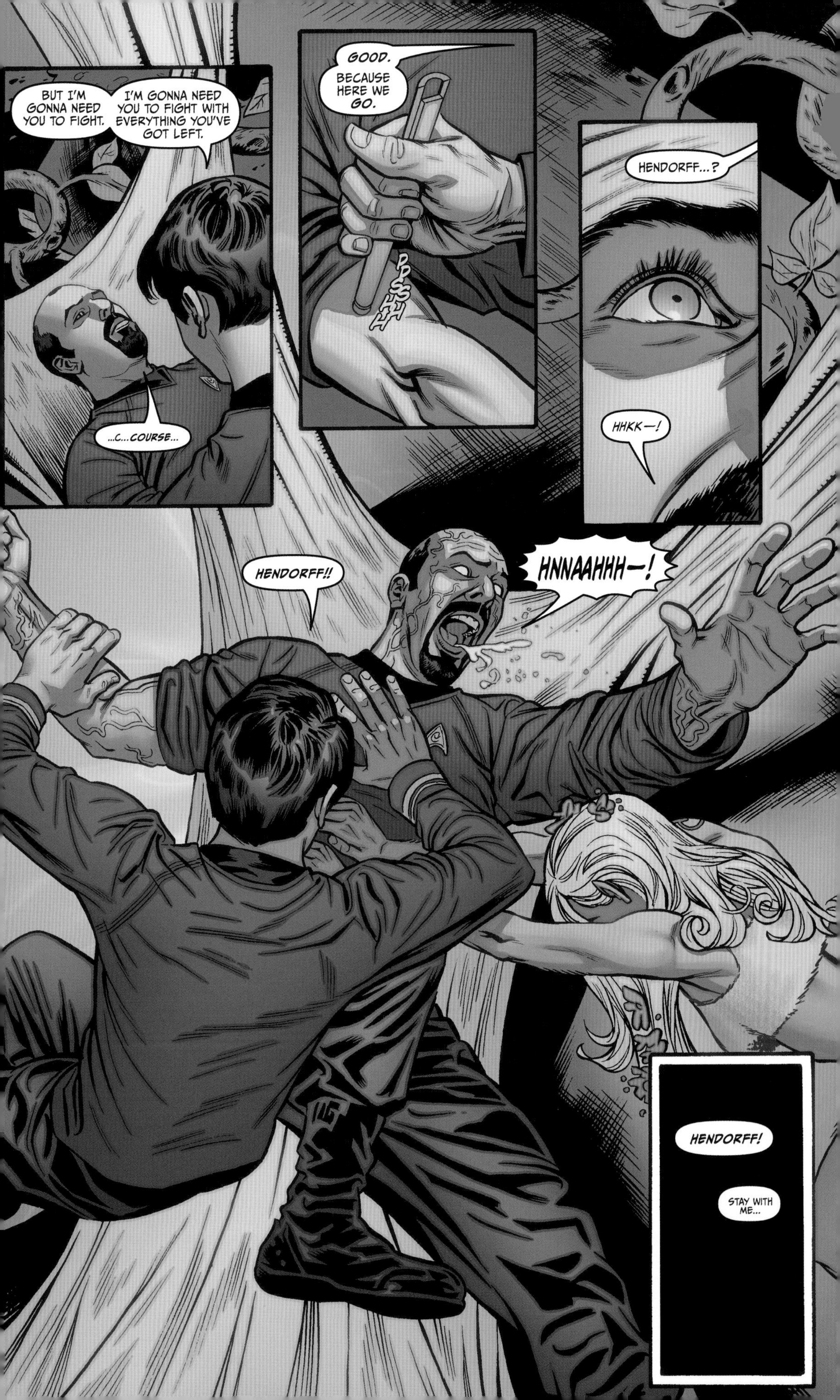

BUT I'M GONNA NEED YOU TO FIGHT.
I'M GONNA NEED YOU TO FIGHT WITH EVERYTHING YOU'VE GOT LEFT.
...C...COURSE...
GOOD.
BECAUSE HERE WE GO.
PSSHH
HENDORFF...?
HHKK—!
HENDORFF!!
HNNAAHHH—!
HENDORFF!
STAY WITH ME...

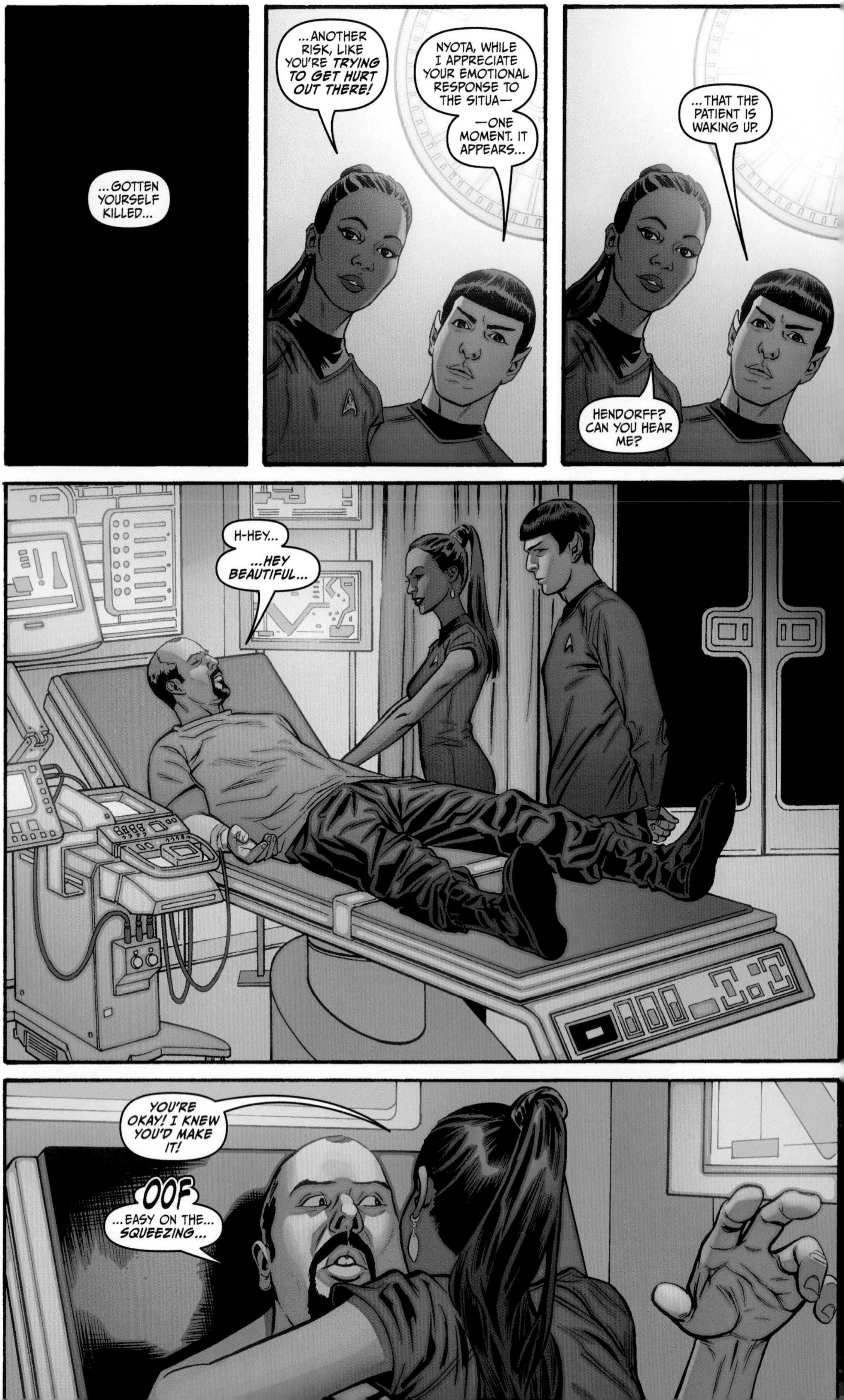

...GOTTEN YOURSELF KILLED...
...ANOTHER RISK, LIKE YOU'RE *TRYING TO GET HURT OUT THERE!*
NYOTA, WHILE I APPRECIATE YOUR EMOTIONAL RESPONSE TO THE SITUA—
—ONE MOMENT. IT APPEARS...
...THAT THE PATIENT IS WAKING UP.
HENDORFF? CAN YOU HEAR ME?
H-HEY...
...*HEY BEAUTIFUL...*
YOU'RE OKAY! I KNEW YOU'D MAKE IT!
OOF
...EASY ON THE... *SQUEEZING...*

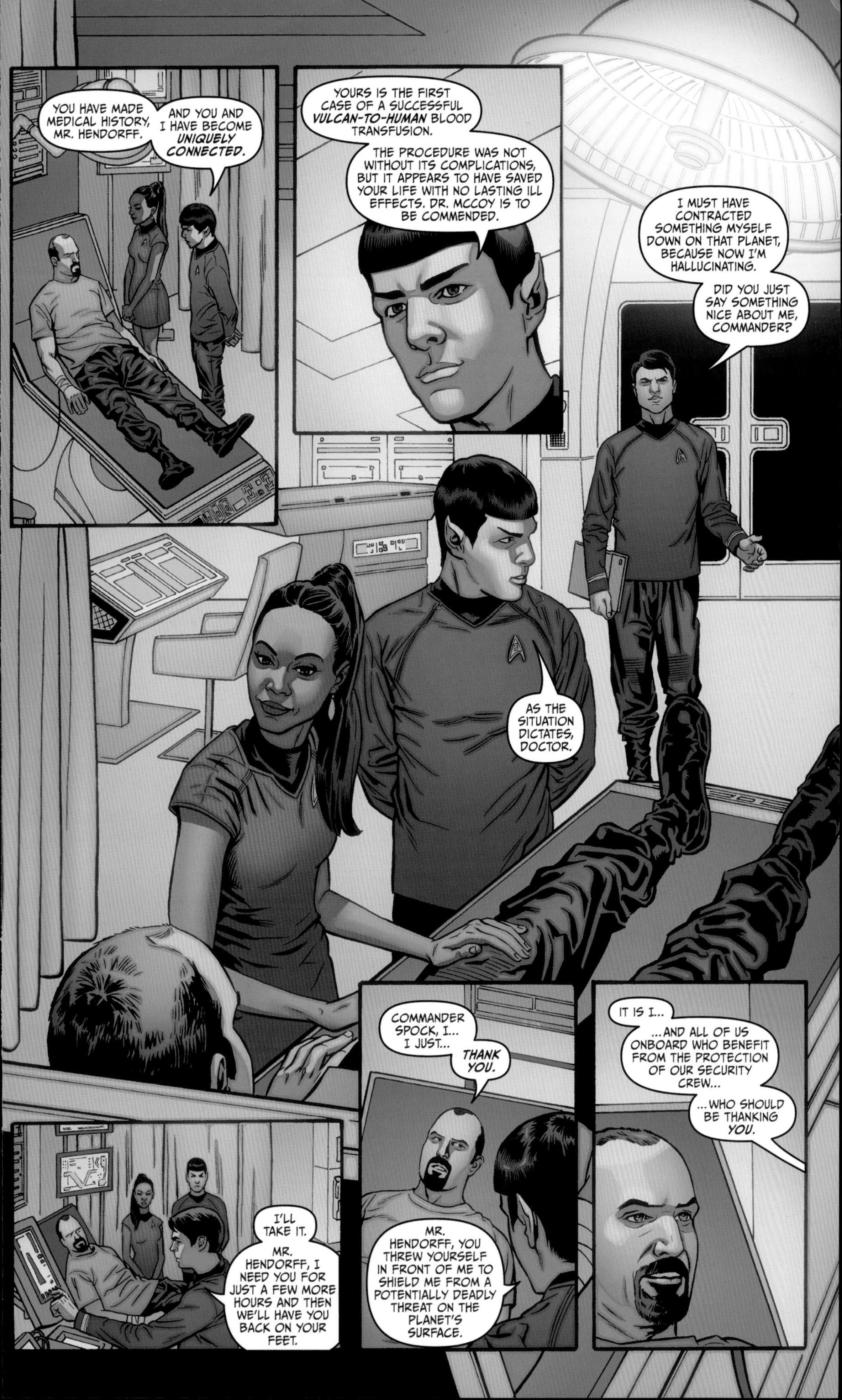

YOU HAVE MADE MEDICAL HISTORY, MR. HENDORFF.
AND YOU AND I HAVE BECOME *UNIQUELY CONNECTED.*
YOURS IS THE FIRST CASE OF A SUCCESSFUL *VULCAN-TO-HUMAN* BLOOD TRANSFUSION.
THE PROCEDURE WAS NOT WITHOUT ITS COMPLICATIONS, BUT IT APPEARS TO HAVE SAVED YOUR LIFE WITH NO LASTING ILL EFFECTS. DR. MCCOY IS TO BE COMMENDED.
I MUST HAVE CONTRACTED SOMETHING MYSELF DOWN ON THAT PLANET, BECAUSE NOW I'M HALLUCINATING.
DID YOU JUST SAY SOMETHING NICE ABOUT ME, COMMANDER?
AS THE SITUATION DICTATES, DOCTOR.
I'LL TAKE IT.
MR. HENDORFF, I NEED YOU FOR JUST A FEW MORE HOURS AND THEN WE'LL HAVE YOU BACK ON YOUR FEET.
COMMANDER SPOCK, I... I JUST... *THANK YOU.*
MR. HENDORFF, YOU THREW YOURSELF IN FRONT OF ME TO SHIELD ME FROM A POTENTIALLY DEADLY THREAT ON THE PLANET'S SURFACE.
IT IS I...
...AND ALL OF US ONBOARD WHO BENEFIT FROM THE PROTECTION OF OUR SECURITY CREW...
...WHO SHOULD BE THANKING *YOU.*

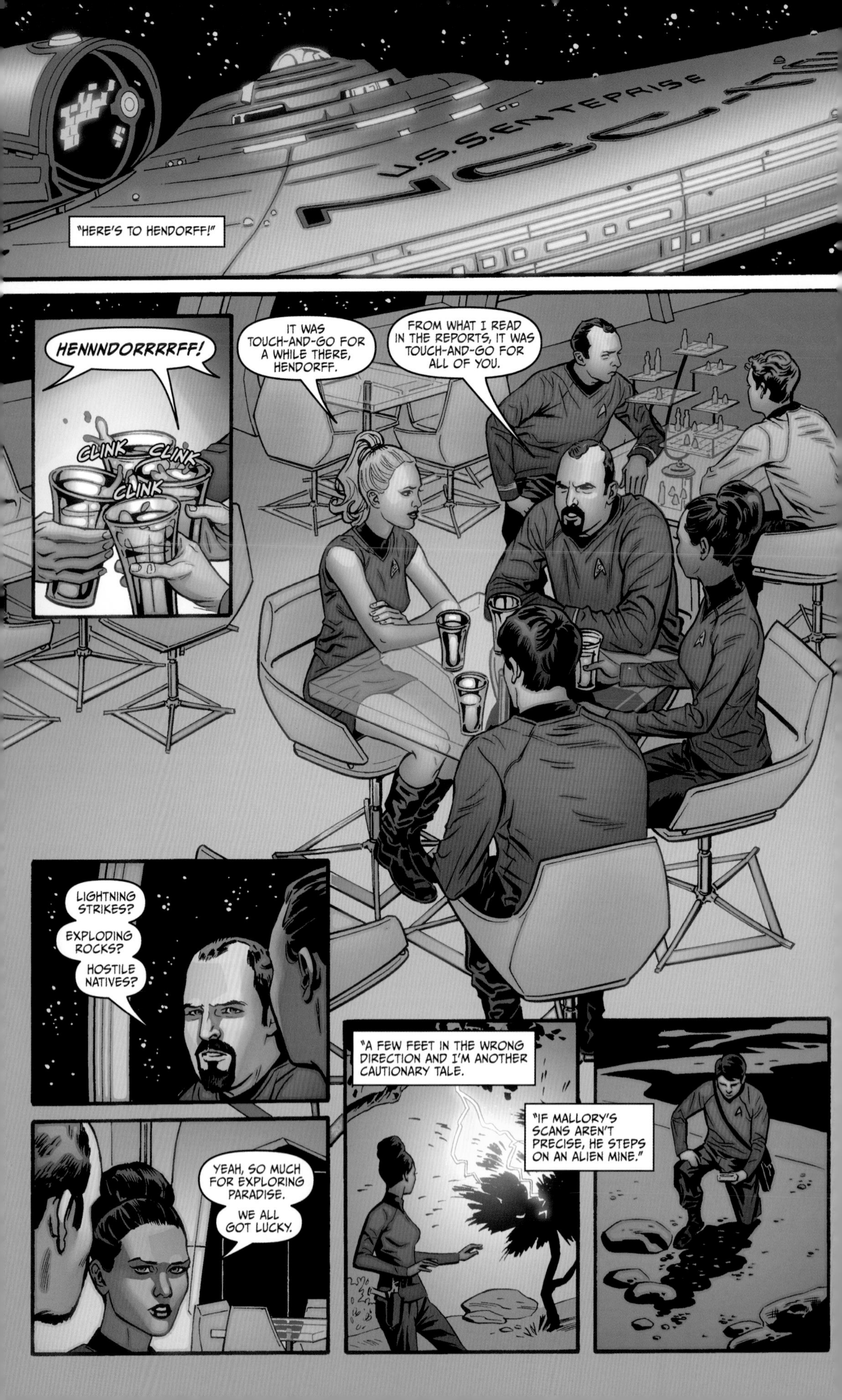
U.S.S. ENTERPRISE
"HERE'S TO HENDORFF!"
HENNNDORRRRFF!
CLINK CLINK CLINK
IT WAS TOUCH-AND-GO FOR A WHILE THERE, HENDORFF.
FROM WHAT I READ IN THE REPORTS, IT WAS TOUCH-AND-GO FOR ALL OF YOU.
LIGHTNING STRIKES?
EXPLODING ROCKS?
HOSTILE NATIVES?
YEAH, SO MUCH FOR EXPLORING PARADISE.
WE ALL GOT LUCKY.
"A FEW FEET IN THE WRONG DIRECTION AND I'M ANOTHER CAUTIONARY TALE.
"IF MALLORY'S SCANS AREN'T PRECISE, HE STEPS ON AN ALIEN MINE."

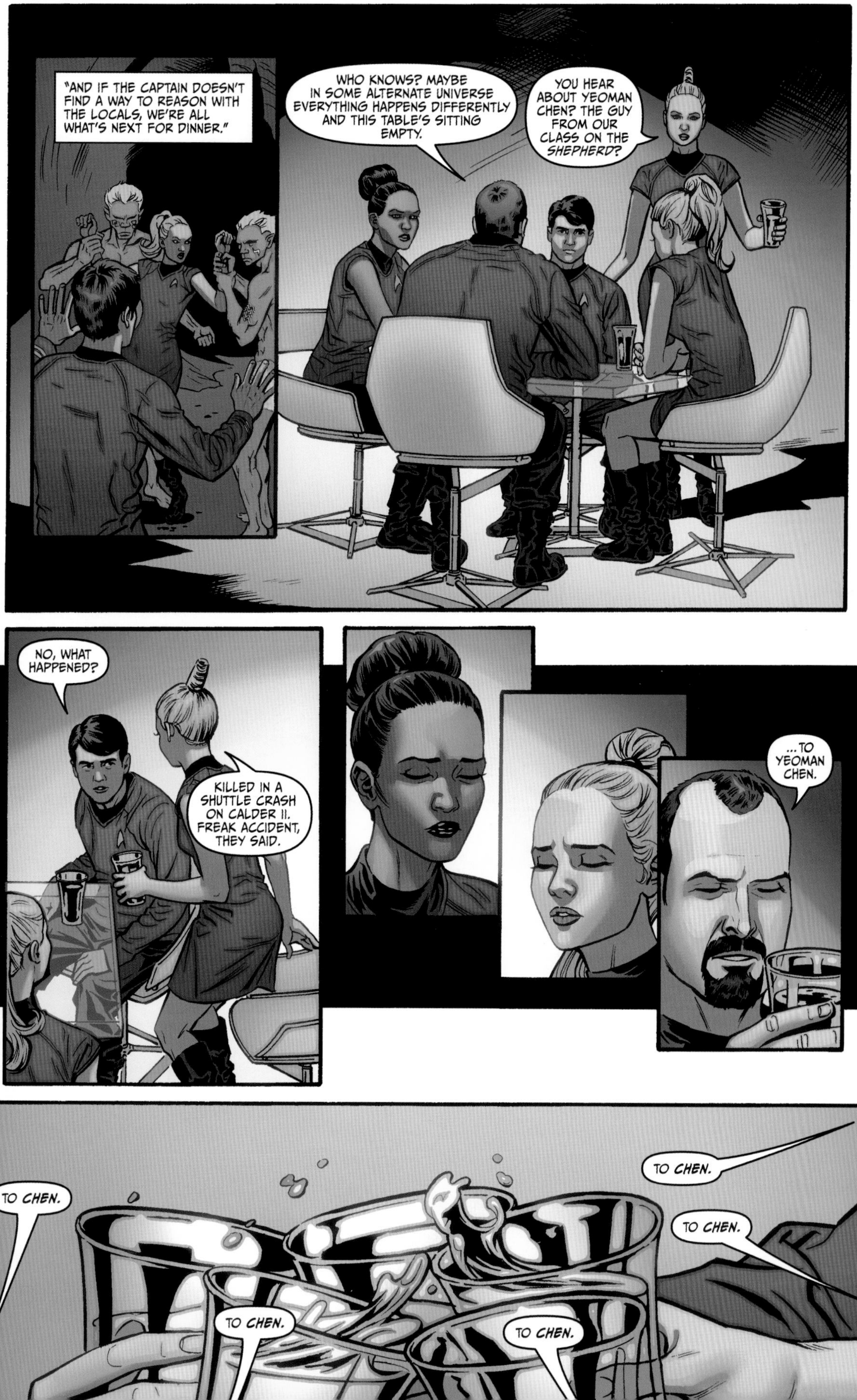
"AND IF THE CAPTAIN DOESN'T FIND A WAY TO REASON WITH THE LOCALS, WE'RE ALL WHAT'S NEXT FOR DINNER."
WHO KNOWS? MAYBE IN SOME ALTERNATE UNIVERSE EVERYTHING HAPPENS DIFFERENTLY AND THIS TABLE'S SITTING EMPTY.
YOU HEAR ABOUT YEOMAN CHEN? THE GUY FROM OUR CLASS ON THE *SHEPHERD*?
NO, WHAT HAPPENED?
KILLED IN A SHUTTLE CRASH ON CALDER II. FREAK ACCIDENT, THEY SAID.
...TO YEOMAN CHEN.
TO *CHEN.*
TO *CHEN.*
TO *CHEN.*
TO *CHEN.*
TO *CHEN.*

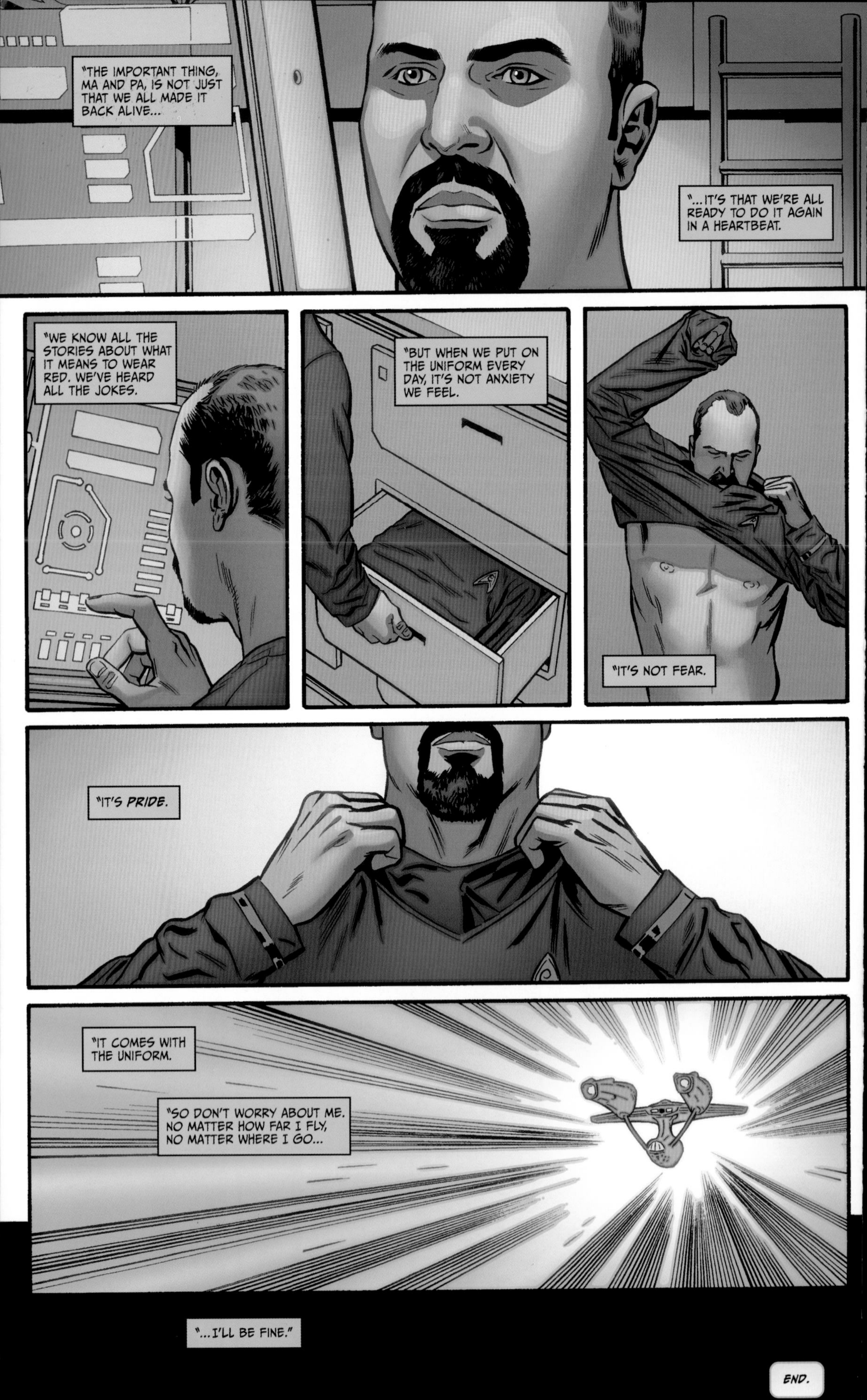
"THE IMPORTANT THING, MA AND PA, IS NOT JUST THAT WE ALL MADE IT BACK ALIVE...
"...IT'S THAT WE'RE ALL READY TO DO IT AGAIN IN A HEARTBEAT.
"WE KNOW ALL THE STORIES ABOUT WHAT IT MEANS TO WEAR RED. WE'VE HEARD ALL THE JOKES.
"BUT WHEN WE PUT ON THE UNIFORM EVERY DAY, IT'S NOT ANXIETY WE FEEL.
"IT'S NOT FEAR.
"IT'S *PRIDE*.
"IT COMES WITH THE UNIFORM.
"SO DON'T WORRY ABOUT ME. NO MATTER HOW FAR I FLY, NO MATTER WHERE I GO...
"...I'LL BE FINE."
END.

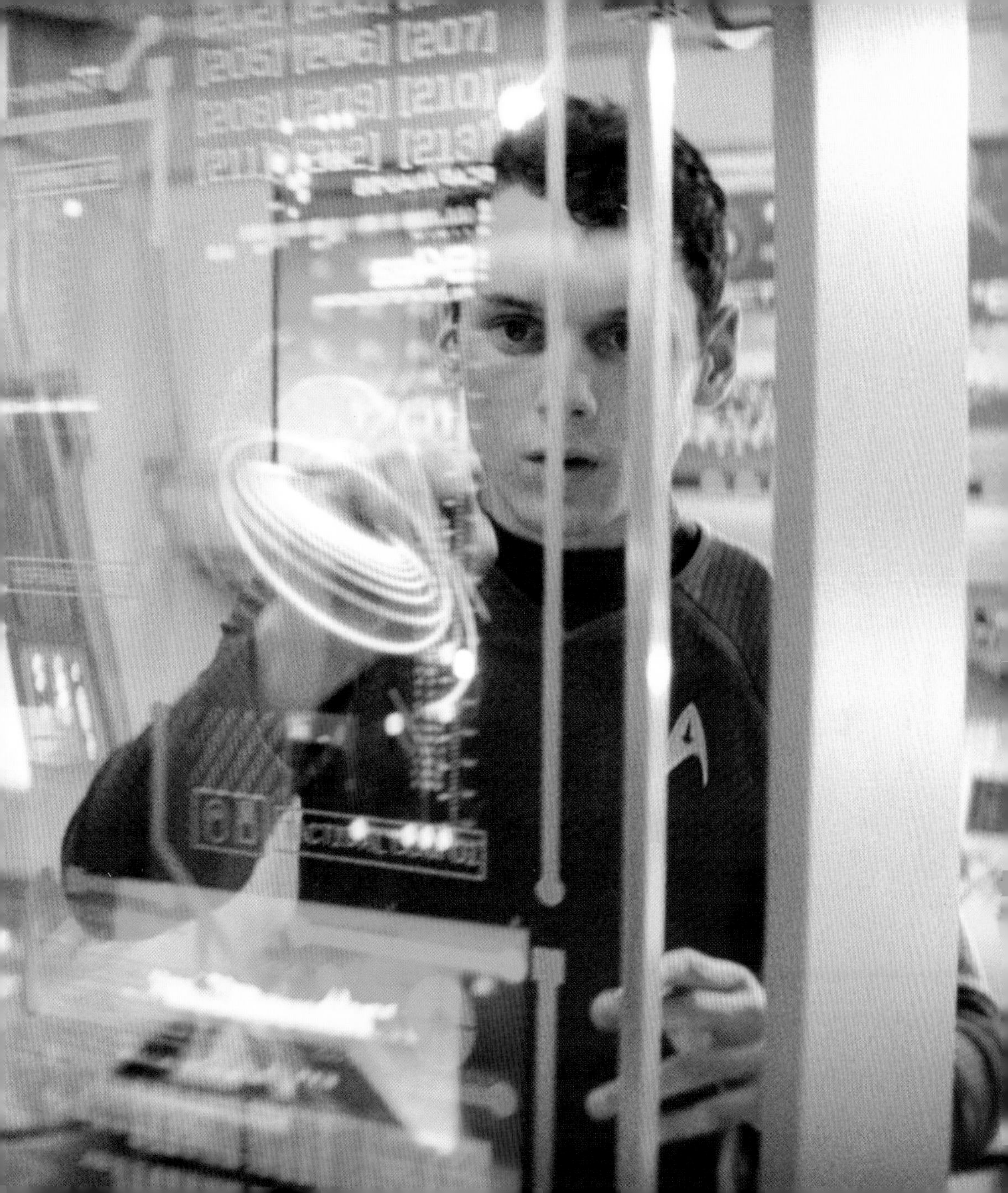

KEENSER'S STORY

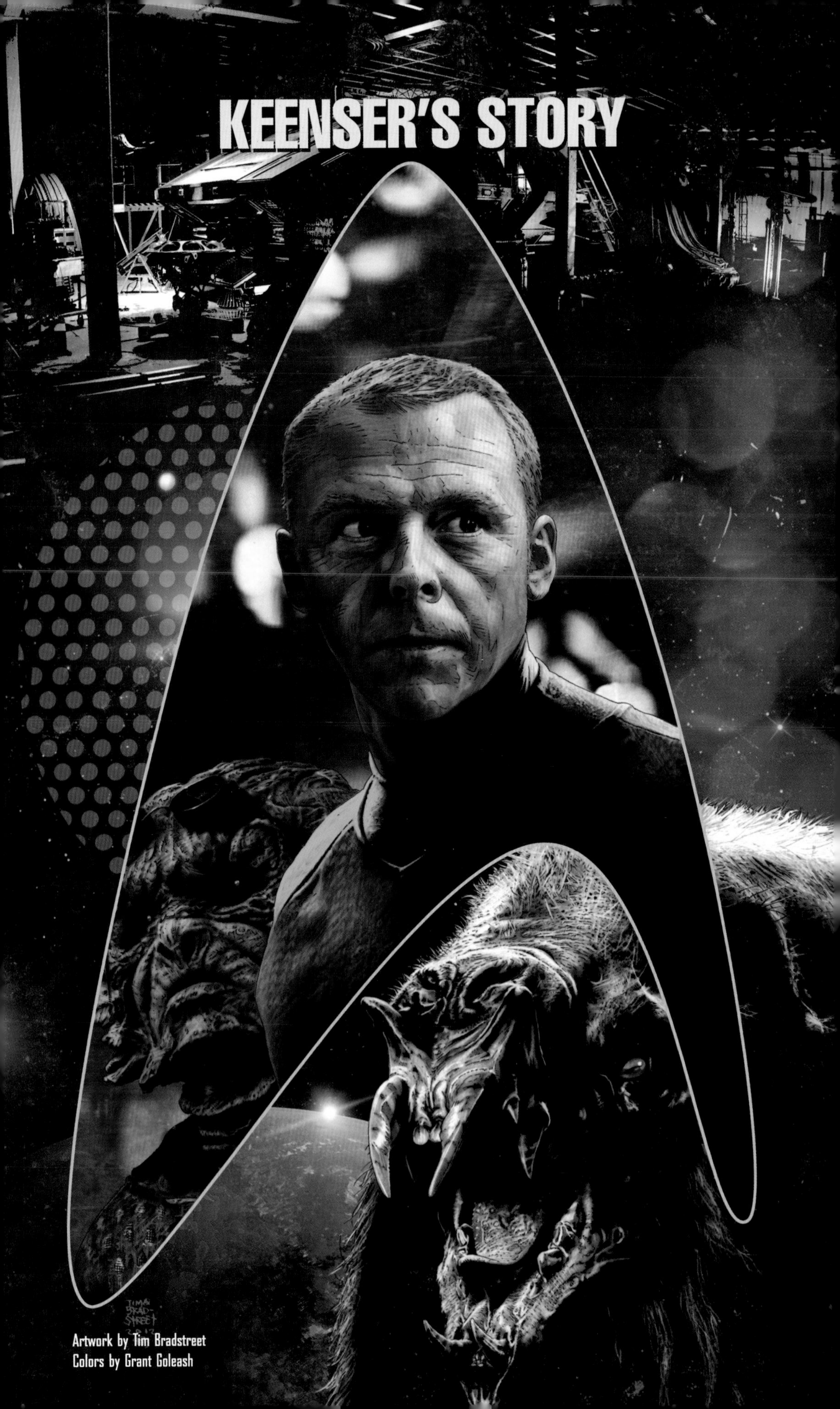

Artwork by Tim Bradstreet
Colors by Grant Goleash

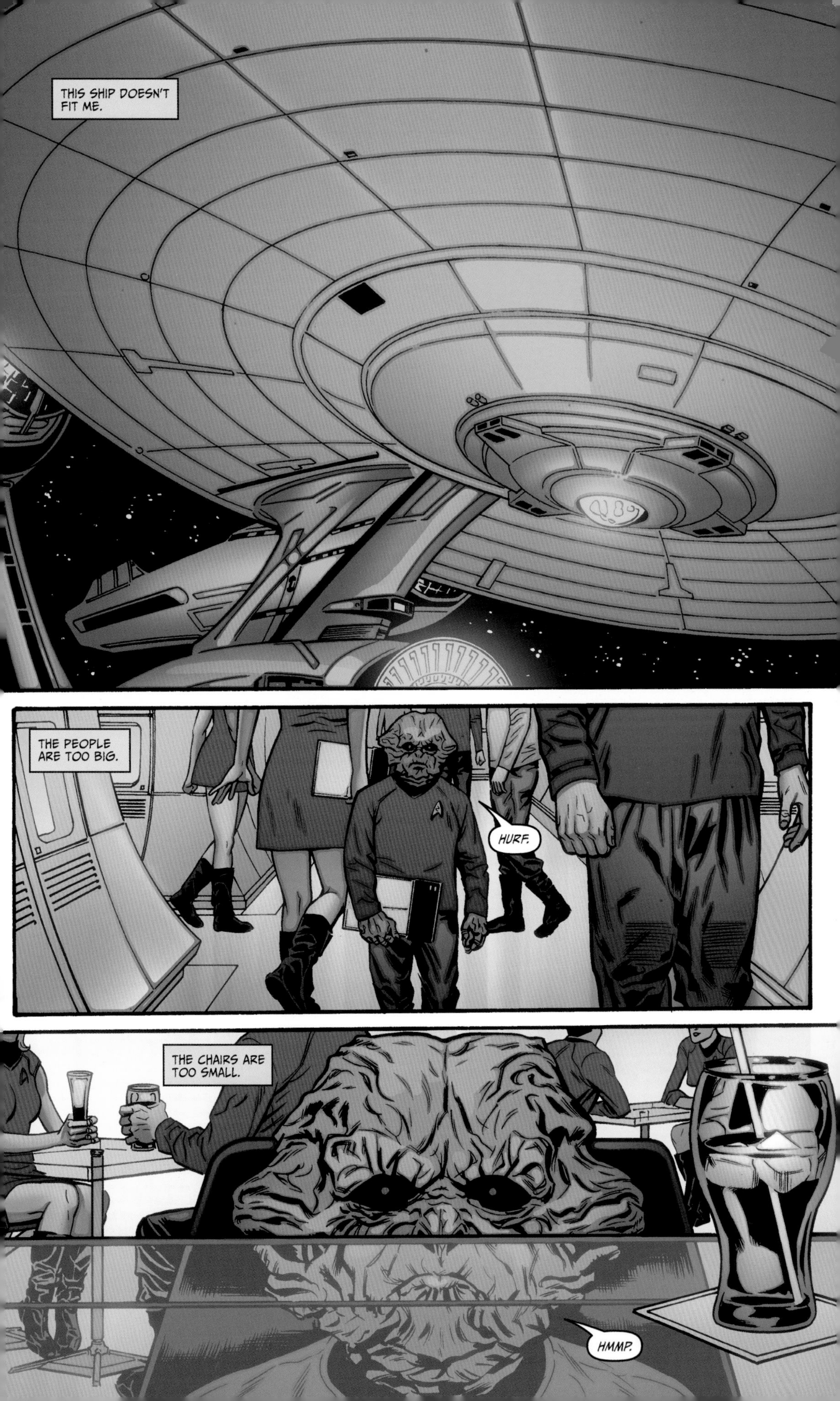
THIS SHIP DOESN'T FIT ME.
THE PEOPLE ARE TOO BIG.
HURF.
THE CHAIRS ARE TOO SMALL.
HMMP.

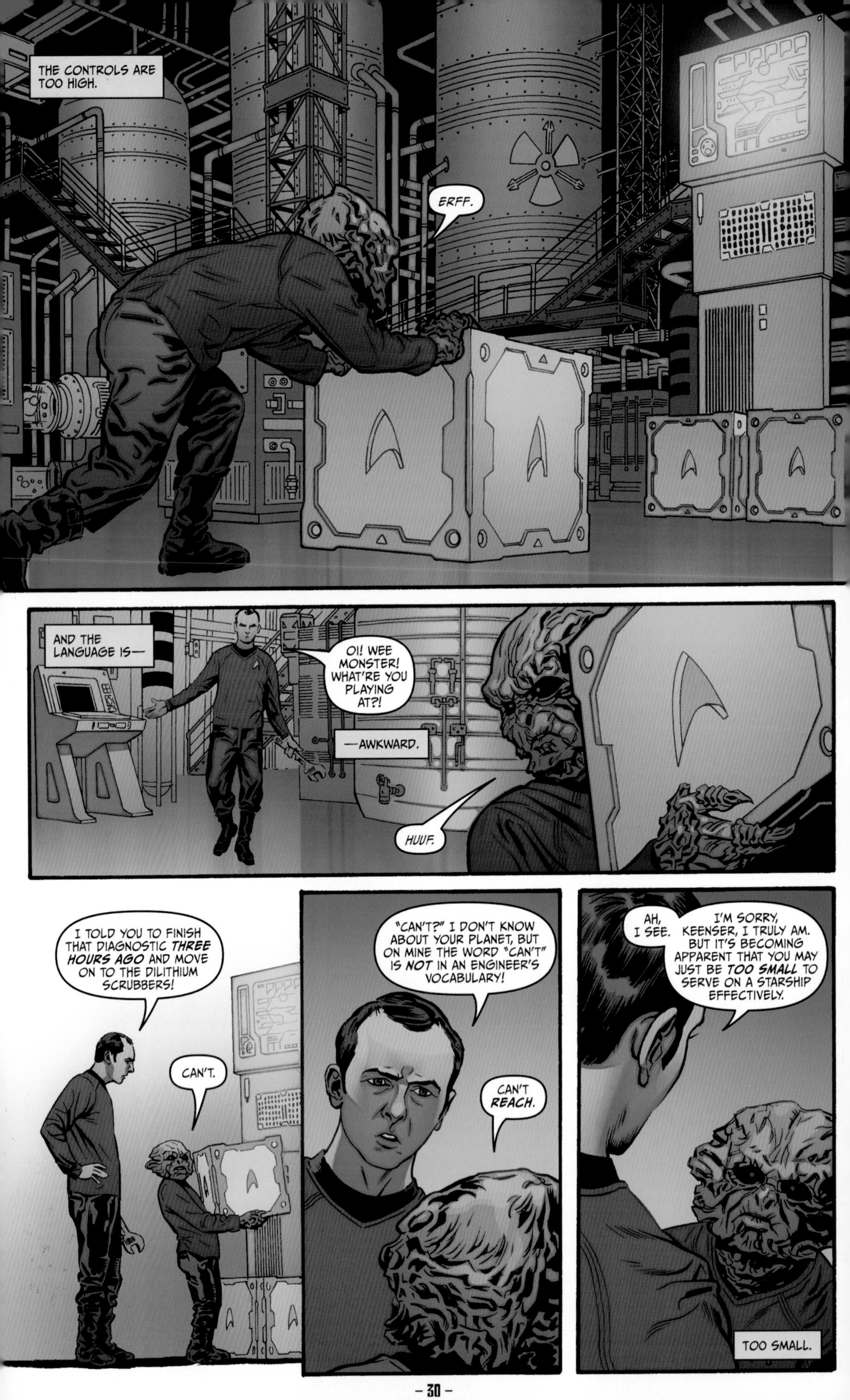
THE CONTROLS ARE TOO HIGH.
ERFF.
AND THE LANGUAGE IS—
OI! WEE MONSTER! WHAT'RE YOU PLAYING AT?!
—AWKWARD.
HUUF.
I TOLD YOU TO FINISH THAT DIAGNOSTIC THREE HOURS AGO AND MOVE ON TO THE DILITHIUM SCRUBBERS!
CAN'T.
"CAN'T?" I DON'T KNOW ABOUT YOUR PLANET, BUT ON MINE THE WORD "CAN'T" IS NOT IN AN ENGINEER'S VOCABULARY!
CAN'T REACH.
AH, I SEE.
I'M SORRY, KEENSER, I TRULY AM. BUT IT'S BECOMING APPARENT THAT YOU MAY JUST BE TOO SMALL TO SERVE ON A STARSHIP EFFECTIVELY.
TOO SMALL.

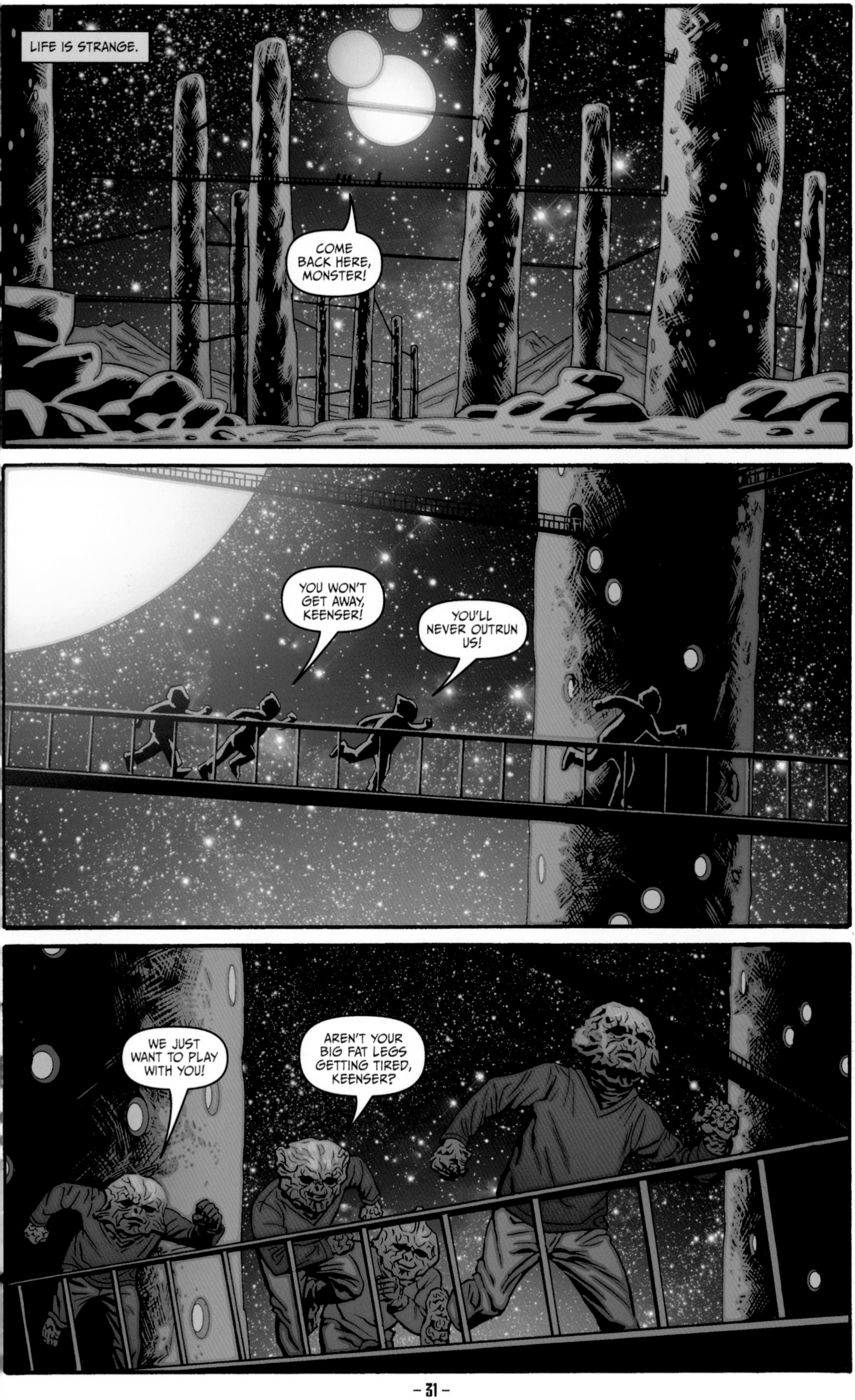
LIFE IS STRANGE.
COME BACK HERE, MONSTER!
YOU WON'T GET AWAY, KEENSER!
YOU'LL NEVER OUTRUN US!
WE JUST WANT TO PLAY WITH YOU!
AREN'T YOUR BIG FAT LEGS GETTING TIRED, KEENSER?

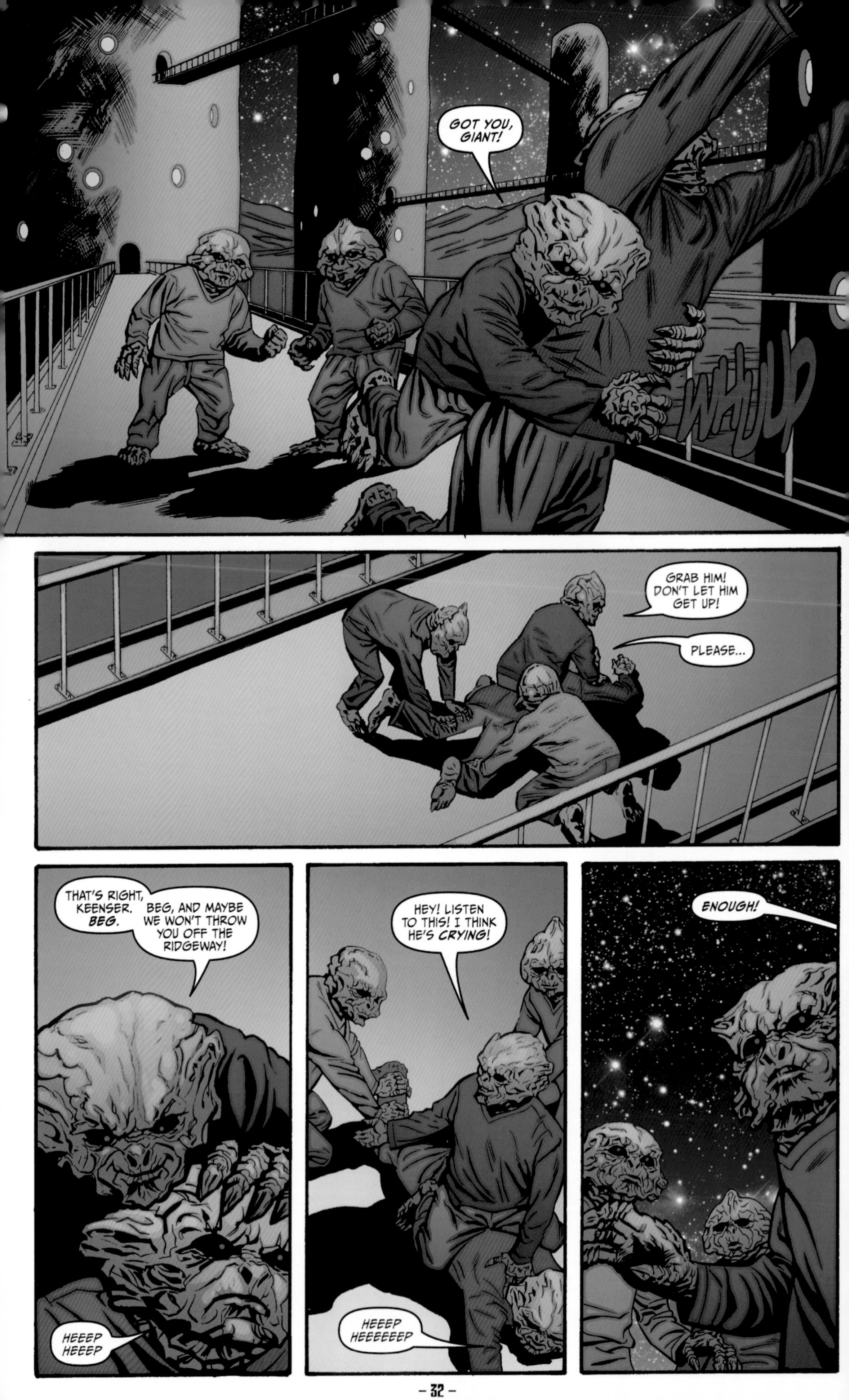
GOT YOU, GIANT!
WHUD
GRAB HIM! DON'T LET HIM GET UP!
PLEASE...
THAT'S RIGHT, KEENSER. *BEG*.
BEG, AND MAYBE WE WON'T THROW YOU OFF THE RIDGEWAY!
HEEEP HEEEP
HEY! LISTEN TO THIS! I THINK HE'S *CRYING*!
HEEEP HEEEEEEP
ENOUGH!

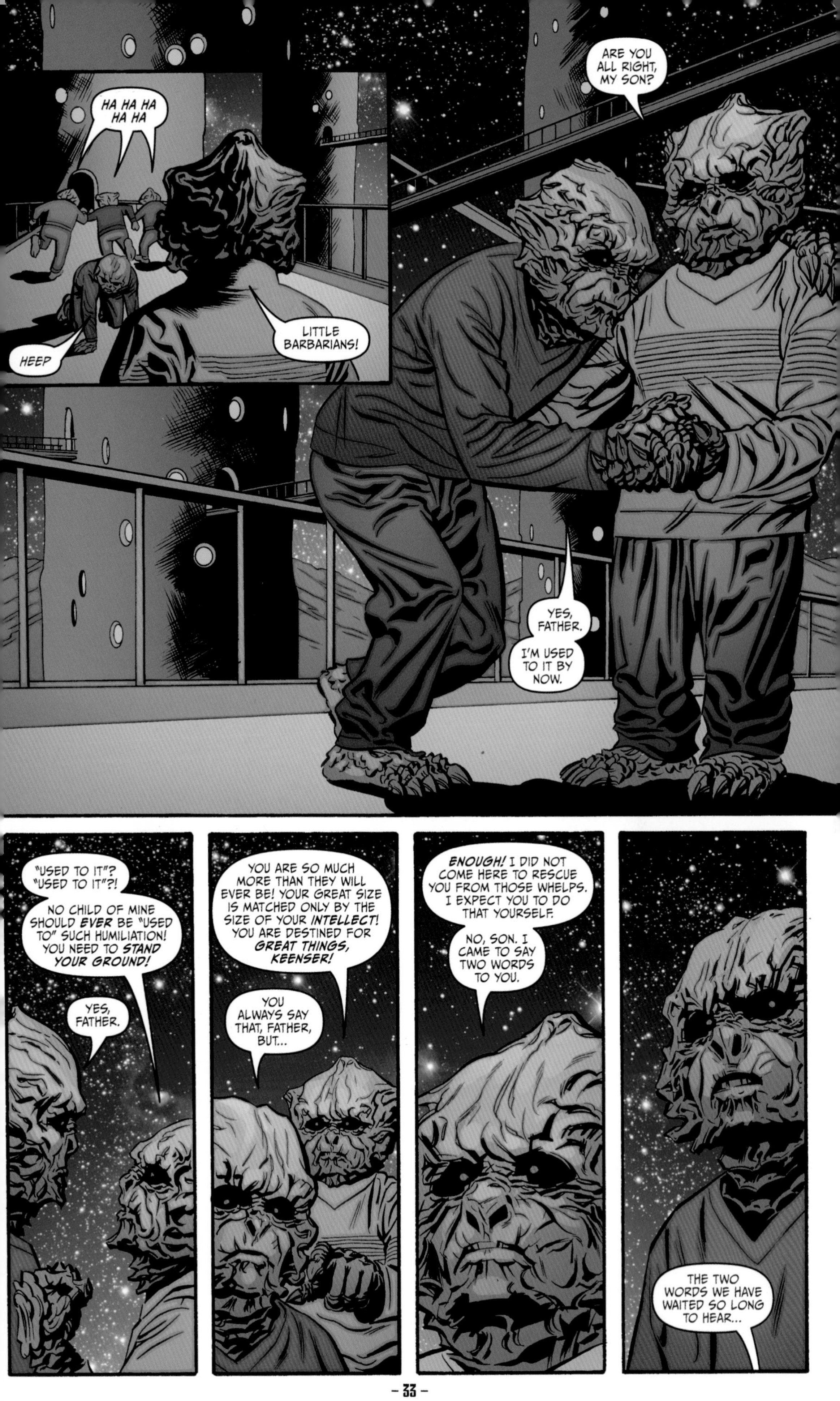
HA HA HA HA HA
HEEP
LITTLE BARBARIANS!
ARE YOU ALL RIGHT, MY SON?
YES, FATHER.
I'M USED TO IT BY NOW.
"USED TO IT"? "USED TO IT"?!
NO CHILD OF MINE SHOULD EVER BE "USED TO" SUCH HUMILIATION! YOU NEED TO STAND YOUR GROUND!
YES, FATHER.
YOU ARE SO MUCH MORE THAN THEY WILL EVER BE! YOUR GREAT SIZE IS MATCHED ONLY BY THE SIZE OF YOUR INTELLECT! YOU ARE DESTINED FOR GREAT THINGS, KEENSER!
YOU ALWAYS SAY THAT, FATHER, BUT...
ENOUGH! I DID NOT COME HERE TO RESCUE YOU FROM THOSE WHELPS. I EXPECT YOU TO DO THAT YOURSELF.
NO, SON. I CAME TO SAY TWO WORDS TO YOU.
THE TWO WORDS WE HAVE WAITED SO LONG TO HEAR...

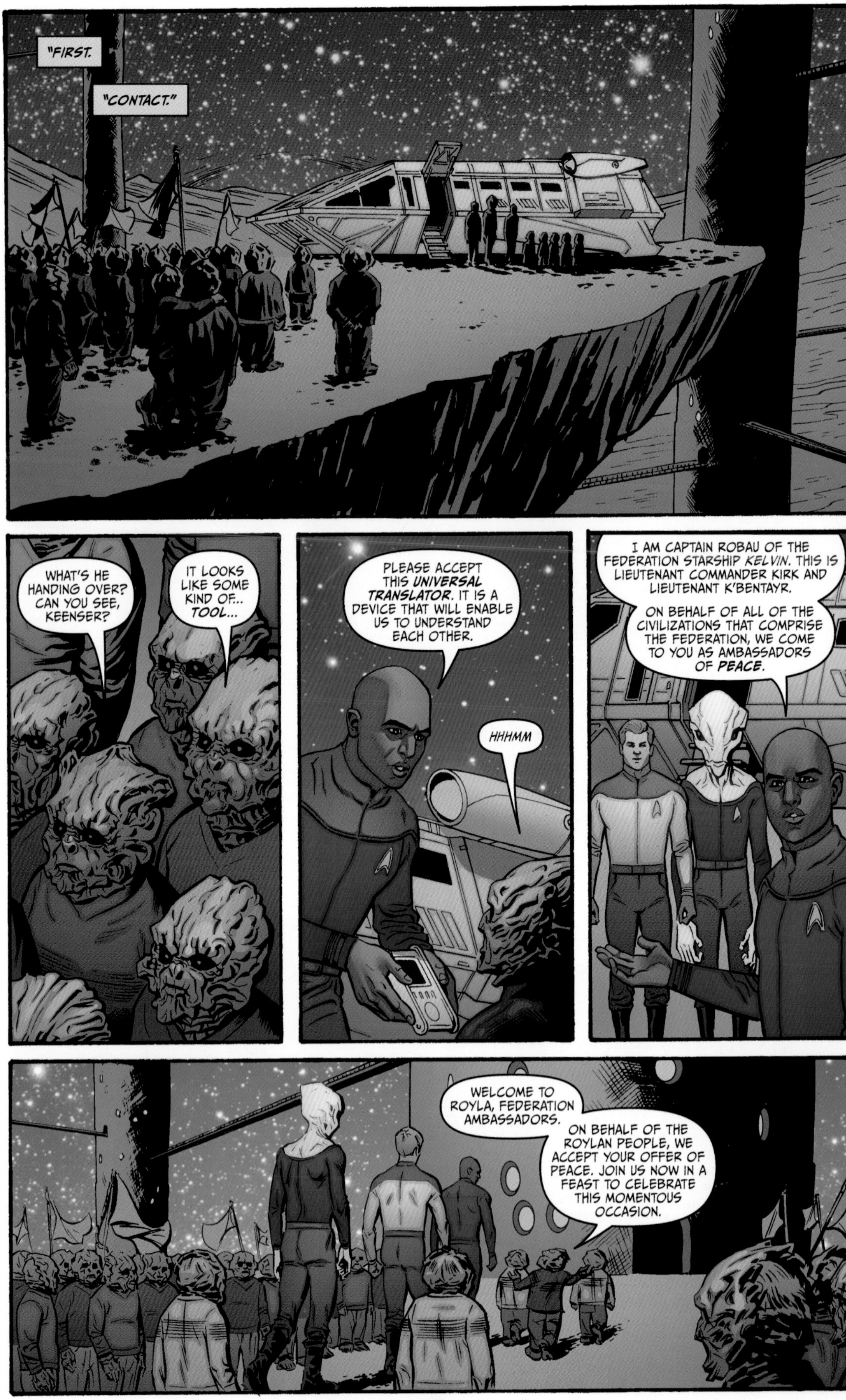
"FIRST.
"CONTACT."
WHAT'S HE HANDING OVER? CAN YOU SEE, KEENSER?
IT LOOKS LIKE SOME KIND OF... TOOL...
PLEASE ACCEPT THIS UNIVERSAL TRANSLATOR. IT IS A DEVICE THAT WILL ENABLE US TO UNDERSTAND EACH OTHER.
HHHMM
I AM CAPTAIN ROBAU OF THE FEDERATION STARSHIP KELVIN. THIS IS LIEUTENANT COMMANDER KIRK AND LIEUTENANT K'BENTAYR.
ON BEHALF OF ALL OF THE CIVILIZATIONS THAT COMPRISE THE FEDERATION, WE COME TO YOU AS AMBASSADORS OF PEACE.
WELCOME TO ROYLA, FEDERATION AMBASSADORS.
ON BEHALF OF THE ROYLAN PEOPLE, WE ACCEPT YOUR OFFER OF PEACE. JOIN US NOW IN A FEAST TO CELEBRATE THIS MOMENTOUS OCCASION.

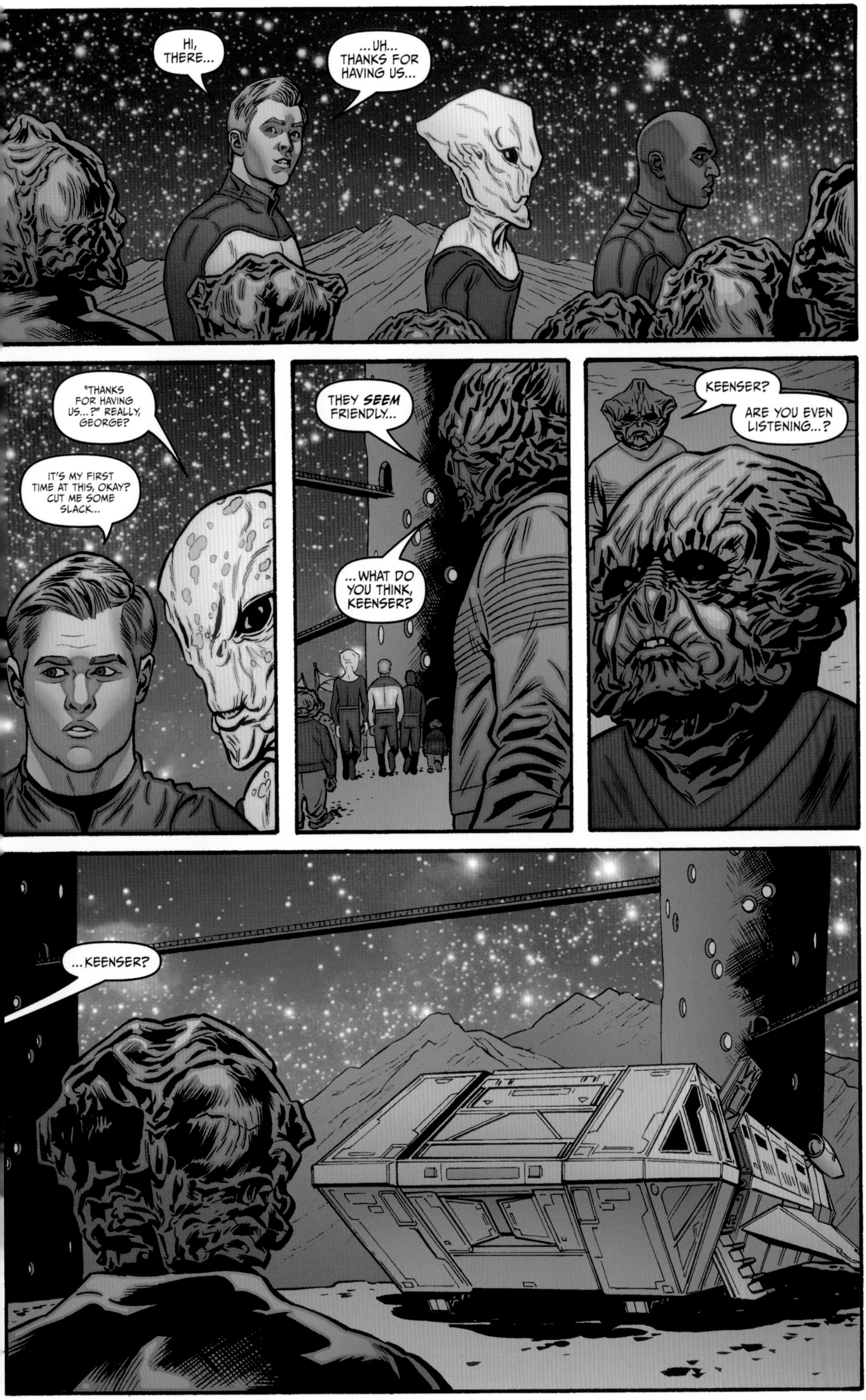
HI, THERE...
...UH... THANKS FOR HAVING US...
"THANKS FOR HAVING US...?" REALLY, GEORGE?
IT'S MY FIRST TIME AT THIS, OKAY? CUT ME SOME SLACK...
THEY SEEM FRIENDLY...
...WHAT DO YOU THINK, KEENSER?
KEENSER?
ARE YOU EVEN LISTENING...?
...KEENSER?

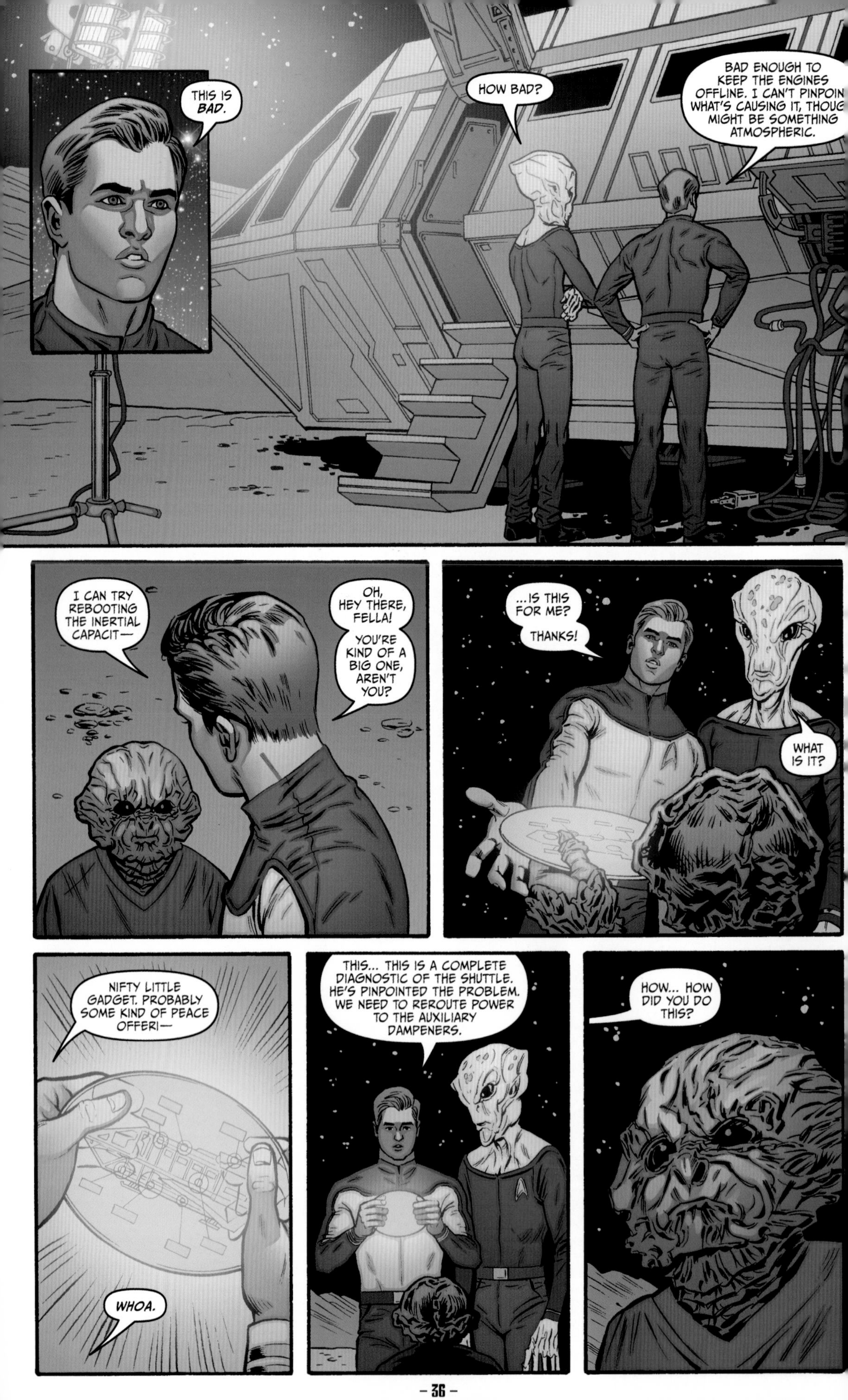
THIS IS BAD.
HOW BAD?
BAD ENOUGH TO KEEP THE ENGINES OFFLINE. I CAN'T PINPOIN WHAT'S CAUSING IT, THOUG MIGHT BE SOMETHING ATMOSPHERIC.
I CAN TRY REBOOTING THE INERTIAL CAPACIT—
OH, HEY THERE, FELLA!
YOU'RE KIND OF A BIG ONE, AREN'T YOU?
...IS THIS FOR ME?
THANKS!
WHAT IS IT?
NIFTY LITTLE GADGET. PROBABLY SOME KIND OF PEACE OFFERI—
WHOA.
THIS... THIS IS A COMPLETE DIAGNOSTIC OF THE SHUTTLE. HE'S PINPOINTED THE PROBLEM. WE NEED TO REROUTE POWER TO THE AUXILIARY DAMPENERS.
HOW... HOW DID YOU DO THIS?

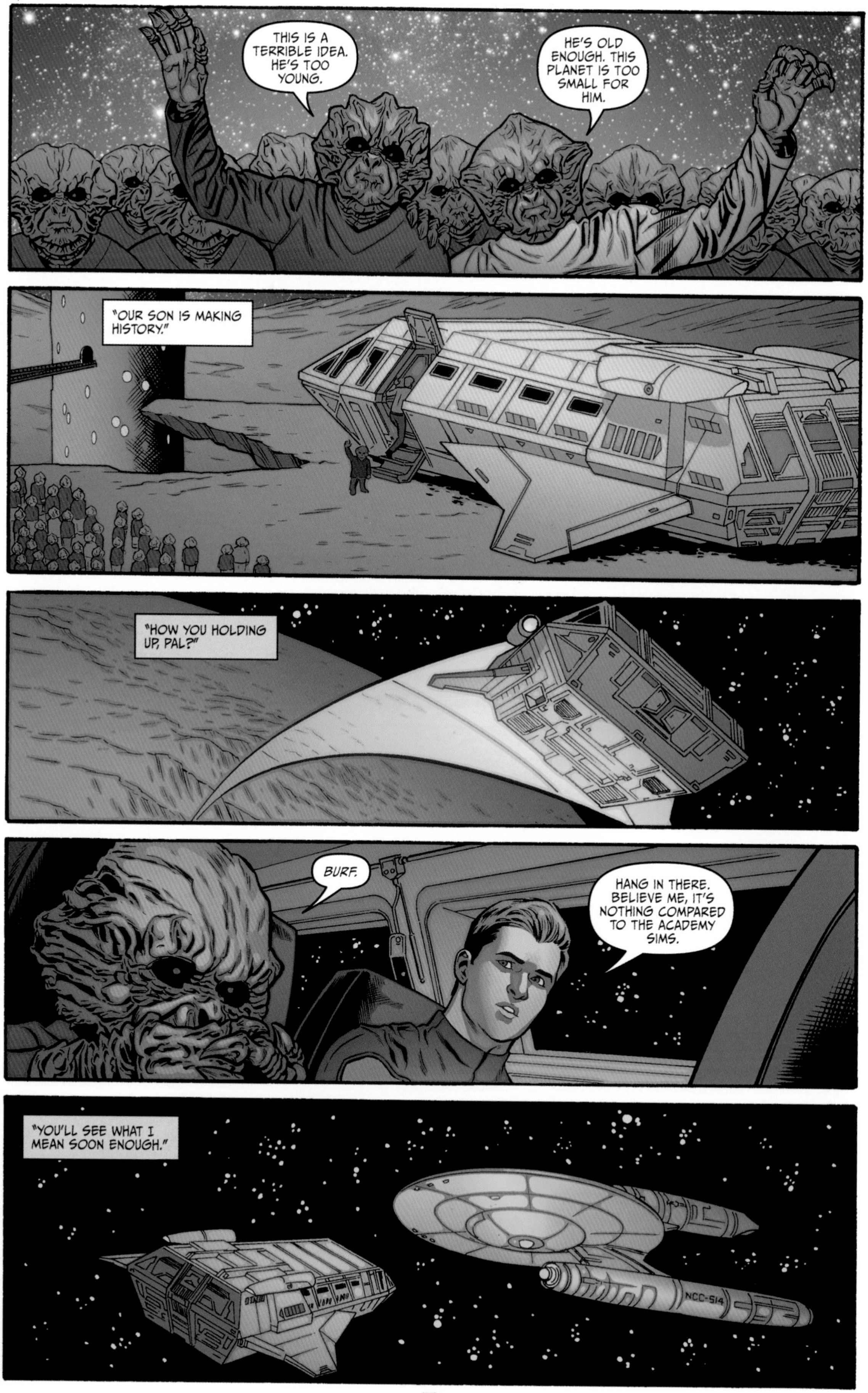
THIS IS A TERRIBLE IDEA. HE'S TOO YOUNG.
HE'S OLD ENOUGH. THIS PLANET IS TOO SMALL FOR HIM.
"OUR SON IS MAKING HISTORY."
"HOW YOU HOLDING UP, PAL?"
BURF.
HANG IN THERE. BELIEVE ME, IT'S NOTHING COMPARED TO THE ACADEMY SIMS.
"YOU'LL SEE WHAT I MEAN SOON ENOUGH."
NCC-514

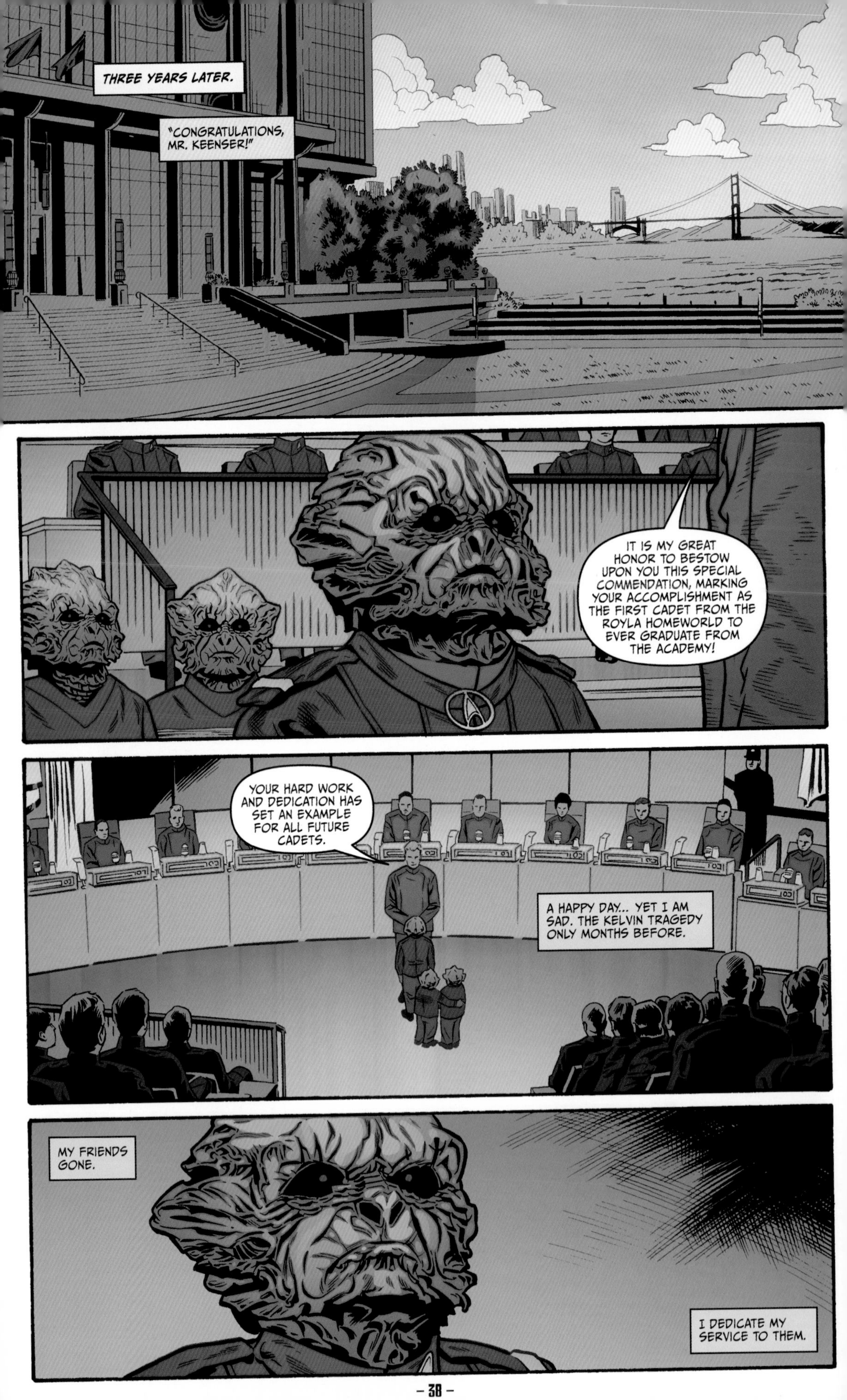
THREE YEARS LATER.
"CONGRATULATIONS, MR. KEENSER!"
IT IS MY GREAT HONOR TO BESTOW UPON YOU THIS SPECIAL COMMENDATION, MARKING YOUR ACCOMPLISHMENT AS THE FIRST CADET FROM THE ROYLA HOMEWORLD TO EVER GRADUATE FROM THE ACADEMY!
YOUR HARD WORK AND DEDICATION HAS SET AN EXAMPLE FOR ALL FUTURE CADETS.
A HAPPY DAY... YET I AM SAD. THE KELVIN TRAGEDY ONLY MONTHS BEFORE.
MY FRIENDS GONE.
I DEDICATE MY SERVICE TO THEM.

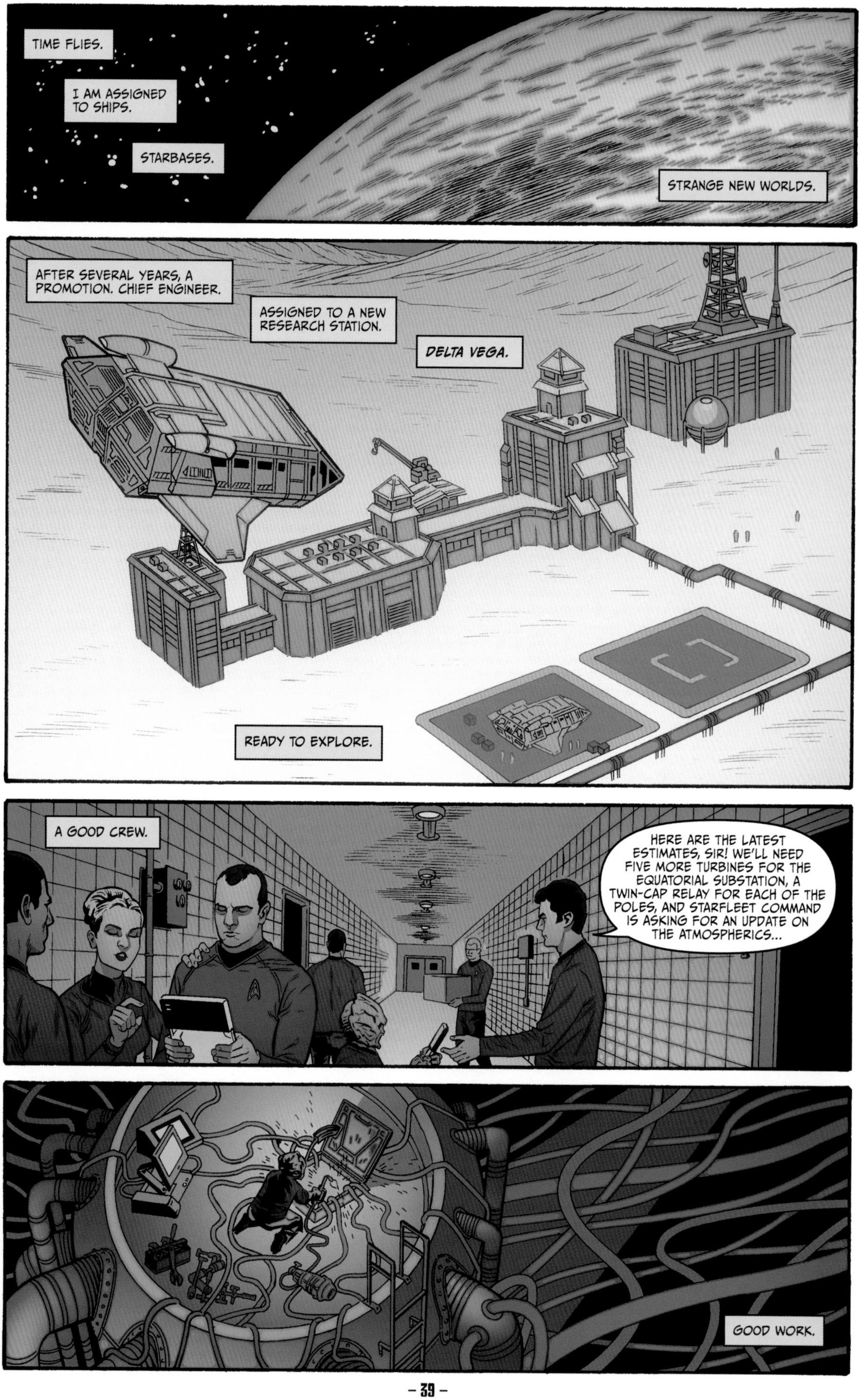
TIME FLIES.
I AM ASSIGNED TO SHIPS.
STARBASES.
STRANGE NEW WORLDS.
AFTER SEVERAL YEARS, A PROMOTION. CHIEF ENGINEER.
ASSIGNED TO A NEW RESEARCH STATION.
DELTA VEGA.
READY TO EXPLORE.
A GOOD CREW.
HERE ARE THE LATEST ESTIMATES, SIR! WE'LL NEED FIVE MORE TURBINES FOR THE EQUATORIAL SUBSTATION, A TWIN-CAP RELAY FOR EACH OF THE POLES, AND STARFLEET COMMAND IS ASKING FOR AN UPDATE ON THE ATMOSPHERICS...
GOOD WORK.

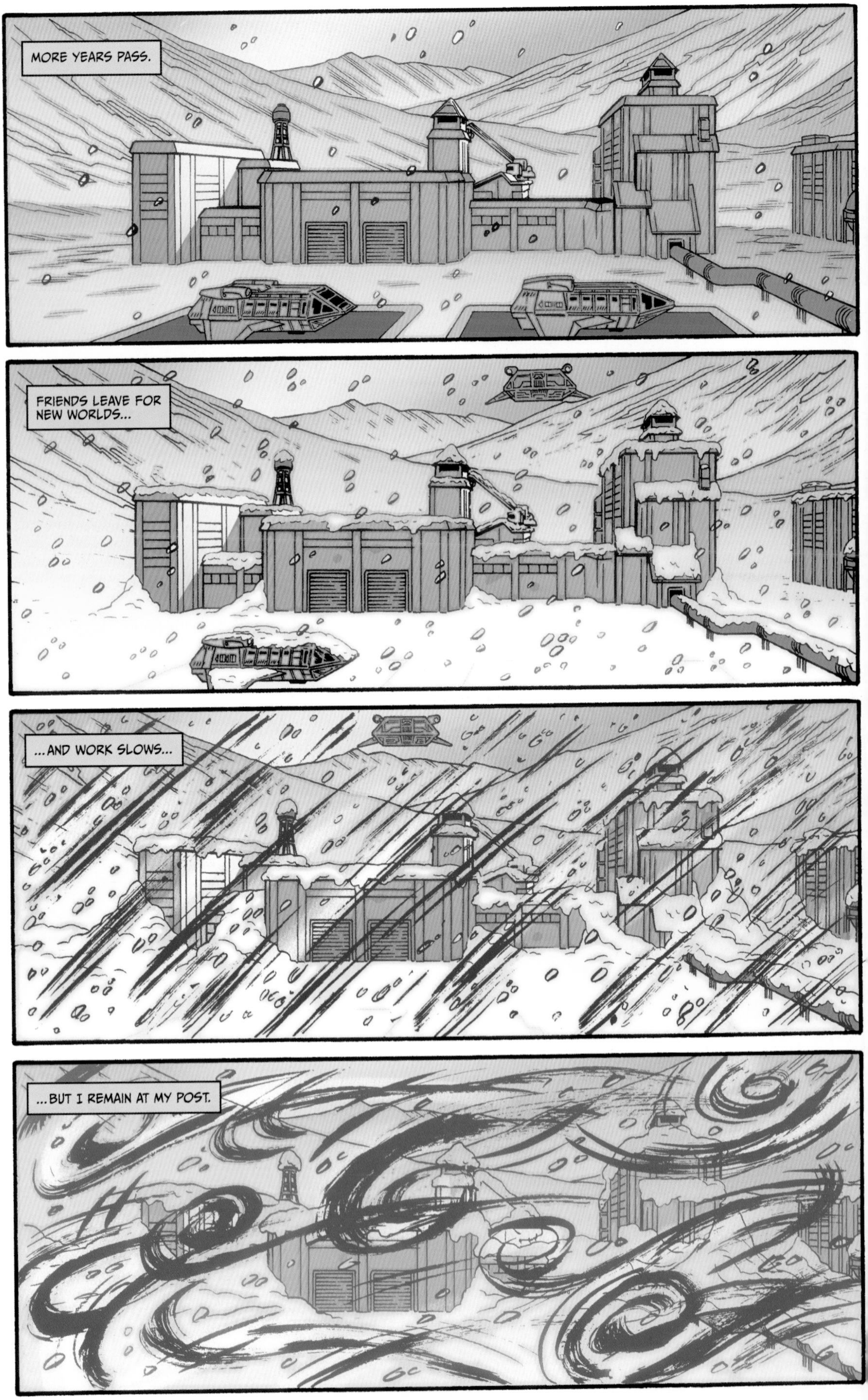
MORE YEARS PASS.
FRIENDS LEAVE FOR NEW WORLDS...
...AND WORK SLOWS...
...BUT I REMAIN AT MY POST.

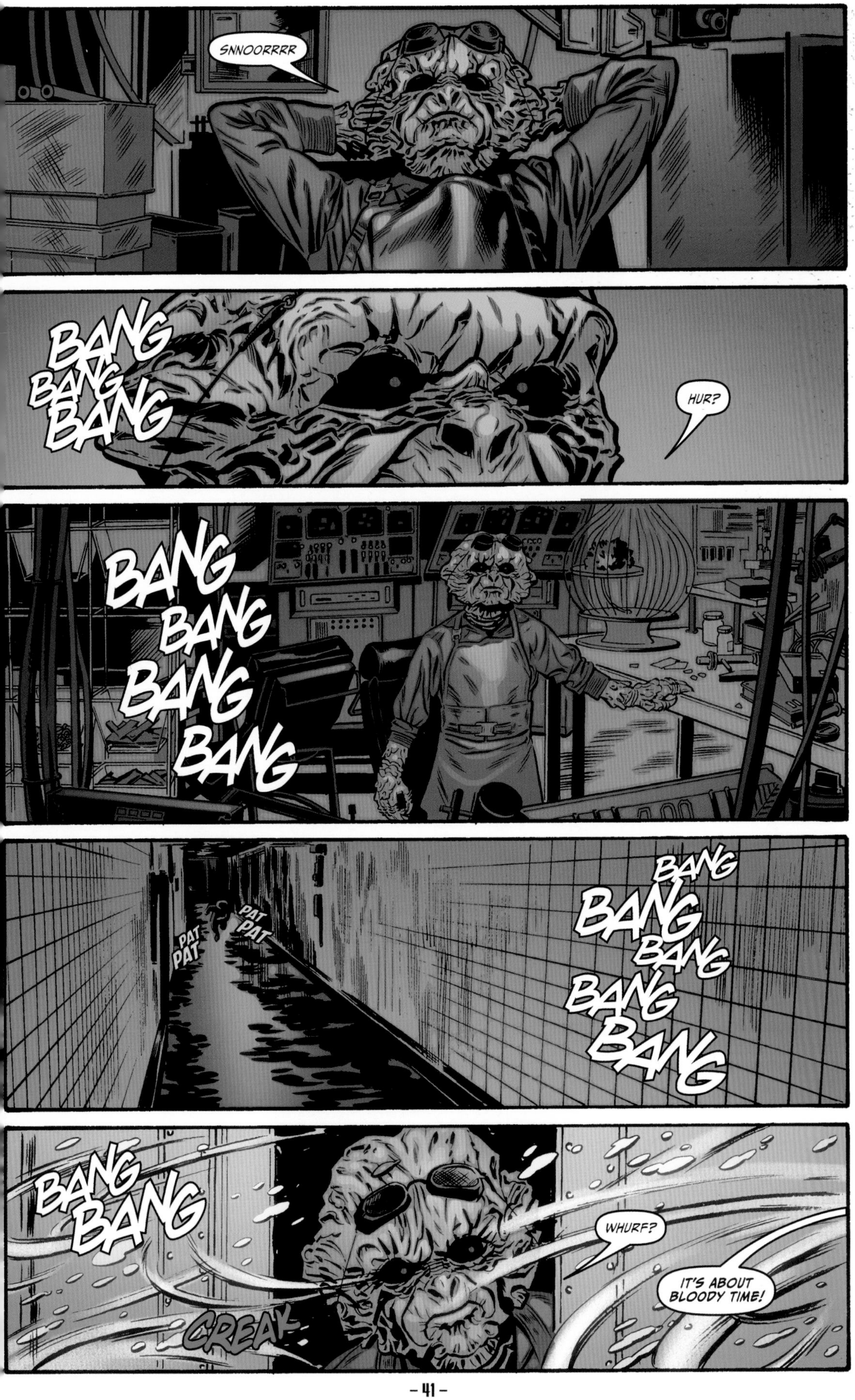
SNNOORRRR
BANG BANG BANG
HUR?
BANG BANG BANG BANG
PAT PAT
PAT PAT
BANG BANG BANG BANG BANG
BANG BANG
CREAK
WHURF?
IT'S ABOUT BLOODY TIME!

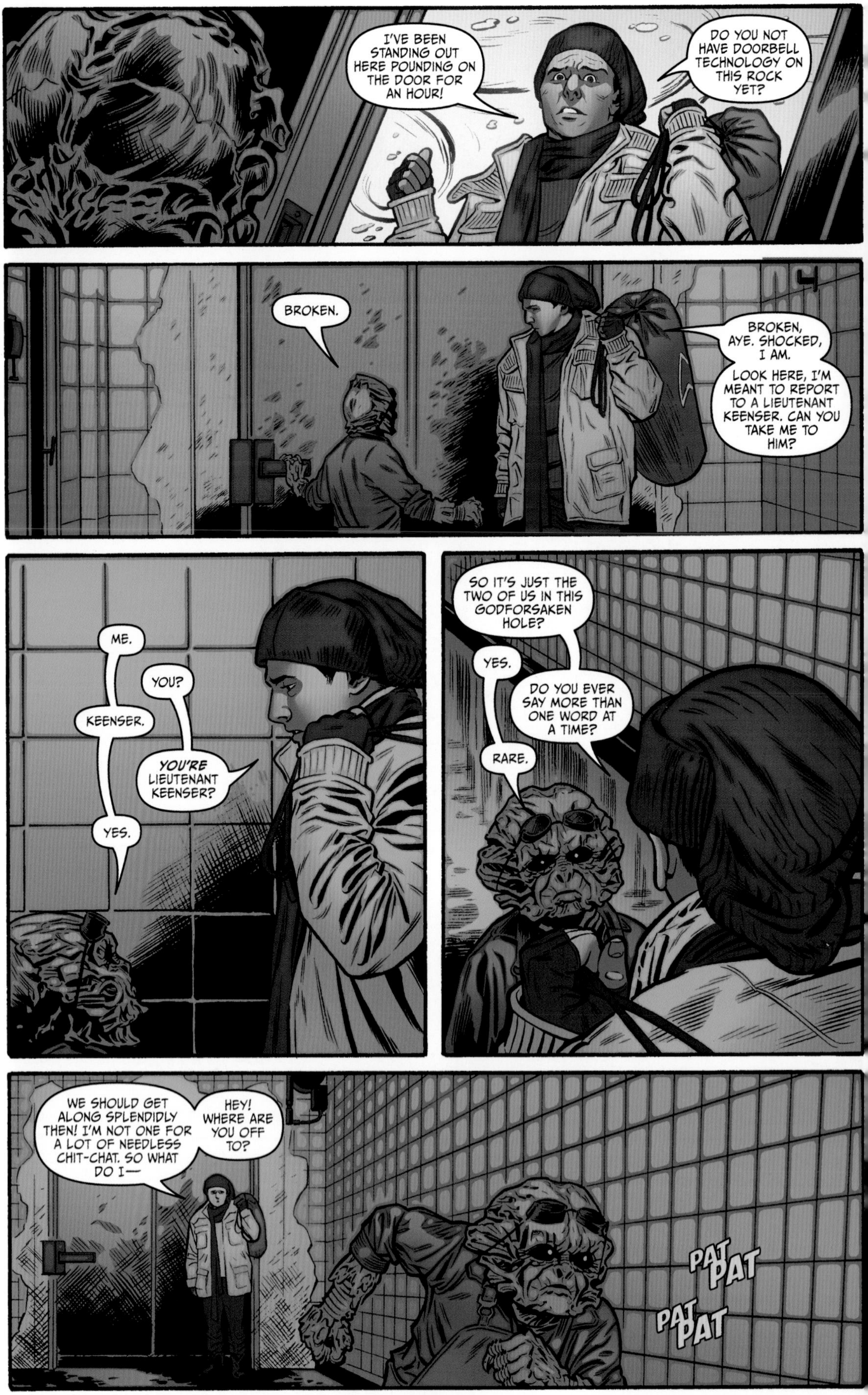
I'VE BEEN STANDING OUT HERE POUNDING ON THE DOOR FOR AN HOUR!
DO YOU NOT HAVE DOORBELL TECHNOLOGY ON THIS ROCK YET?
BROKEN.
BROKEN, AYE. SHOCKED, I AM.
LOOK HERE, I'M MEANT TO REPORT TO A LIEUTENANT KEENSER. CAN YOU TAKE ME TO HIM?
ME.
YOU?
KEENSER.
YOU'RE LIEUTENANT KEENSER?
YES.
SO IT'S JUST THE TWO OF US IN THIS GODFORSAKEN HOLE?
YES.
DO YOU EVER SAY MORE THAN ONE WORD AT A TIME?
RARE.
WE SHOULD GET ALONG SPLENDIDLY THEN! I'M NOT ONE FOR A LOT OF NEEDLESS CHIT-CHAT. SO WHAT DO I—
HEY! WHERE ARE YOU OFF TO?
PAT PAT
PAT PAT

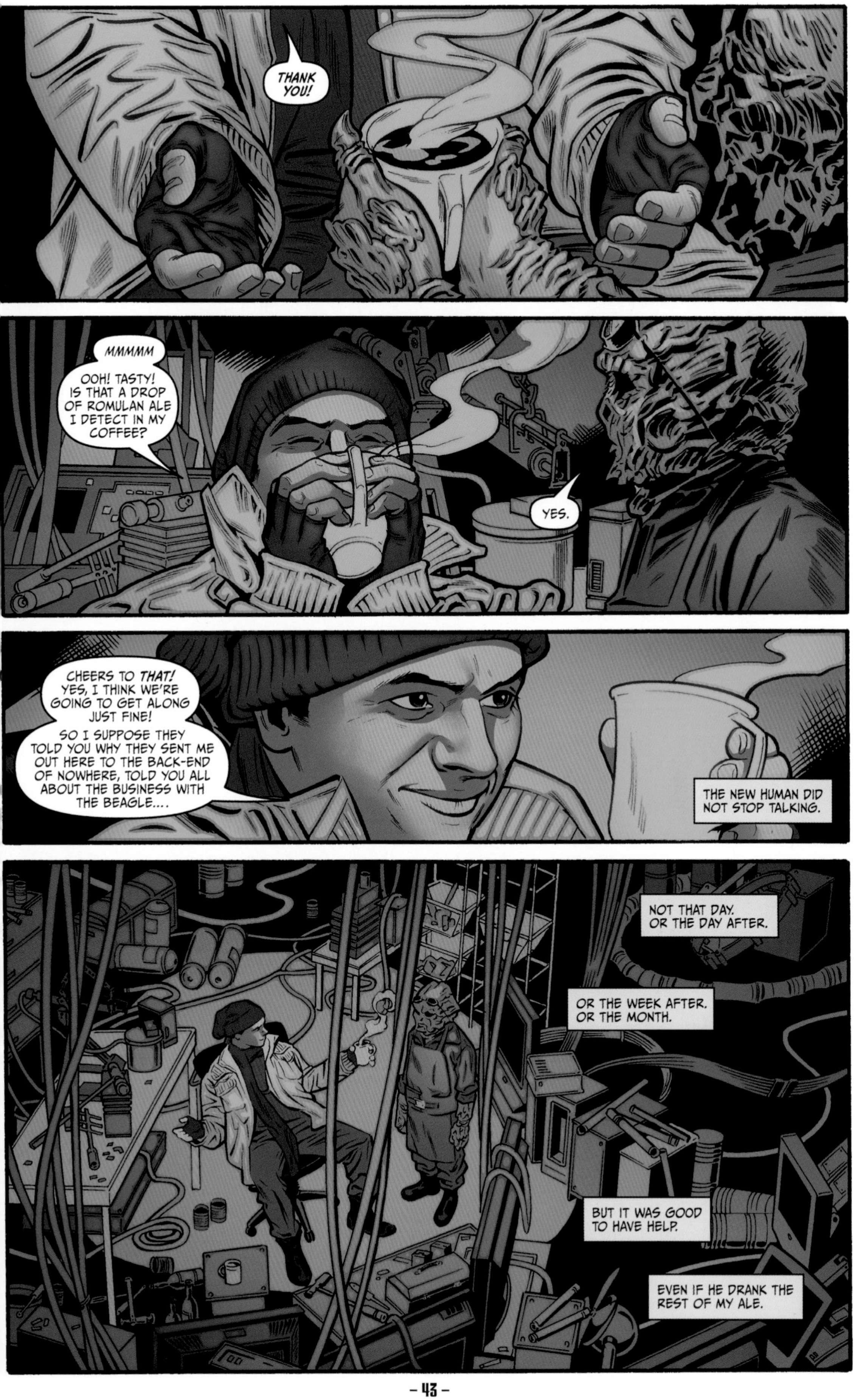
THANK YOU!
MMMMM
OOH! TASTY! IS THAT A DROP OF ROMULAN ALE I DETECT IN MY COFFEE?
YES.
CHEERS TO *THAT!* YES, I THINK WE'RE GOING TO GET ALONG JUST FINE!
SO I SUPPOSE THEY TOLD YOU WHY THEY SENT ME OUT HERE TO THE BACK-END OF NOWHERE, TOLD YOU ALL ABOUT THE BUSINESS WITH THE BEAGLE....
THE NEW HUMAN DID NOT STOP TALKING.
NOT THAT DAY. OR THE DAY AFTER.
OR THE WEEK AFTER. OR THE MONTH.
BUT IT WAS GOOD TO HAVE HELP.
EVEN IF HE DRANK THE REST OF MY ALE.

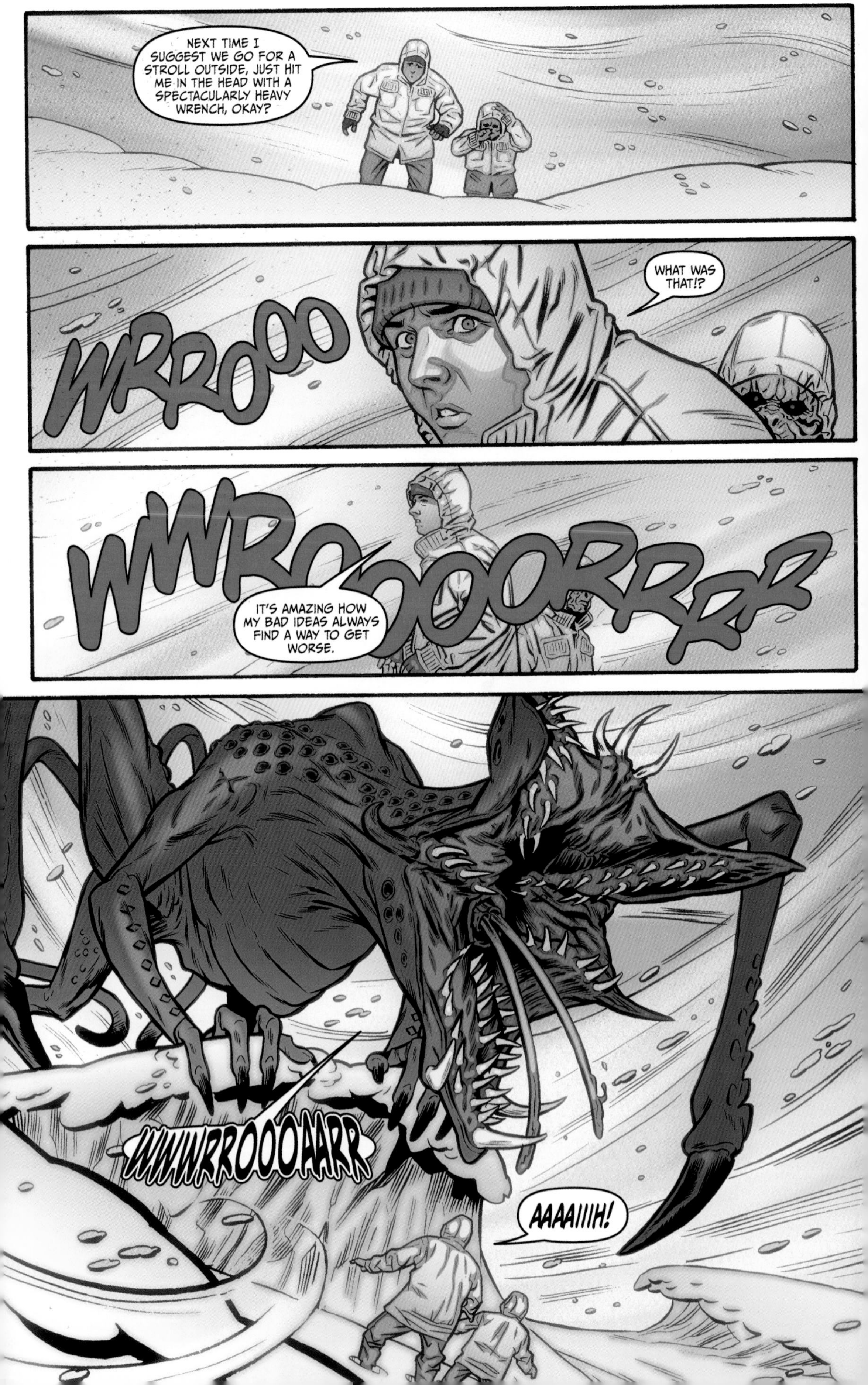
NEXT TIME I SUGGEST WE GO FOR A STROLL OUTSIDE, JUST HIT ME IN THE HEAD WITH A SPECTACULARLY HEAVY WRENCH, OKAY?
WRROOO
WHAT WAS THAT!?
WWROOOORRRR
IT'S AMAZING HOW MY BAD IDEAS ALWAYS FIND A WAY TO GET WORSE.
WWWRROOOAARR
AAAAIIIH!

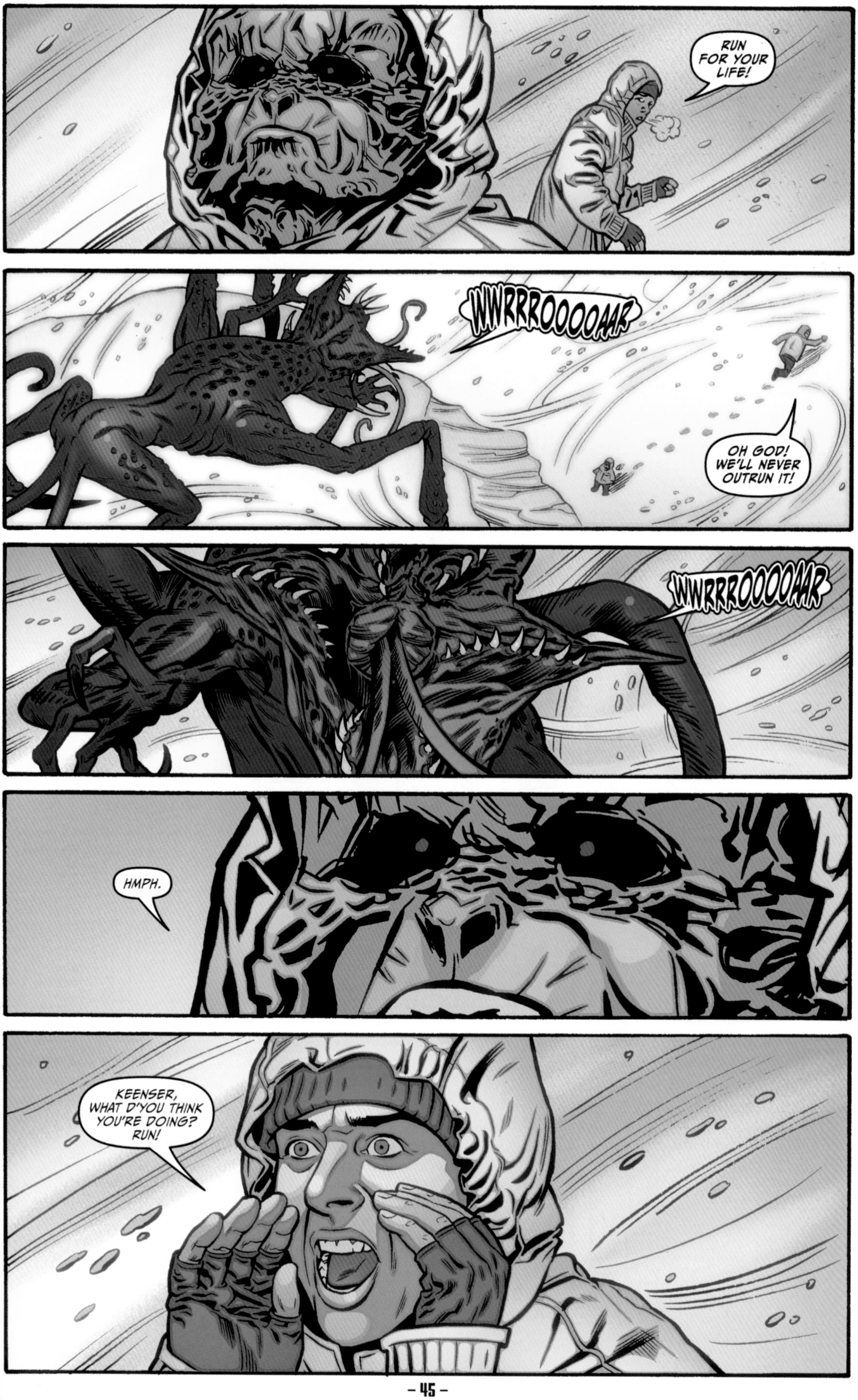
RUN FOR YOUR LIFE!
WWRRROOOOAAR
OH GOD! WE'LL NEVER OUTRUN IT!
WWRRROOOOAAR
HMPH.
KEENSER, WHAT D'YOU THINK YOU'RE DOING? RUN!

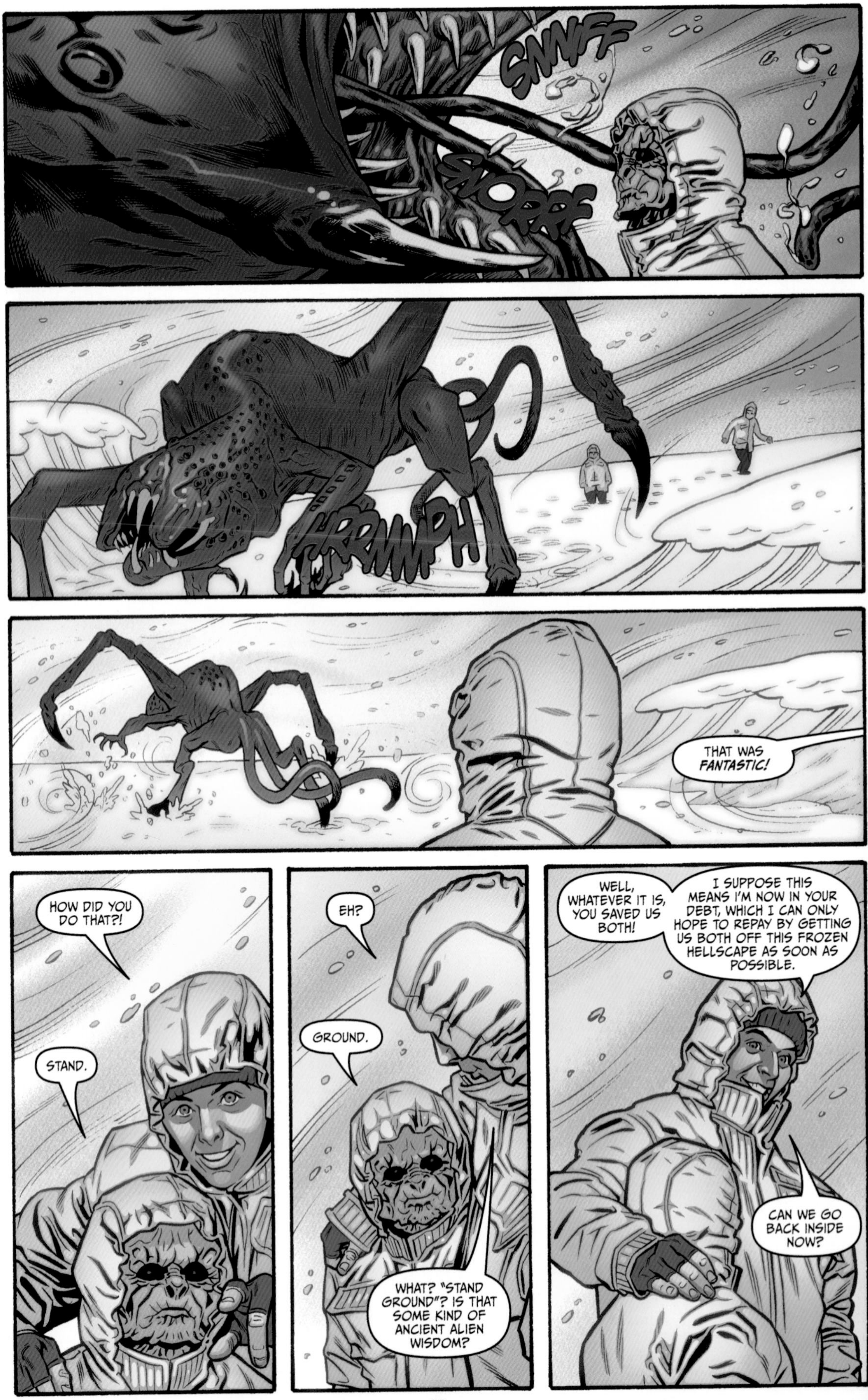
SNNIFF
SNORRF
HRRMMPH
THAT WAS FANTASTIC!
HOW DID YOU DO THAT?!
STAND.
EH?
GROUND.
WHAT? "STAND GROUND"? IS THAT SOME KIND OF ANCIENT ALIEN WISDOM?
WELL, WHATEVER IT IS, YOU SAVED US BOTH!
I SUPPOSE THIS MEANS I'M NOW IN YOUR DEBT, WHICH I CAN ONLY HOPE TO REPAY BY GETTING US BOTH OFF THIS FROZEN HELLSCAPE AS SOON AS POSSIBLE.
CAN WE GO BACK INSIDE NOW?

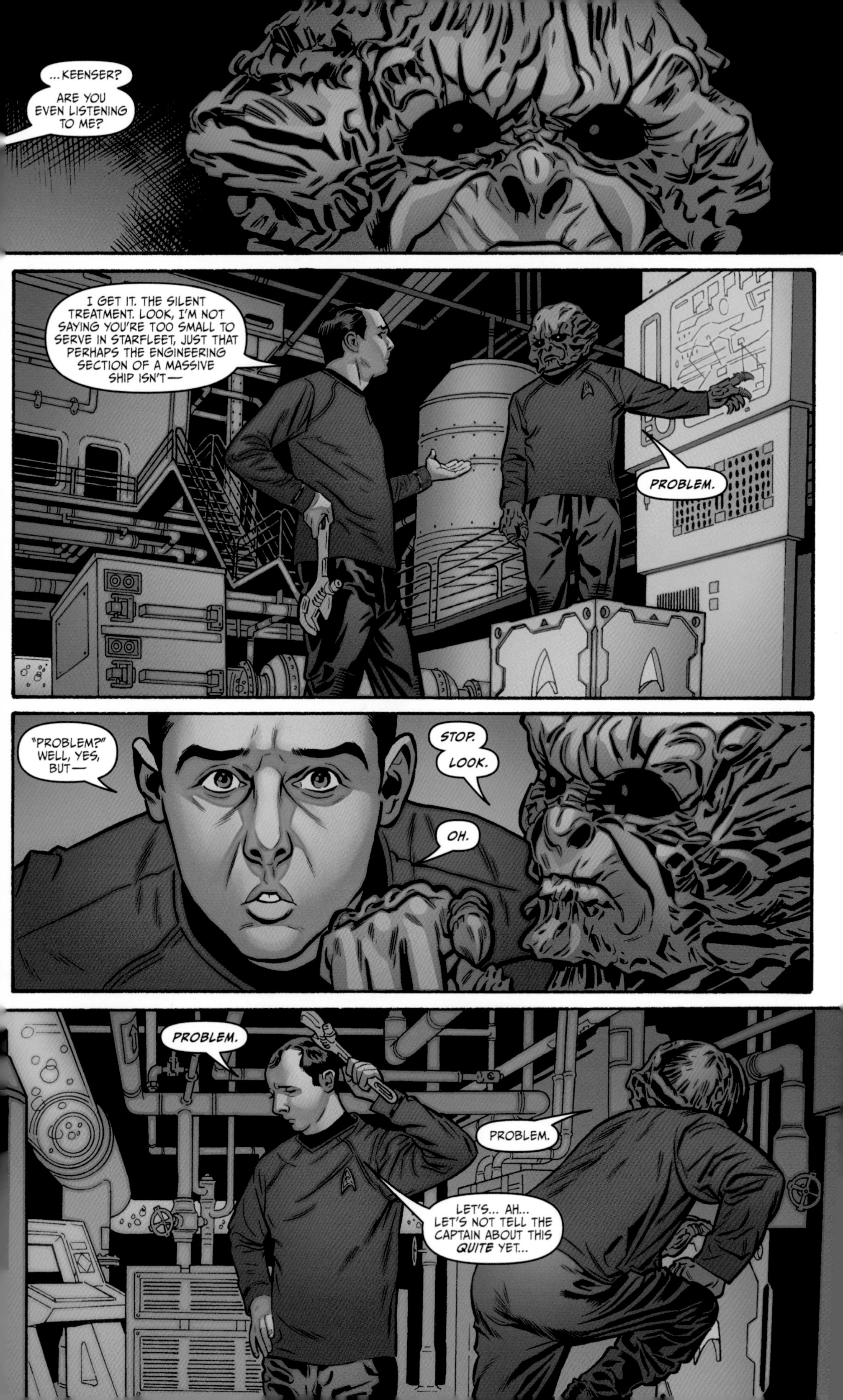
...KEENSER?
ARE YOU EVEN LISTENING TO ME?
I GET IT. THE SILENT TREATMENT. LOOK, I'M NOT SAYING YOU'RE TOO SMALL TO SERVE IN STARFLEET, JUST THAT PERHAPS THE ENGINEERING SECTION OF A MASSIVE SHIP ISN'T—
PROBLEM.
"PROBLEM?" WELL, YES, BUT—
STOP.
LOOK.
OH.
PROBLEM.
PROBLEM.
LET'S... AH... LET'S NOT TELL THE CAPTAIN ABOUT THIS QUITE YET...

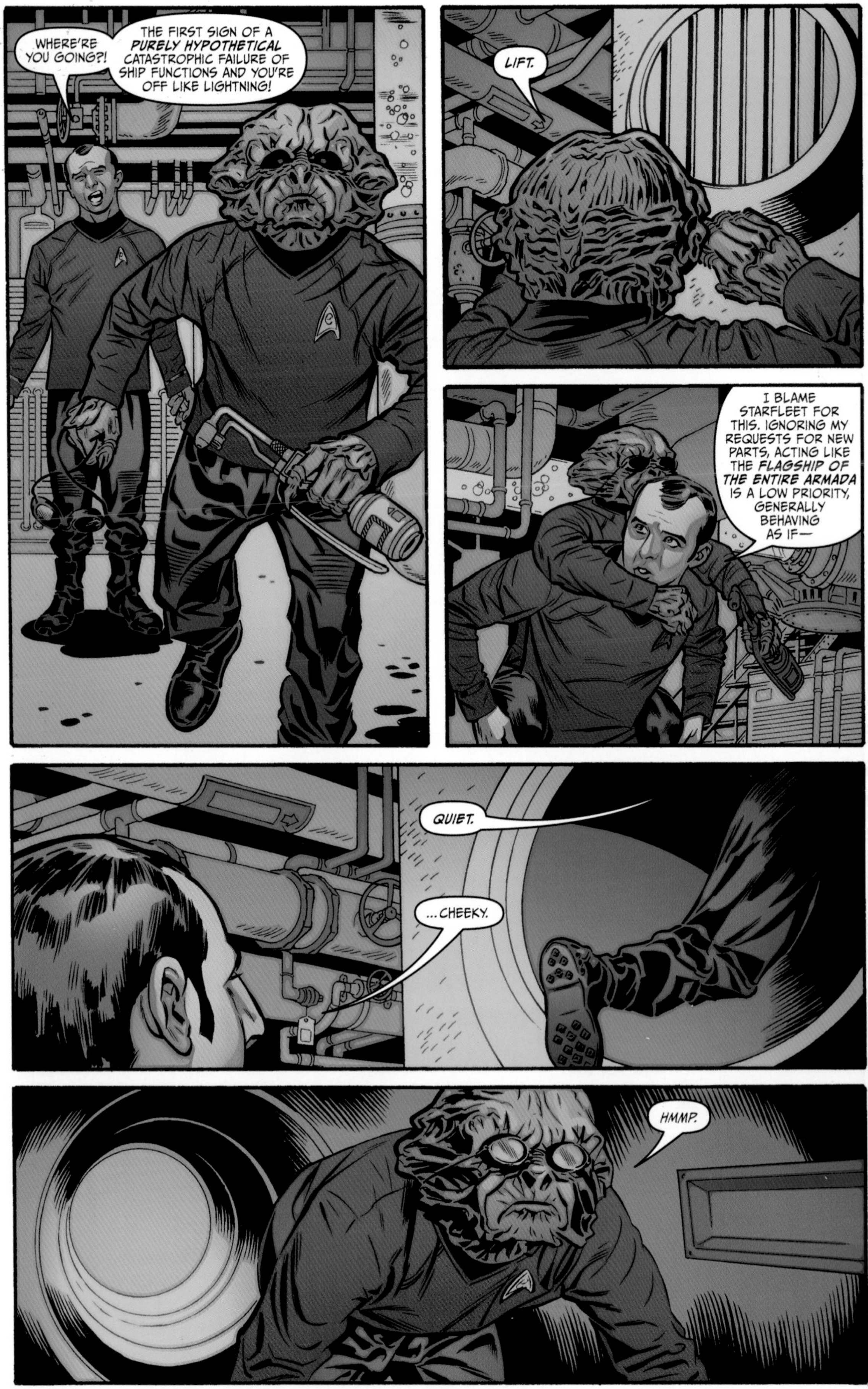
WHERE'RE YOU GOING?!
THE FIRST SIGN OF A PURELY HYPOTHETICAL CATASTROPHIC FAILURE OF SHIP FUNCTIONS AND YOU'RE OFF LIKE LIGHTNING!
LIFT.
I BLAME STARFLEET FOR THIS. IGNORING MY REQUESTS FOR NEW PARTS, ACTING LIKE THE FLAGSHIP OF THE ENTIRE ARMADA IS A LOW PRIORITY, GENERALLY BEHAVING AS IF—
QUIET.
...CHEEKY.
HMMP.

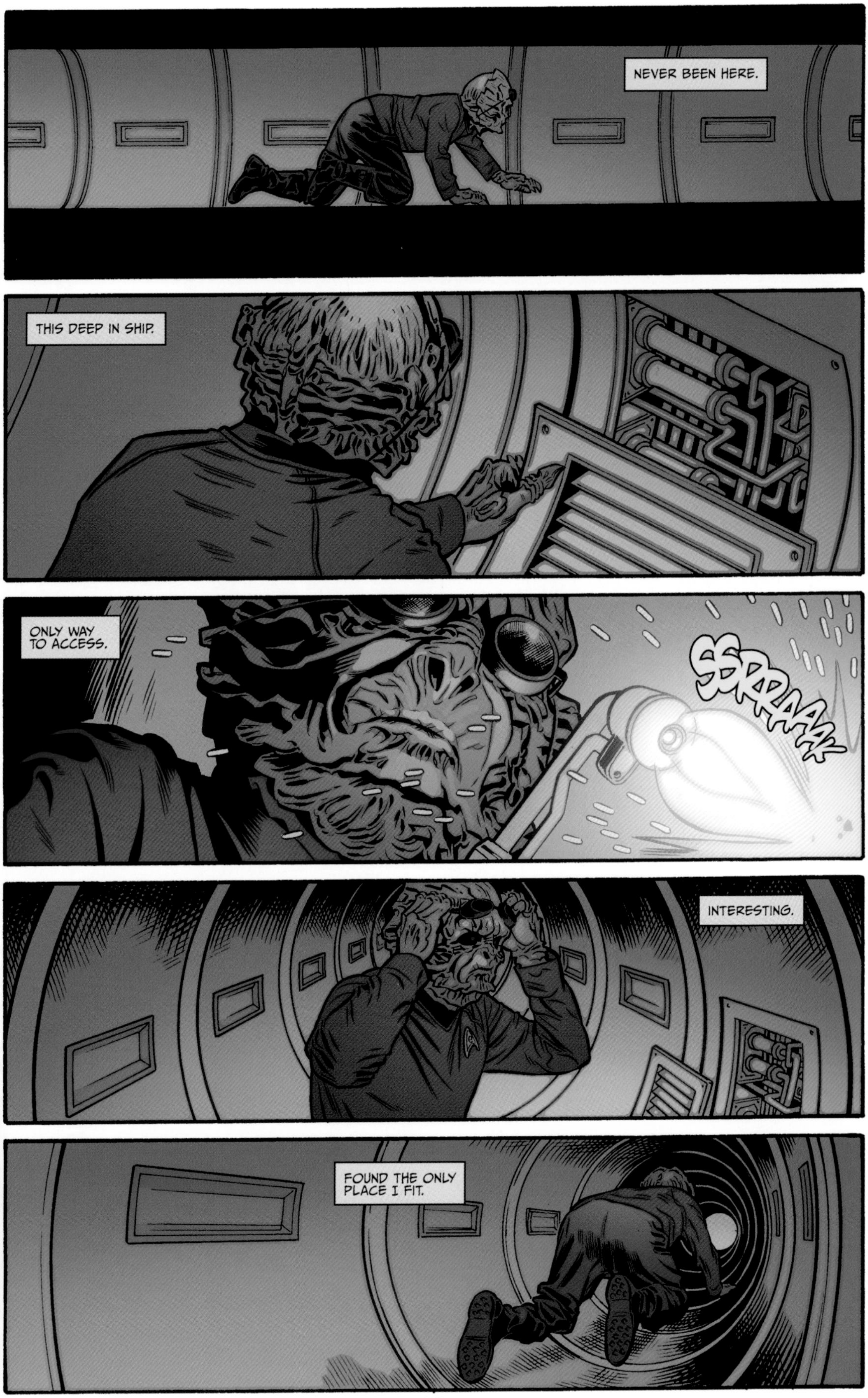

NEVER BEEN HERE.
THIS DEEP IN SHIP.
ONLY WAY TO ACCESS.
SSRRAAAK
INTERESTING.
FOUND THE ONLY PLACE I FIT.

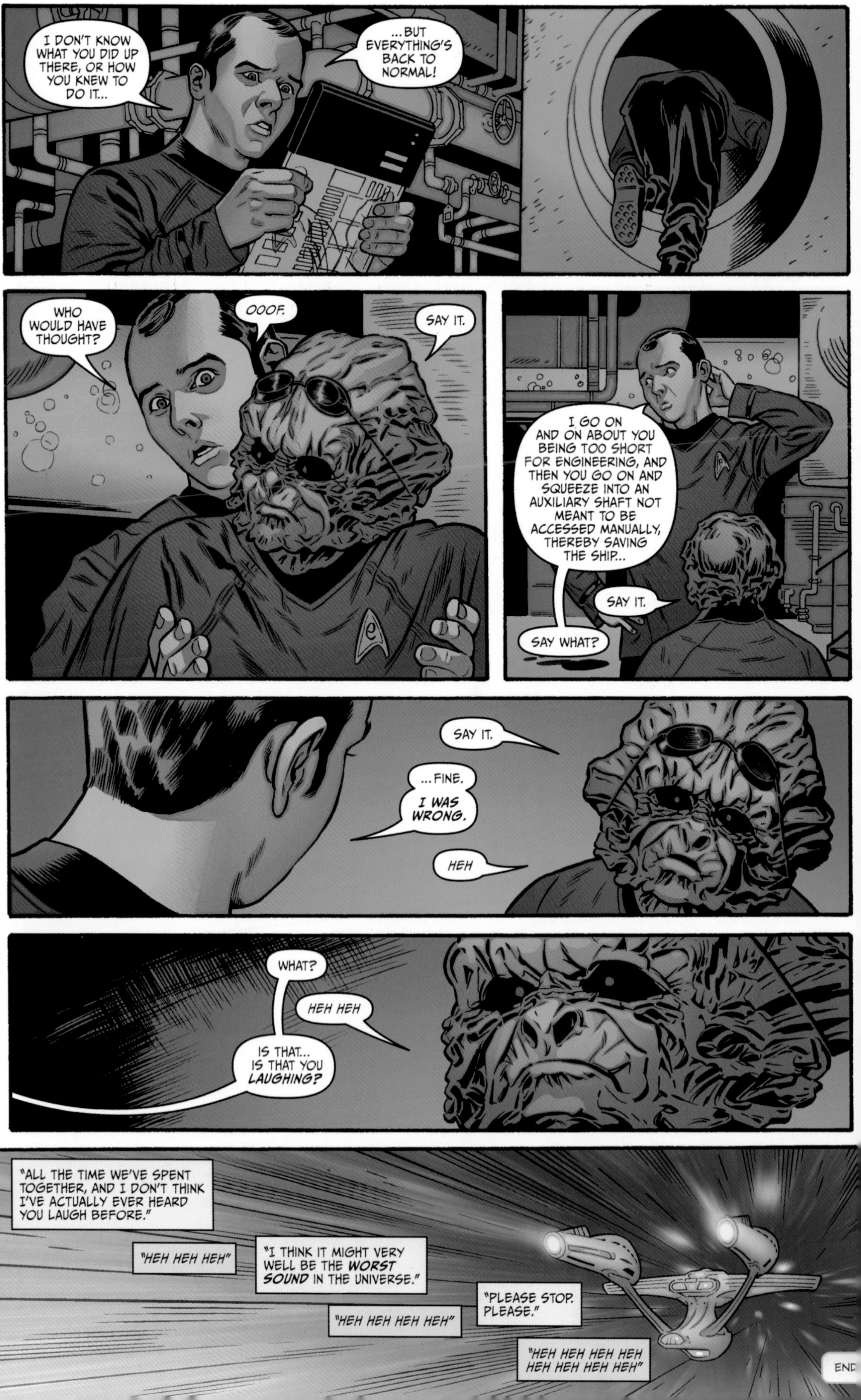
I DON'T KNOW WHAT YOU DID UP THERE, OR HOW YOU KNEW TO DO IT...
...BUT EVERYTHING'S BACK TO NORMAL!
WHO WOULD HAVE THOUGHT?
OOOF.
SAY IT.
I GO ON AND ON ABOUT YOU BEING TOO SHORT FOR ENGINEERING, AND THEN YOU GO ON AND SQUEEZE INTO AN AUXILIARY SHAFT NOT MEANT TO BE ACCESSED MANUALLY, THEREBY SAVING THE SHIP...
SAY IT.
SAY WHAT?
SAY IT.
...FINE. I WAS WRONG.
HEH
WHAT?
HEH HEH
IS THAT... IS THAT YOU LAUGHING?
"ALL THE TIME WE'VE SPENT TOGETHER, AND I DON'T THINK I'VE ACTUALLY EVER HEARD YOU LAUGH BEFORE."
"HEH HEH HEH"
"I THINK IT MIGHT VERY WELL BE THE WORST SOUND IN THE UNIVERSE."
"HEH HEH HEH HEH"
"PLEASE STOP. PLEASE."
"HEH HEH HEH HEH HEH HEH HEH HEH"
END

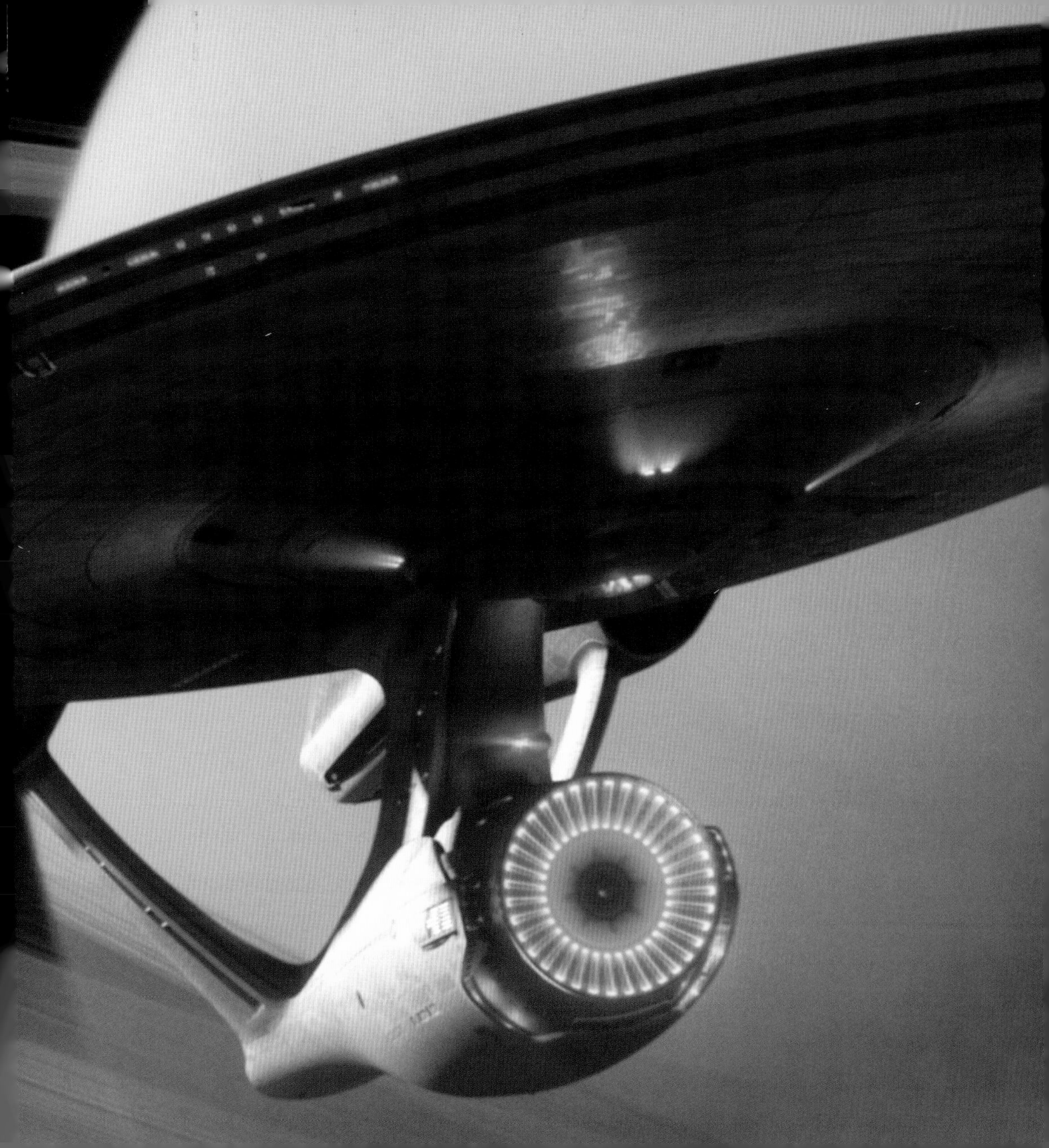

MIRRORED

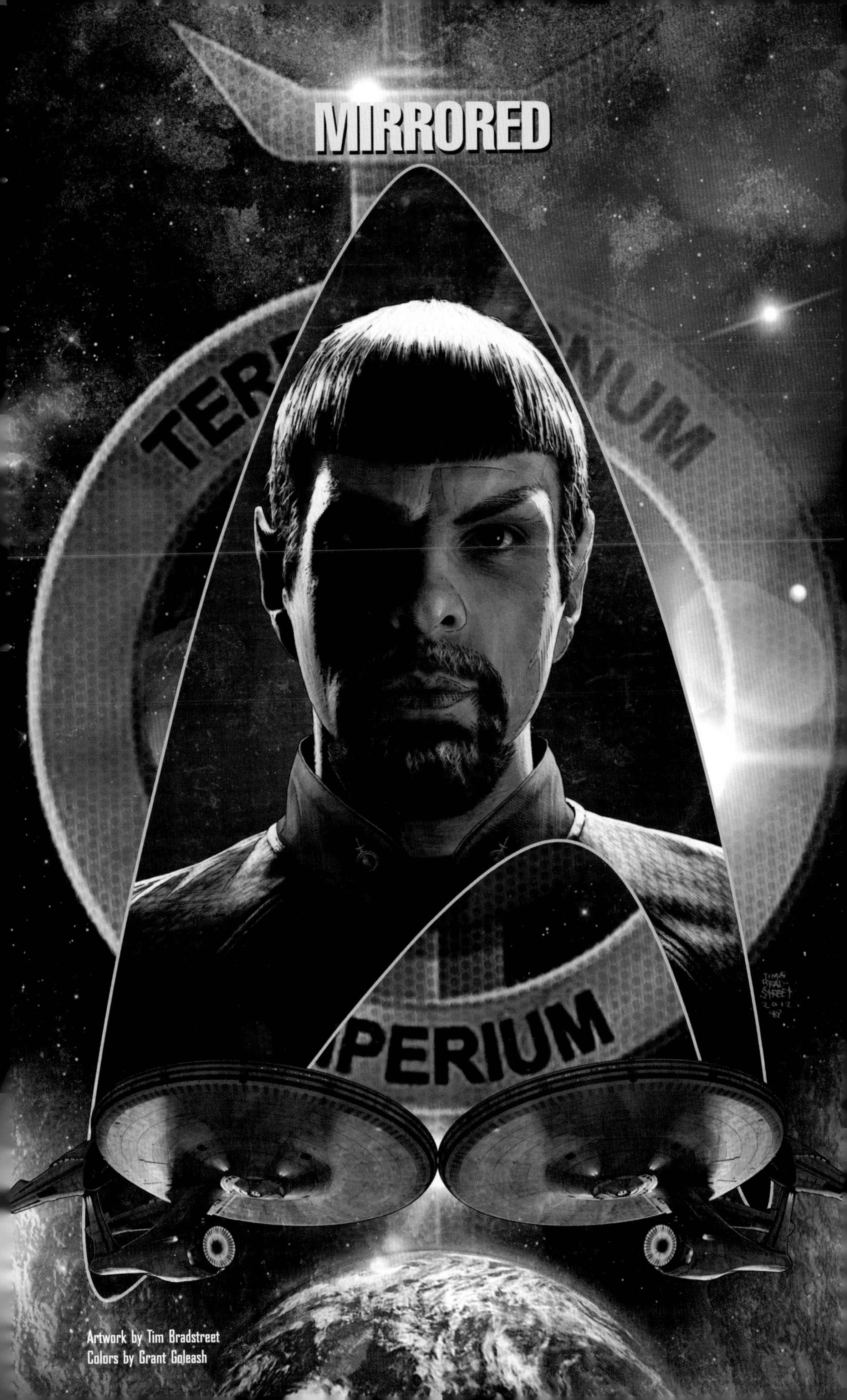

Artwork by Tim Bradstreet
Colors by Grant Goleash

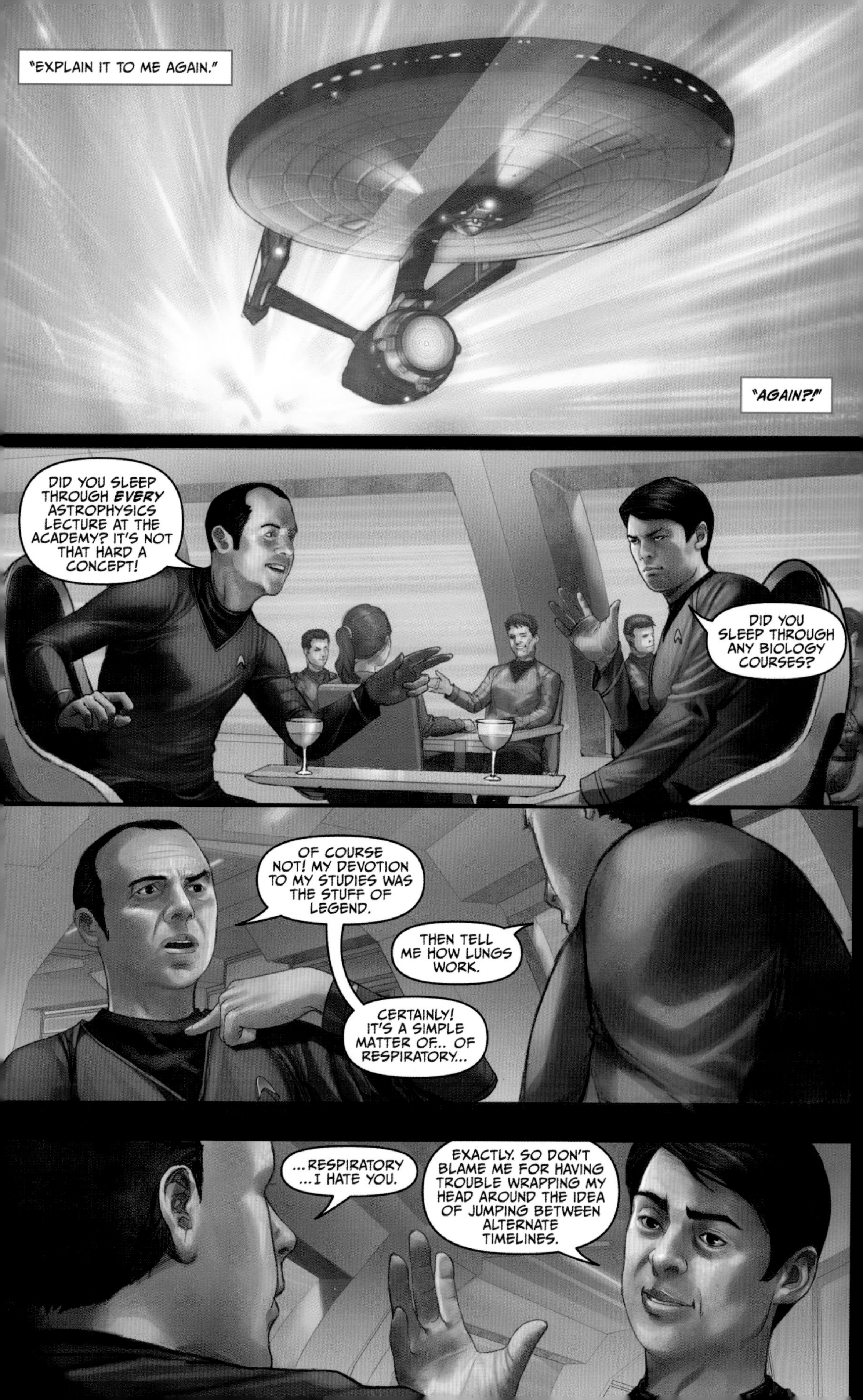
"EXPLAIN IT TO ME AGAIN."
"AGAIN?!"
DID YOU SLEEP THROUGH EVERY ASTROPHYSICS LECTURE AT THE ACADEMY? IT'S NOT THAT HARD A CONCEPT!
DID YOU SLEEP THROUGH ANY BIOLOGY COURSES?
OF COURSE NOT! MY DEVOTION TO MY STUDIES WAS THE STUFF OF LEGEND.
THEN TELL ME HOW LUNGS WORK.
CERTAINLY! IT'S A SIMPLE MATTER OF... OF RESPIRATORY...
...RESPIRATORY ...I HATE YOU.
EXACTLY. SO DON'T BLAME ME FOR HAVING TROUBLE WRAPPING MY HEAD AROUND THE IDEA OF JUMPING BETWEEN ALTERNATE TIMELINES.

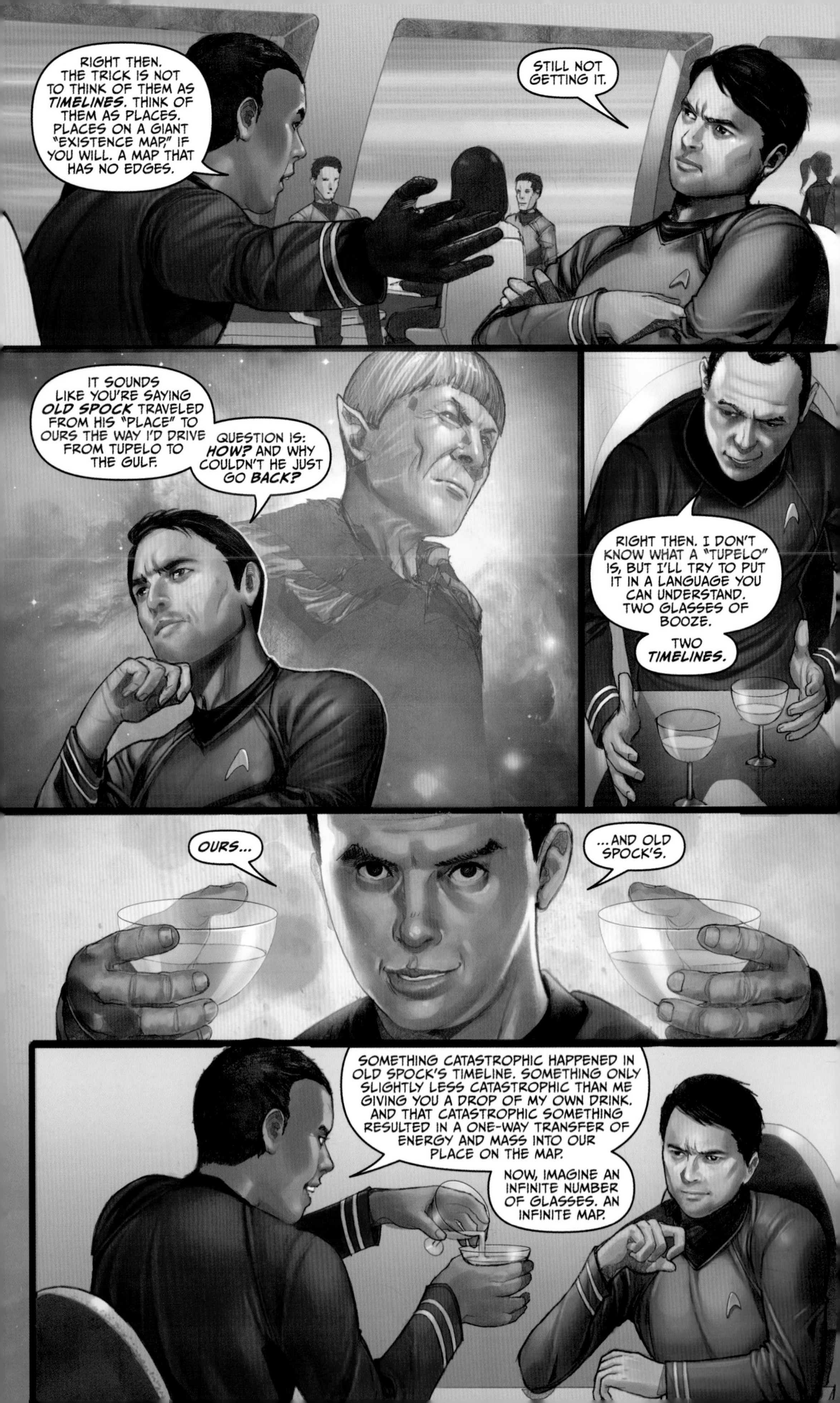
RIGHT THEN. THE TRICK IS NOT TO THINK OF THEM AS *TIMELINES*. THINK OF THEM AS PLACES. PLACES ON A GIANT "EXISTENCE MAP," IF YOU WILL. A MAP THAT HAS NO EDGES.
STILL NOT GETTING IT.
IT SOUNDS LIKE YOU'RE SAYING *OLD SPOCK* TRAVELED FROM HIS "PLACE" TO OURS THE WAY I'D DRIVE FROM TUPELO TO THE GULF.
QUESTION IS: *HOW?* AND WHY COULDN'T HE JUST GO *BACK?*
RIGHT THEN. I DON'T KNOW WHAT A "TUPELO" IS, BUT I'LL TRY TO PUT IT IN A LANGUAGE YOU CAN UNDERSTAND. TWO GLASSES OF BOOZE.
TWO *TIMELINES.*
OURS...
...AND OLD SPOCK'S.
SOMETHING CATASTROPHIC HAPPENED IN OLD SPOCK'S TIMELINE. SOMETHING ONLY SLIGHTLY LESS CATASTROPHIC THAN ME GIVING YOU A DROP OF MY OWN DRINK. AND THAT CATASTROPHIC SOMETHING RESULTED IN A ONE-WAY TRANSFER OF ENERGY AND MASS INTO OUR PLACE ON THE MAP.
NOW, IMAGINE AN INFINITE NUMBER OF GLASSES. AN INFINITE MAP.

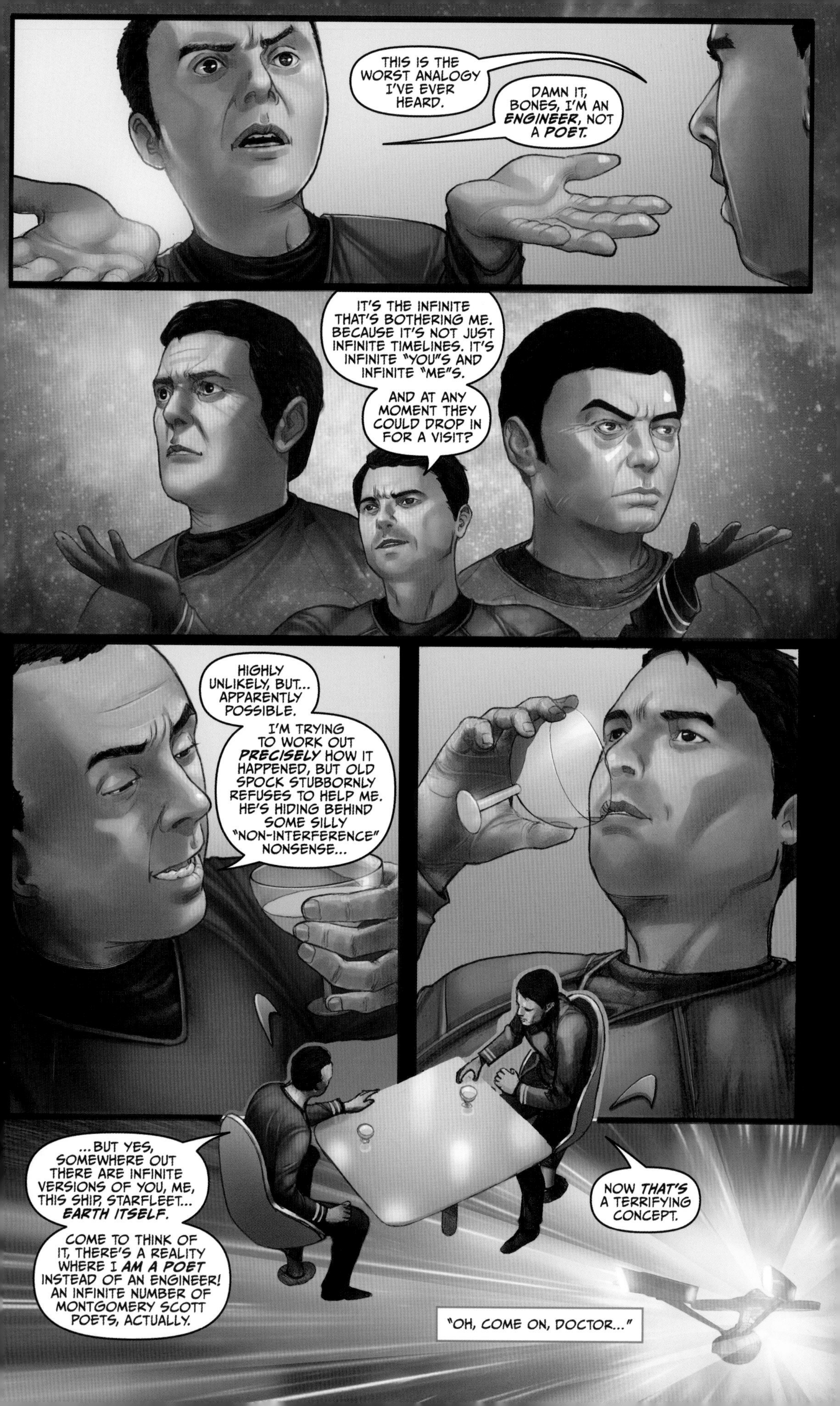
THIS IS THE WORST ANALOGY I'VE EVER HEARD.
DAMN IT, BONES, I'M AN ***ENGINEER***, NOT A ***POET***.
IT'S THE INFINITE THAT'S BOTHERING ME. BECAUSE IT'S NOT JUST INFINITE TIMELINES. IT'S INFINITE "YOU"S AND INFINITE "ME"S.
AND AT ANY MOMENT THEY COULD DROP IN FOR A VISIT?
HIGHLY UNLIKELY, BUT... APPARENTLY POSSIBLE.
I'M TRYING TO WORK OUT ***PRECISELY*** HOW IT HAPPENED, BUT OLD SPOCK STUBBORNLY REFUSES TO HELP ME. HE'S HIDING BEHIND SOME SILLY "NON-INTERFERENCE" NONSENSE...
...BUT YES, SOMEWHERE OUT THERE ARE INFINITE VERSIONS OF YOU, ME, THIS SHIP, STARFLEET... ***EARTH ITSELF***.
COME TO THINK OF IT, THERE'S A REALITY WHERE I ***AM A POET*** INSTEAD OF AN ENGINEER! AN INFINITE NUMBER OF MONTGOMERY SCOTT POETS, ACTUALLY.
NOW ***THAT'S*** A TERRIFYING CONCEPT.
"OH, COME ON, DOCTOR..."

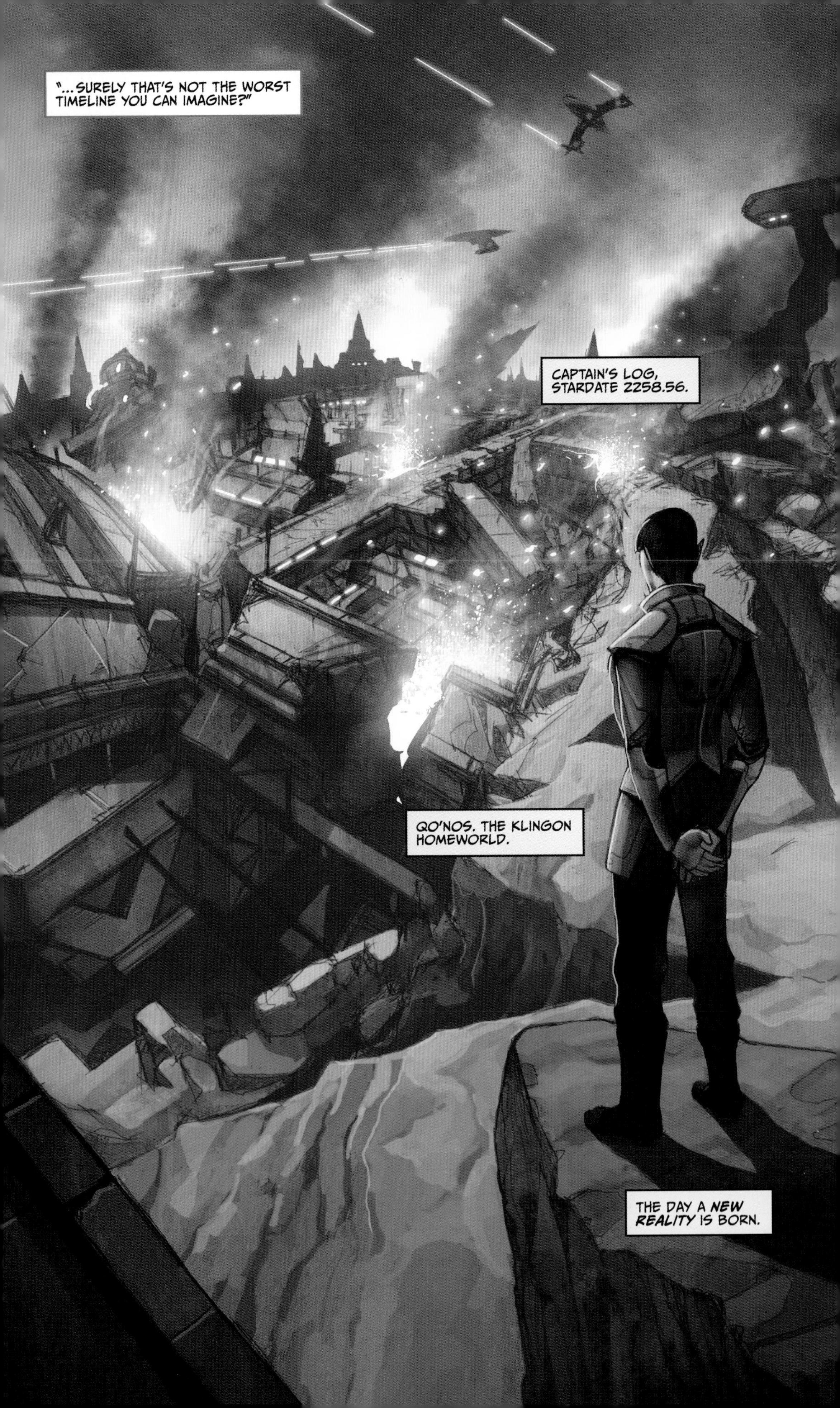
"...SURELY THAT'S NOT THE WORST TIMELINE YOU CAN IMAGINE?"
CAPTAIN'S LOG, STARDATE 2258.56.
QO'NOS. THE KLINGON HOMEWORLD.
THE DAY A *NEW REALITY* IS BORN.

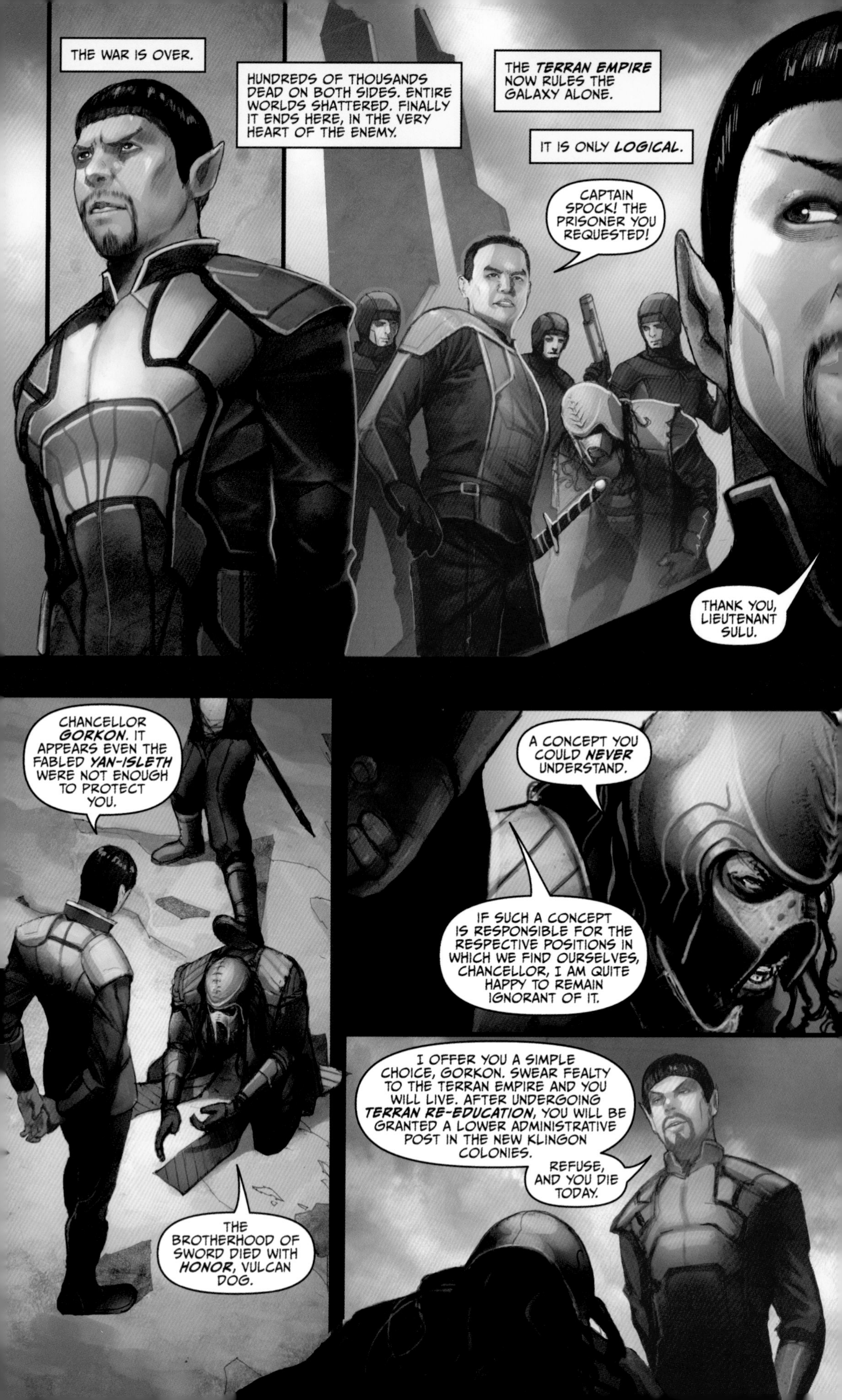

THE WAR IS OVER.
HUNDREDS OF THOUSANDS DEAD ON BOTH SIDES. ENTIRE WORLDS SHATTERED. FINALLY IT ENDS HERE, IN THE VERY HEART OF THE ENEMY.
THE TERRAN EMPIRE NOW RULES THE GALAXY ALONE.
IT IS ONLY LOGICAL.
CAPTAIN SPOCK! THE PRISONER YOU REQUESTED!
THANK YOU, LIEUTENANT SULU.
CHANCELLOR GORKON. IT APPEARS EVEN THE FABLED YAN-ISLETH WERE NOT ENOUGH TO PROTECT YOU.
THE BROTHERHOOD OF SWORD DIED WITH HONOR, VULCAN DOG.
A CONCEPT YOU COULD NEVER UNDERSTAND.
IF SUCH A CONCEPT IS RESPONSIBLE FOR THE RESPECTIVE POSITIONS IN WHICH WE FIND OURSELVES, CHANCELLOR, I AM QUITE HAPPY TO REMAIN IGNORANT OF IT.
I OFFER YOU A SIMPLE CHOICE, GORKON. SWEAR FEALTY TO THE TERRAN EMPIRE AND YOU WILL LIVE. AFTER UNDERGOING TERRAN RE-EDUCATION, YOU WILL BE GRANTED A LOWER ADMINISTRATIVE POST IN THE NEW KLINGON COLONIES.
REFUSE, AND YOU DIE TODAY.

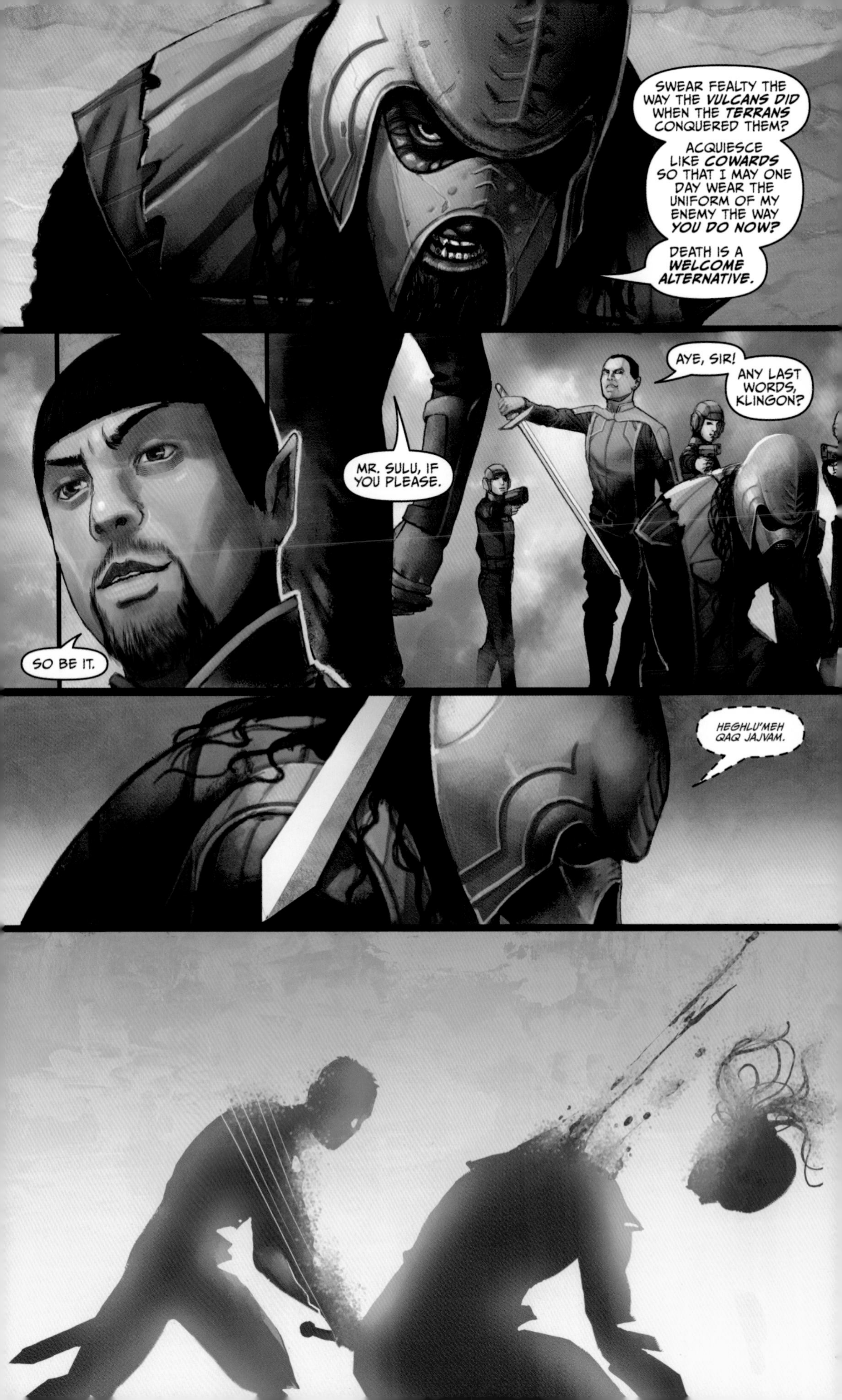

SWEAR FEALTY THE WAY THE VULCANS DID WHEN THE TERRANS CONQUERED THEM?
ACQUIESCE LIKE COWARDS SO THAT I MAY ONE DAY WEAR THE UNIFORM OF MY ENEMY THE WAY YOU DO NOW?
DEATH IS A WELCOME ALTERNATIVE.
MR. SULU, IF YOU PLEASE.
AYE, SIR!
ANY LAST WORDS, KLINGON?
SO BE IT.
HEGHLU'MEH QAQ JAJVAM.

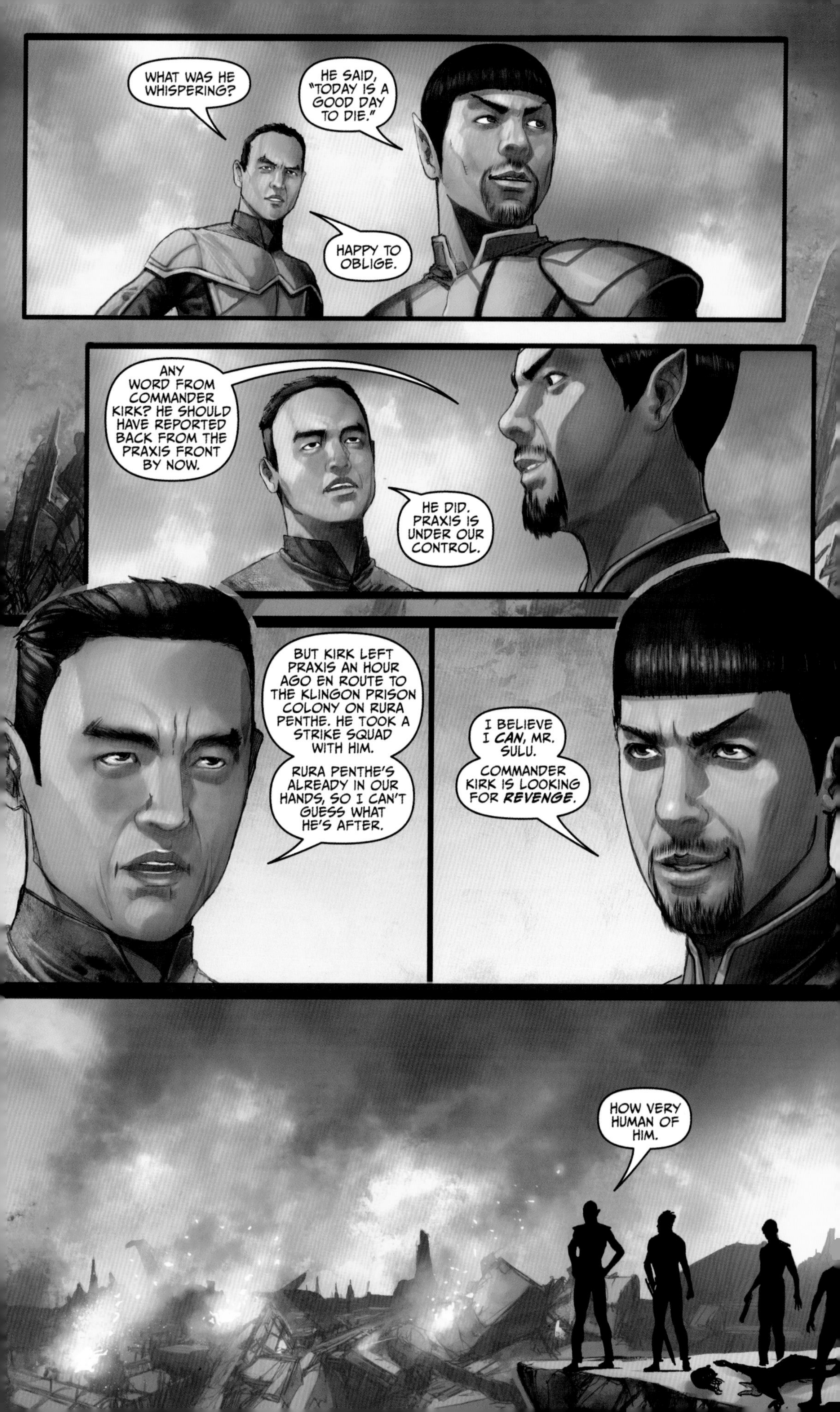
WHAT WAS HE WHISPERING?
HE SAID, "TODAY IS A GOOD DAY TO DIE."
HAPPY TO OBLIGE.
ANY WORD FROM COMMANDER KIRK? HE SHOULD HAVE REPORTED BACK FROM THE PRAXIS FRONT BY NOW.
HE DID. PRAXIS IS UNDER OUR CONTROL.
BUT KIRK LEFT PRAXIS AN HOUR AGO EN ROUTE TO THE KLINGON PRISON COLONY ON RURA PENTHE. HE TOOK A STRIKE SQUAD WITH HIM.
RURA PENTHE'S ALREADY IN OUR HANDS, SO I CAN'T GUESS WHAT HE'S AFTER.
I BELIEVE I *CAN*, MR. SULU.
COMMANDER KIRK IS LOOKING FOR ***REVENGE***.
HOW VERY HUMAN OF HIM.

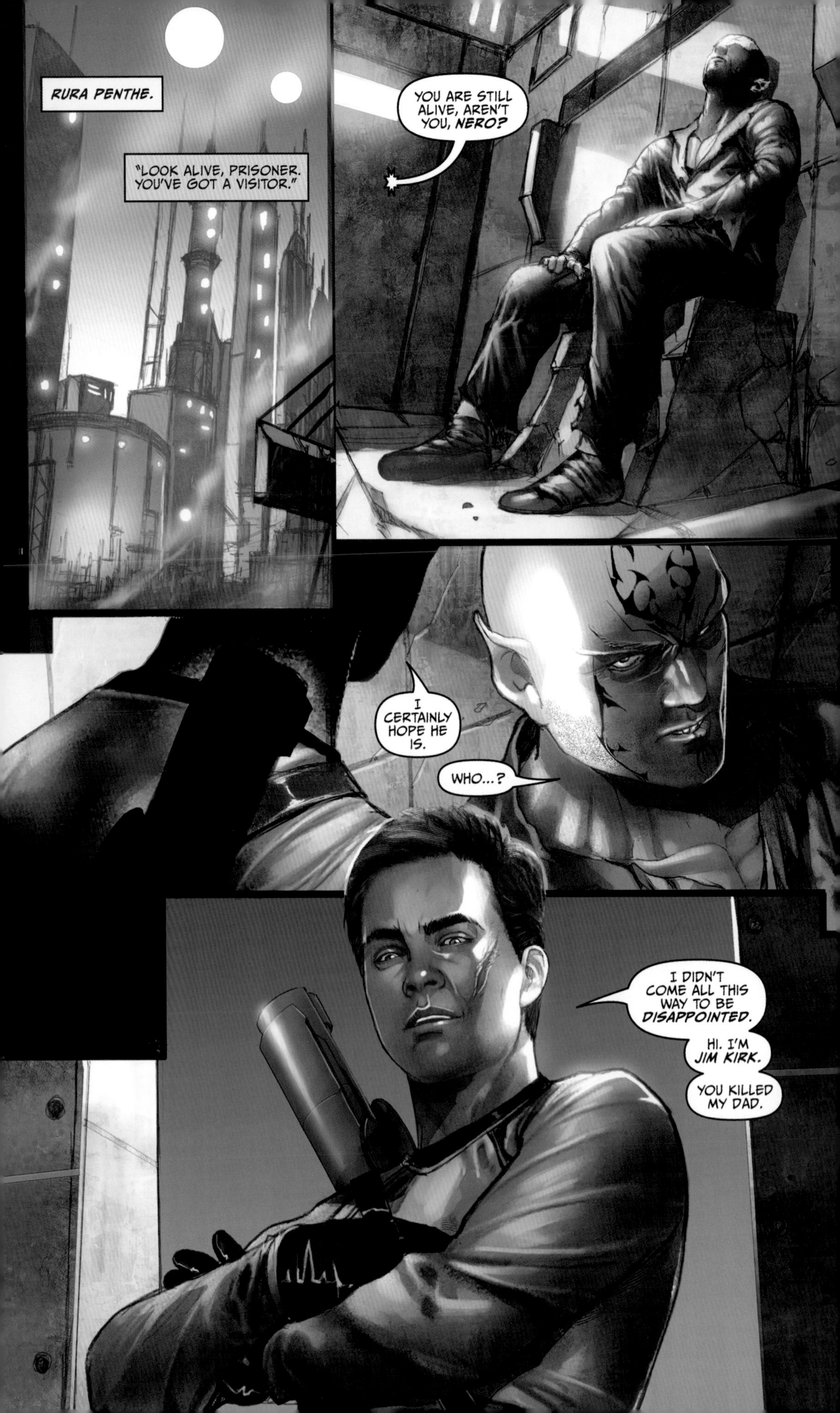
RURA PENTHE.
"LOOK ALIVE, PRISONER. YOU'VE GOT A VISITOR."
YOU ARE STILL ALIVE, AREN'T YOU, *NERO?*
I CERTAINLY HOPE HE IS.
WHO...?
I DIDN'T COME ALL THIS WAY TO BE *DISAPPOINTED*.
HI. I'M *JIM KIRK*.
YOU KILLED MY DAD.

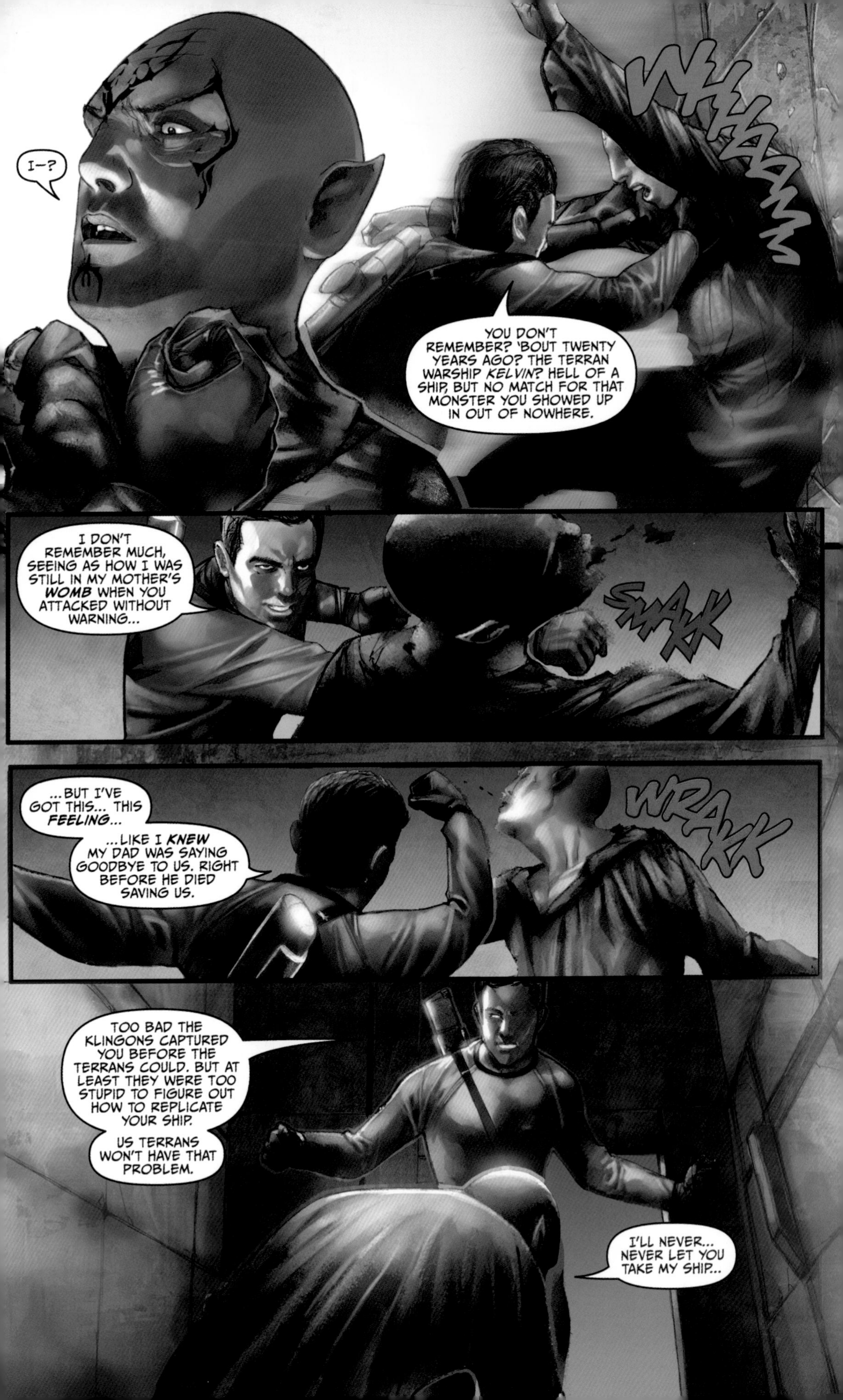
I–?
WHHAAMM
YOU DON'T REMEMBER? 'BOUT TWENTY YEARS AGO? THE TERRAN WARSHIP *KELVIN*? HELL OF A SHIP, BUT NO MATCH FOR THAT MONSTER YOU SHOWED UP IN OUT OF NOWHERE.
I DON'T REMEMBER MUCH, SEEING AS HOW I WAS STILL IN MY MOTHER'S **WOMB** WHEN YOU ATTACKED WITHOUT WARNING...
SMAKK
...BUT I'VE GOT THIS... THIS **FEELING**...
...LIKE I **KNEW** MY DAD WAS SAYING GOODBYE TO US. RIGHT BEFORE HE DIED SAVING US.
WRAKK
TOO BAD THE KLINGONS CAPTURED YOU BEFORE THE TERRANS COULD. BUT AT LEAST THEY WERE TOO STUPID TO FIGURE OUT HOW TO REPLICATE YOUR SHIP.
US TERRANS WON'T HAVE THAT PROBLEM.
I'LL NEVER... NEVER LET YOU TAKE MY SHIP...

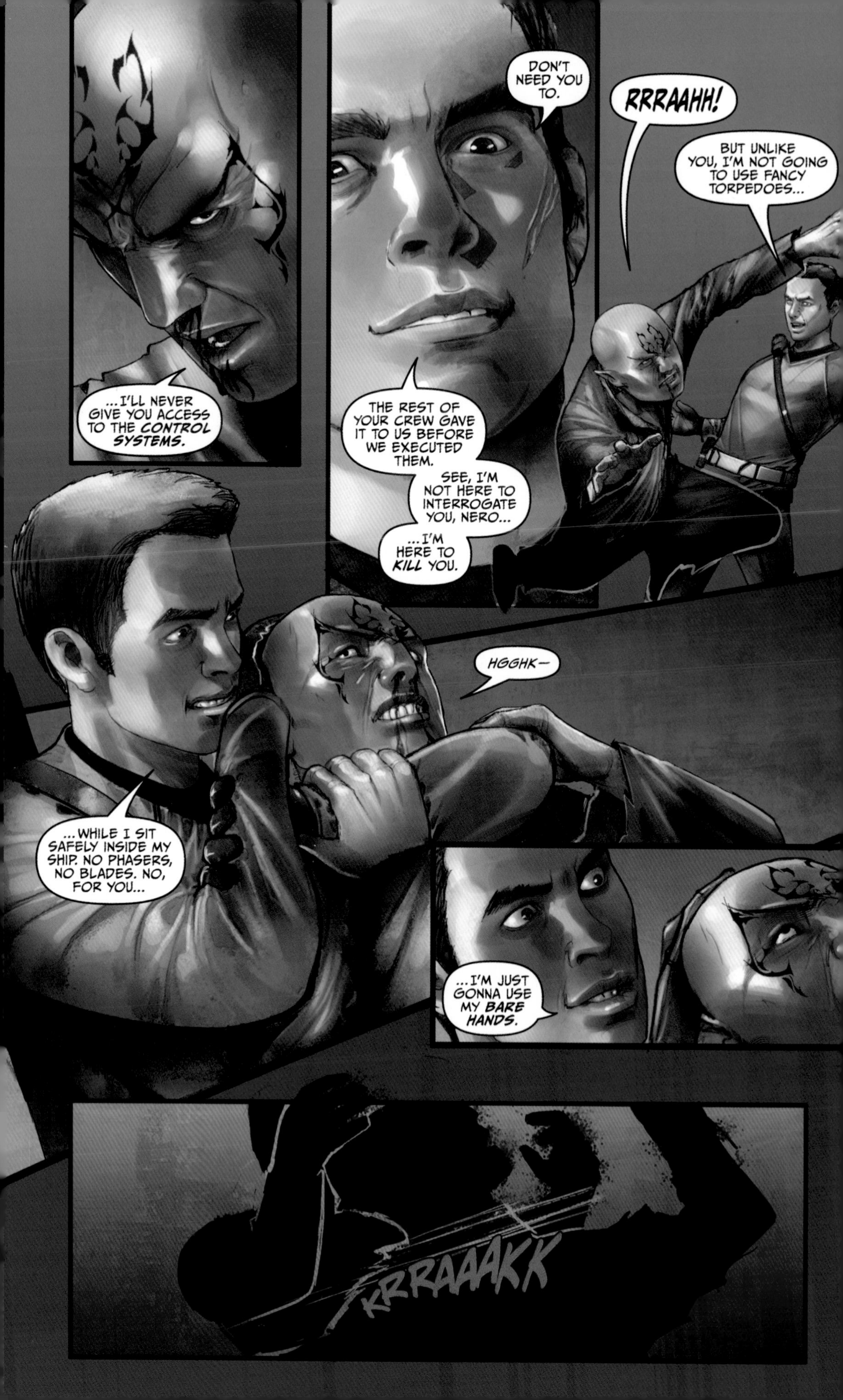

...I'LL NEVER GIVE YOU ACCESS TO THE CONTROL SYSTEMS.
DON'T NEED YOU TO.
THE REST OF YOUR CREW GAVE IT TO US BEFORE WE EXECUTED THEM.
SEE, I'M NOT HERE TO INTERROGATE YOU, NERO...
...I'M HERE TO KILL YOU.
RRRAAHH!
BUT UNLIKE YOU, I'M NOT GOING TO USE FANCY TORPEDOES...
HGGHK—
...WHILE I SIT SAFELY INSIDE MY SHIP. NO PHASERS, NO BLADES. NO, FOR YOU...
...I'M JUST GONNA USE MY BARE HANDS.
KRRAAAKK

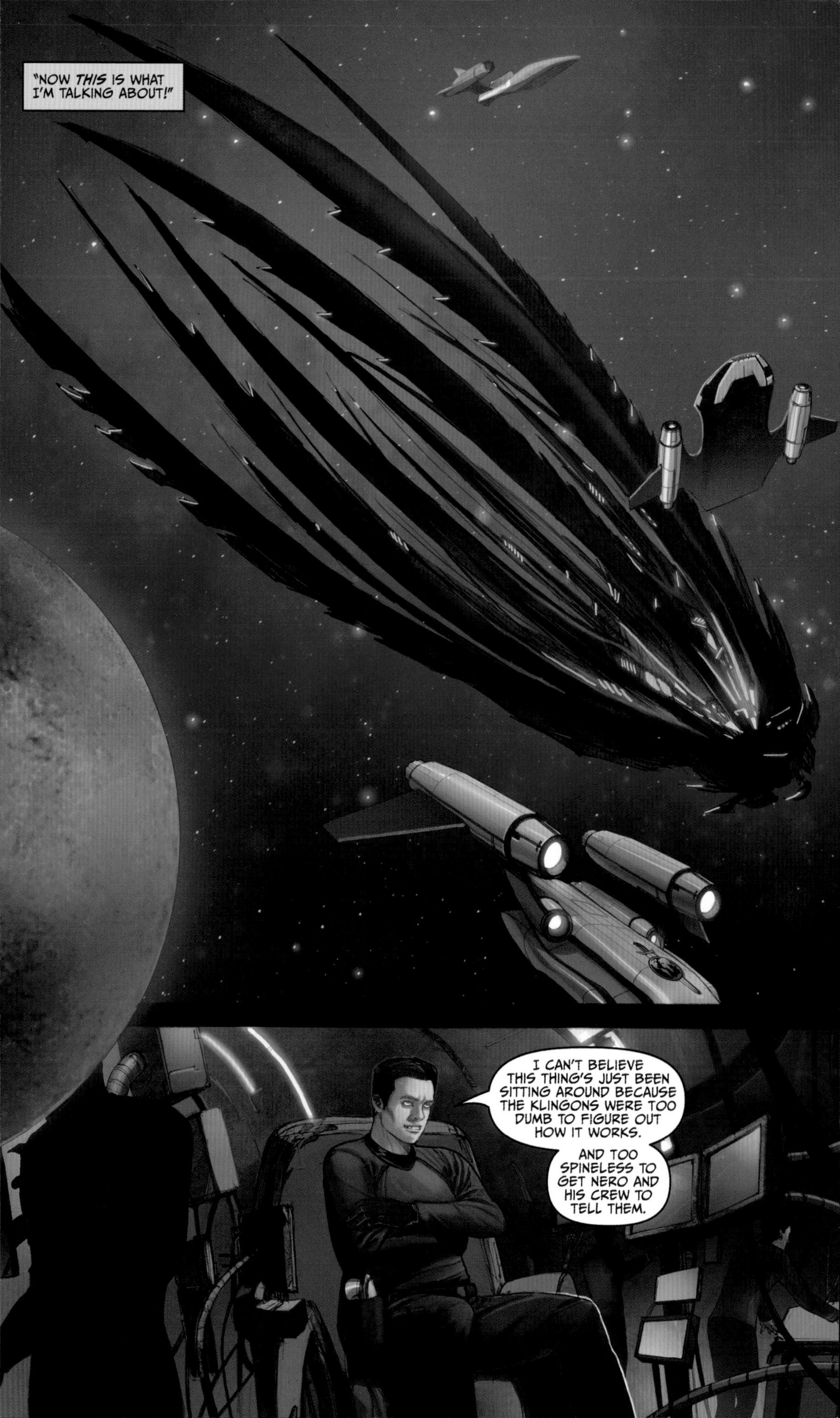
"NOW THIS IS WHAT I'M TALKING ABOUT!"
I CAN'T BELIEVE THIS THING'S JUST BEEN SITTING AROUND BECAUSE THE KLINGONS WERE TOO DUMB TO FIGURE OUT HOW IT WORKS.
AND TOO SPINELESS TO GET NERO AND HIS CREW TO TELL THEM.

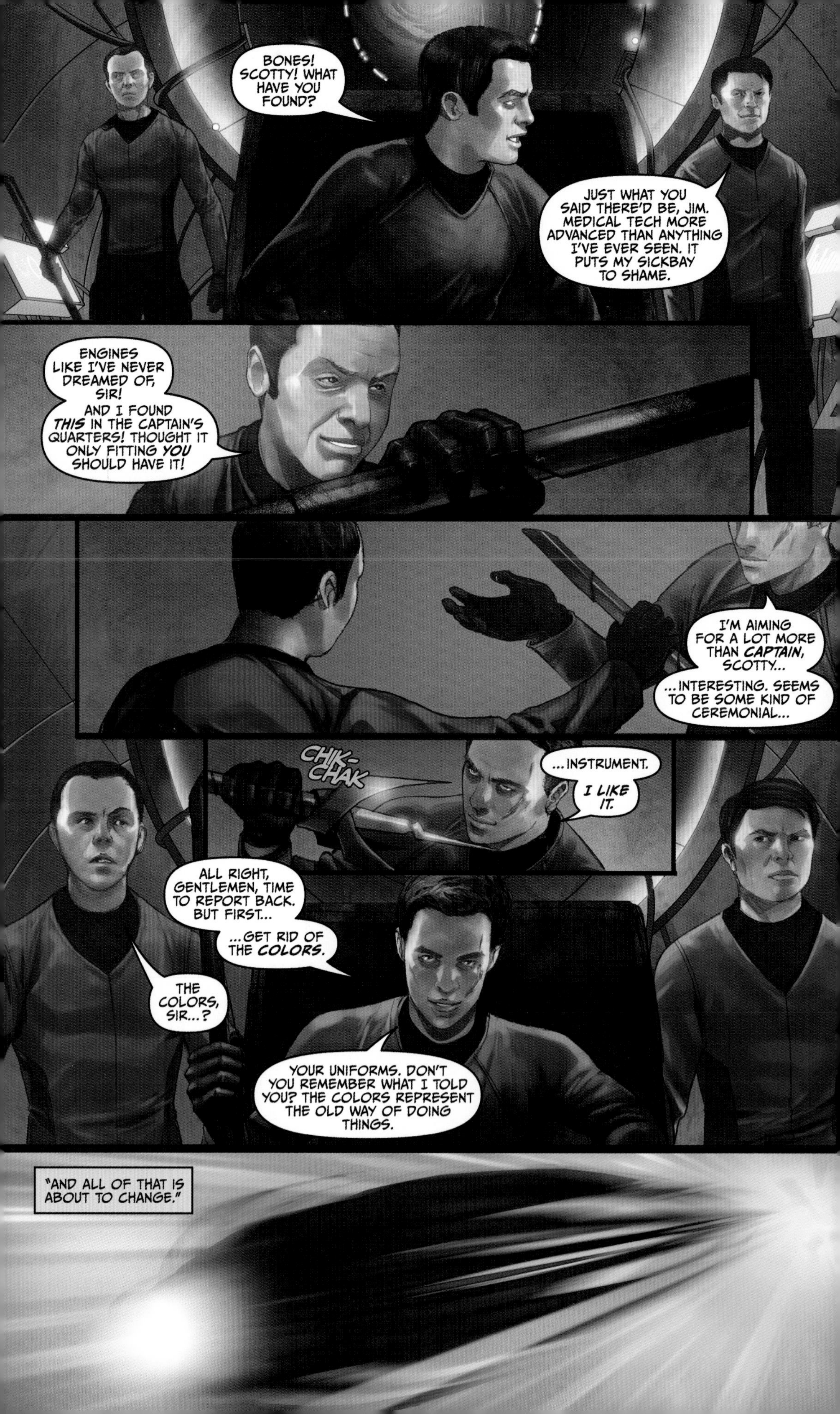
BONES! SCOTTY! WHAT HAVE YOU FOUND?
JUST WHAT YOU SAID THERE'D BE, JIM. MEDICAL TECH MORE ADVANCED THAN ANYTHING I'VE EVER SEEN. IT PUTS MY SICKBAY TO SHAME.
ENGINES LIKE I'VE NEVER DREAMED OF, SIR!
AND I FOUND *THIS* IN THE CAPTAIN'S QUARTERS! THOUGHT IT ONLY FITTING *YOU* SHOULD HAVE IT!
I'M AIMING FOR A LOT MORE THAN *CAPTAIN*, SCOTTY...
...INTERESTING. SEEMS TO BE SOME KIND OF CEREMONIAL...
CHIK-CHAK
...INSTRUMENT.
I LIKE IT.
ALL RIGHT, GENTLEMEN, TIME TO REPORT BACK. BUT FIRST...
...GET RID OF THE *COLORS*.
THE COLORS, SIR...?
YOUR UNIFORMS. DON'T YOU REMEMBER WHAT I TOLD YOU? THE COLORS REPRESENT THE OLD WAY OF DOING THINGS.
"AND ALL OF THAT IS ABOUT TO CHANGE."

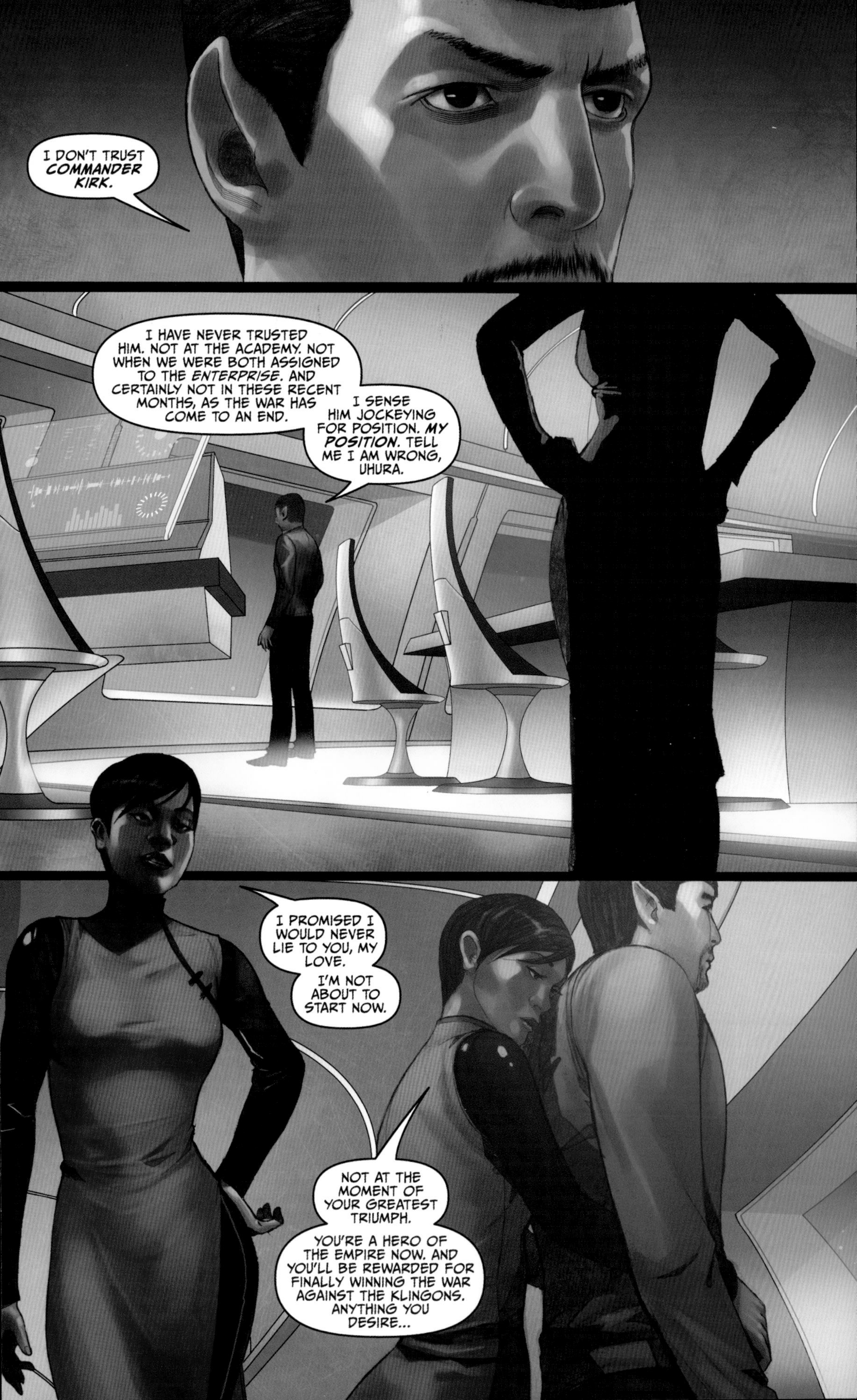
I DON'T TRUST *COMMANDER KIRK.*
I HAVE NEVER TRUSTED HIM. NOT AT THE ACADEMY. NOT WHEN WE WERE BOTH ASSIGNED TO THE *ENTERPRISE*. AND CERTAINLY NOT IN THESE RECENT MONTHS, AS THE WAR HAS COME TO AN END.
I SENSE HIM JOCKEYING FOR POSITION. *MY POSITION.* TELL ME I AM WRONG, UHURA.
I PROMISED I WOULD NEVER LIE TO YOU, MY LOVE.
I'M NOT ABOUT TO START NOW.
NOT AT THE MOMENT OF YOUR GREATEST TRIUMPH.
YOU'RE A HERO OF THE EMPIRE NOW. AND YOU'LL BE REWARDED FOR FINALLY WINNING THE WAR AGAINST THE KLINGONS. ANYTHING YOU DESIRE...

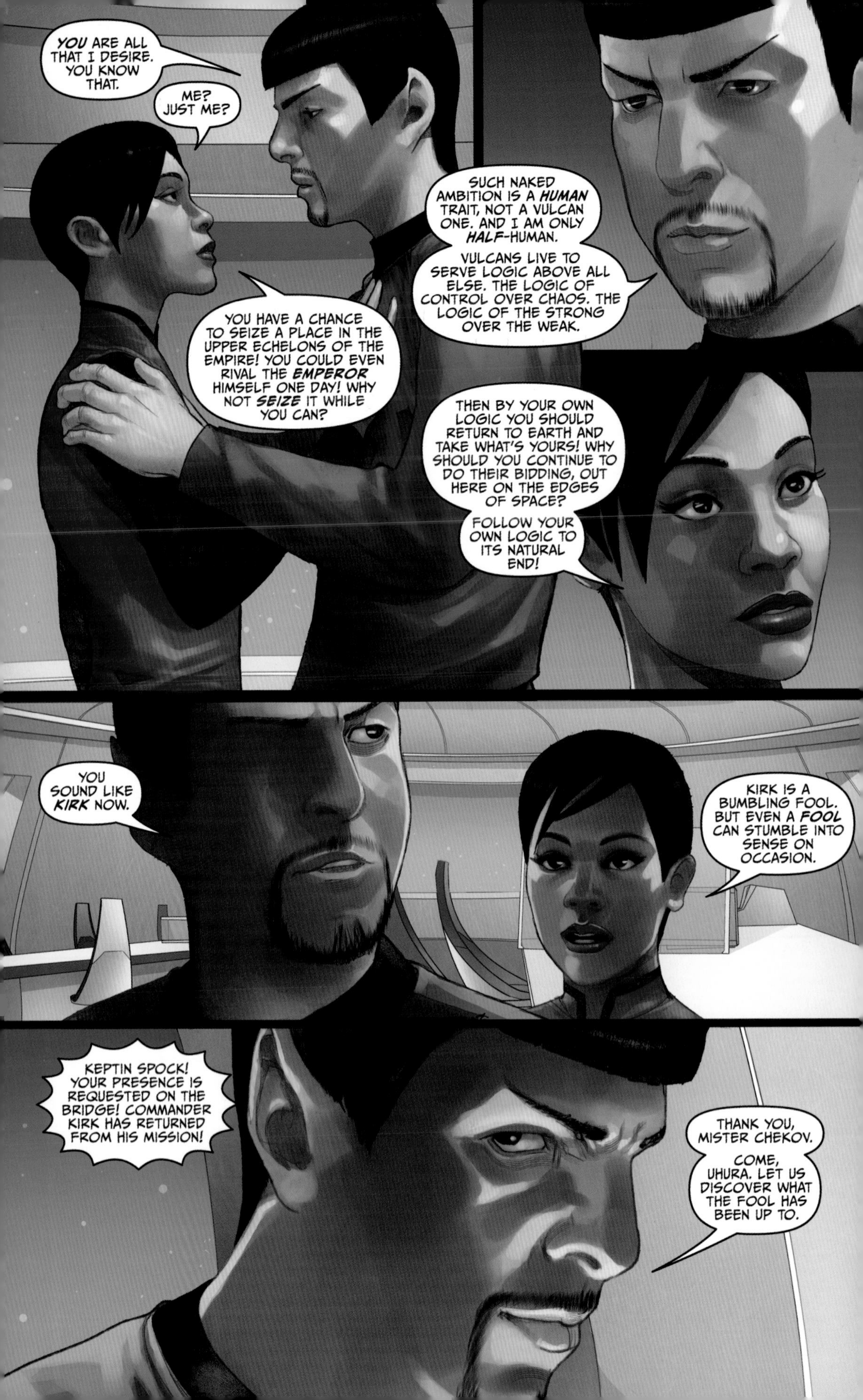
YOU ARE ALL THAT I DESIRE. YOU KNOW THAT.
ME? JUST ME?
YOU HAVE A CHANCE TO SEIZE A PLACE IN THE UPPER ECHELONS OF THE EMPIRE! YOU COULD EVEN RIVAL THE EMPEROR HIMSELF ONE DAY! WHY NOT SEIZE IT WHILE YOU CAN?
SUCH NAKED AMBITION IS A HUMAN TRAIT, NOT A VULCAN ONE. AND I AM ONLY HALF-HUMAN.
VULCANS LIVE TO SERVE LOGIC ABOVE ALL ELSE. THE LOGIC OF CONTROL OVER CHAOS. THE LOGIC OF THE STRONG OVER THE WEAK.
THEN BY YOUR OWN LOGIC YOU SHOULD RETURN TO EARTH AND TAKE WHAT'S YOURS! WHY SHOULD YOU CONTINUE TO DO THEIR BIDDING, OUT HERE ON THE EDGES OF SPACE?
FOLLOW YOUR OWN LOGIC TO ITS NATURAL END!
YOU SOUND LIKE KIRK NOW.
KIRK IS A BUMBLING FOOL. BUT EVEN A FOOL CAN STUMBLE INTO SENSE ON OCCASION.
KEPTIN SPOCK! YOUR PRESENCE IS REQUESTED ON THE BRIDGE! COMMANDER KIRK HAS RETURNED FROM HIS MISSION!
THANK YOU, MISTER CHEKOV.
COME, UHURA. LET US DISCOVER WHAT THE FOOL HAS BEEN UP TO.

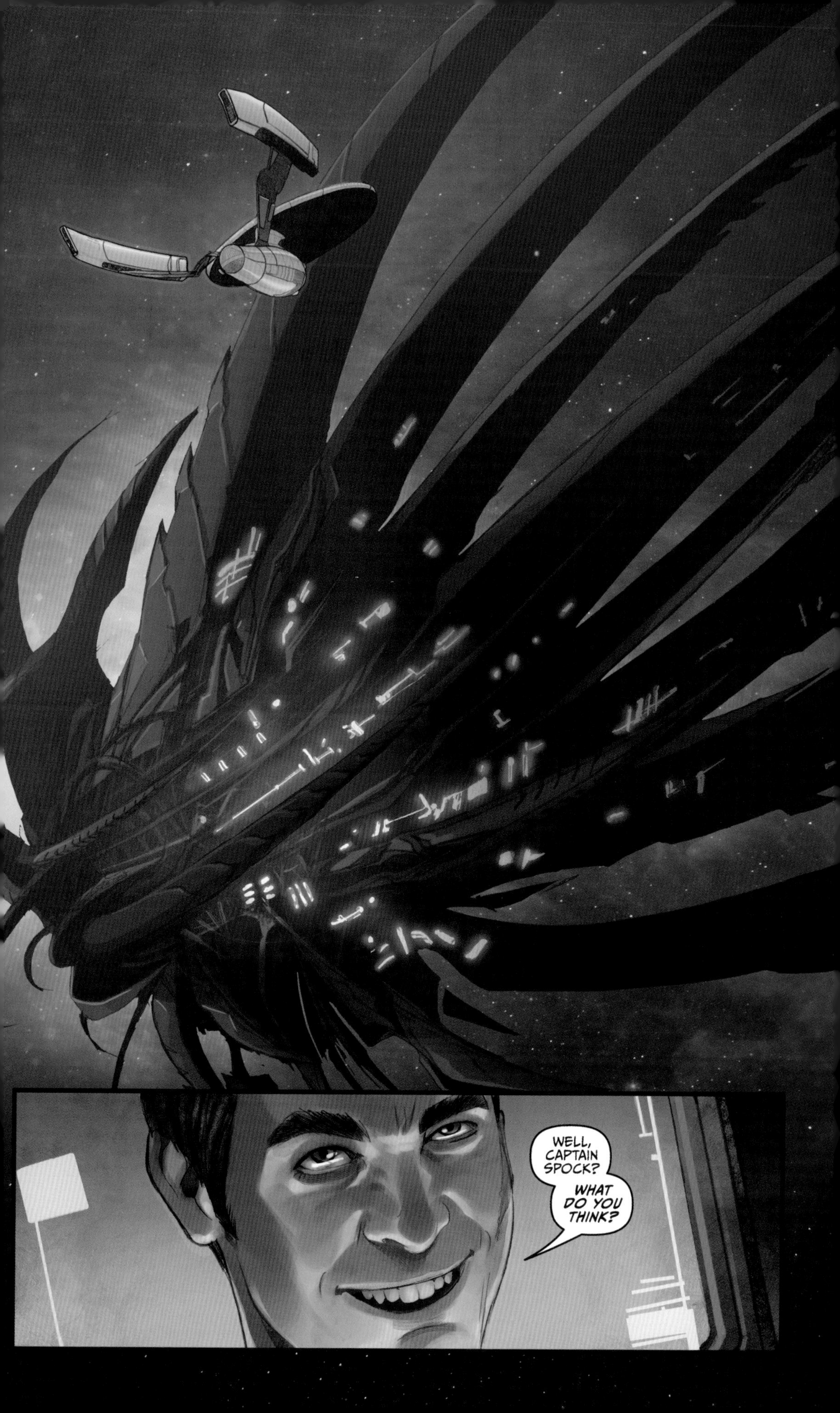
WELL, CAPTAIN SPOCK?
WHAT DO YOU THINK?

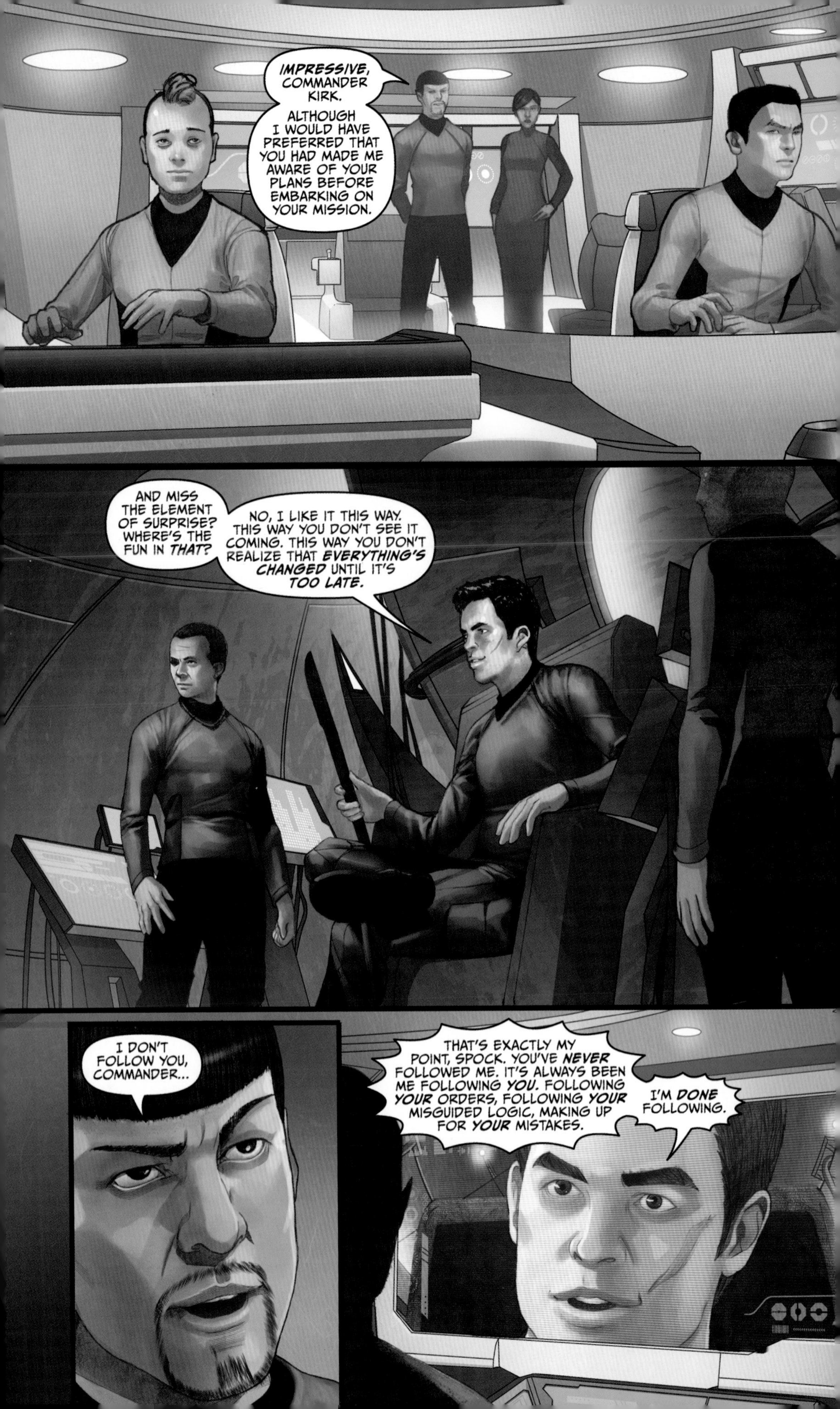

IMPRESSIVE, COMMANDER KIRK.
ALTHOUGH I WOULD HAVE PREFERRED THAT YOU HAD MADE ME AWARE OF YOUR PLANS BEFORE EMBARKING ON YOUR MISSION.
AND MISS THE ELEMENT OF SURPRISE? WHERE'S THE FUN IN THAT?
NO, I LIKE IT THIS WAY. THIS WAY YOU DON'T SEE IT COMING. THIS WAY YOU DON'T REALIZE THAT EVERYTHING'S CHANGED UNTIL IT'S TOO LATE.
I DON'T FOLLOW YOU, COMMANDER...
THAT'S EXACTLY MY POINT, SPOCK. YOU'VE NEVER FOLLOWED ME. IT'S ALWAYS BEEN ME FOLLOWING YOU. FOLLOWING YOUR ORDERS, FOLLOWING YOUR MISGUIDED LOGIC, MAKING UP FOR YOUR MISTAKES.
I'M DONE FOLLOWING.

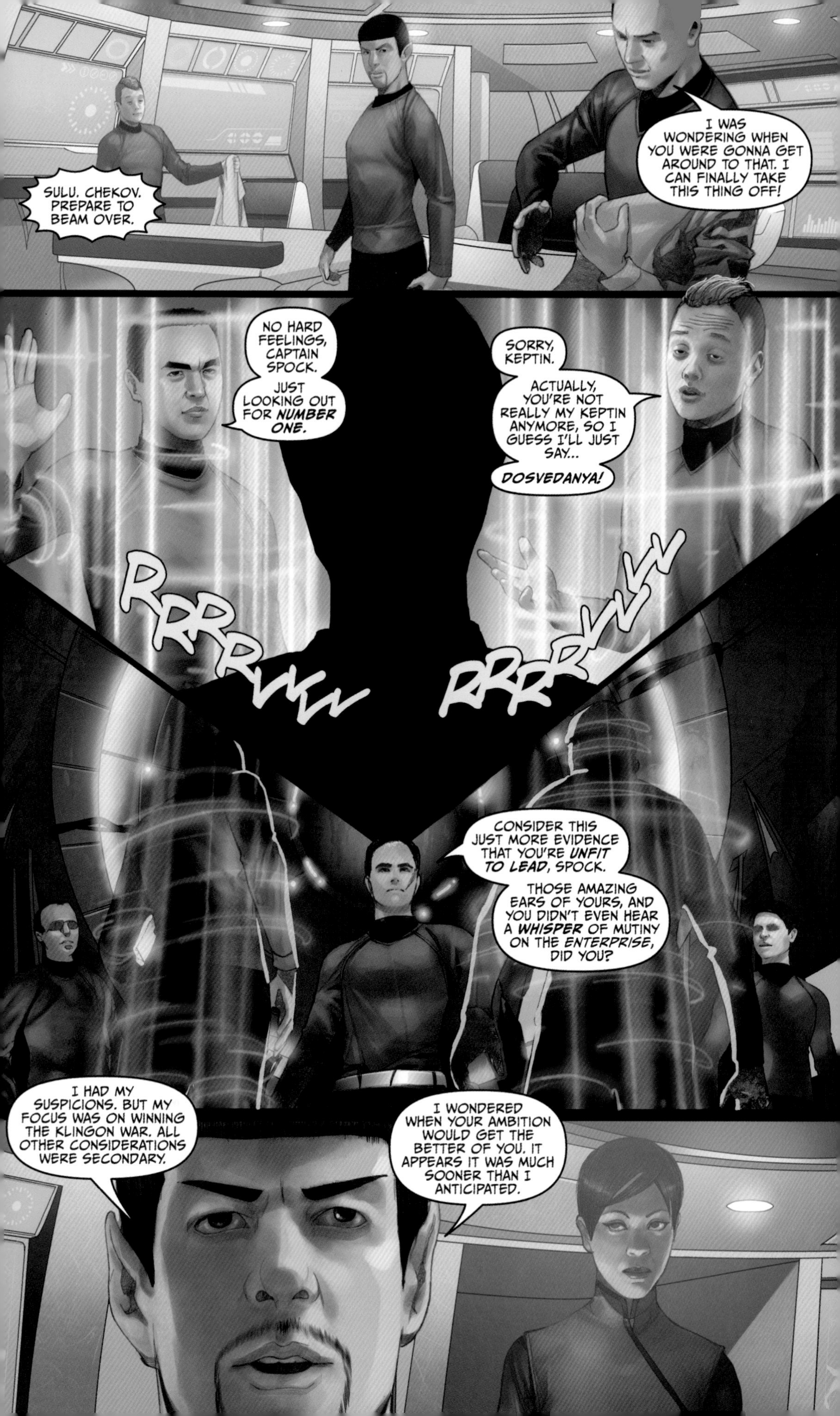
SULU. CHEKOV. PREPARE TO BEAM OVER.
I WAS WONDERING WHEN YOU WERE GONNA GET AROUND TO THAT. I CAN FINALLY TAKE THIS THING OFF!
NO HARD FEELINGS, CAPTAIN SPOCK.
JUST LOOKING OUT FOR NUMBER ONE.
SORRY, KEPTIN.
ACTUALLY, YOU'RE NOT REALLY MY KEPTIN ANYMORE, SO I GUESS I'LL JUST SAY...
DOSVEDANYA!
RRRRVKN
RRRRVVVN
CONSIDER THIS JUST MORE EVIDENCE THAT YOU'RE UNFIT TO LEAD, SPOCK.
THOSE AMAZING EARS OF YOURS, AND YOU DIDN'T EVEN HEAR A WHISPER OF MUTINY ON THE ENTERPRISE, DID YOU?
I HAD MY SUSPICIONS. BUT MY FOCUS WAS ON WINNING THE KLINGON WAR. ALL OTHER CONSIDERATIONS WERE SECONDARY.
I WONDERED WHEN YOUR AMBITION WOULD GET THE BETTER OF YOU. IT APPEARS IT WAS MUCH SOONER THAN I ANTICIPATED.

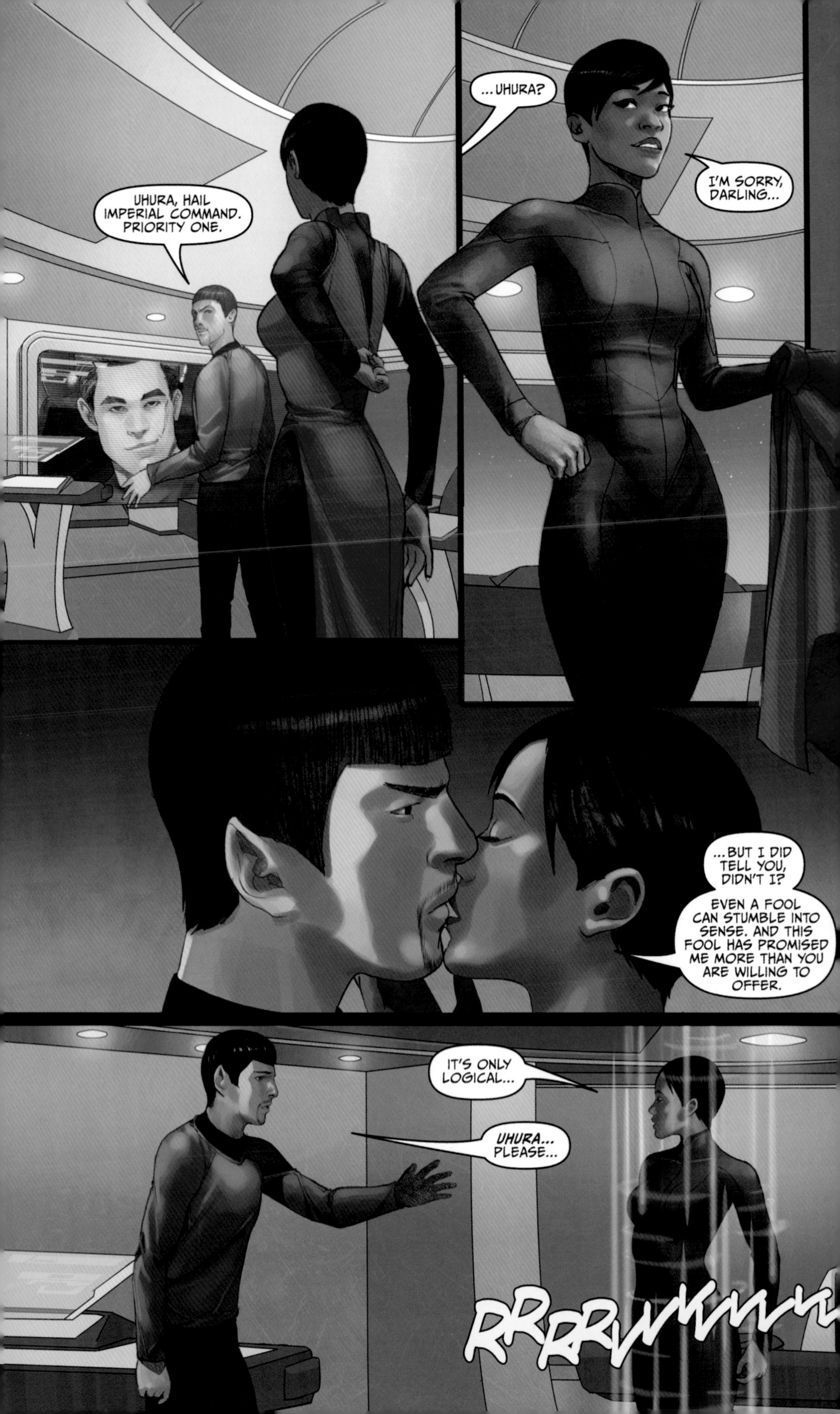
UHURA, HAIL IMPERIAL COMMAND. PRIORITY ONE.
...UHURA?
I'M SORRY, DARLING...
...BUT I DID TELL YOU, DIDN'T I?
EVEN A FOOL CAN STUMBLE INTO SENSE. AND THIS FOOL HAS PROMISED ME MORE THAN YOU ARE WILLING TO OFFER.
IT'S ONLY LOGICAL...
UHURA... PLEASE...
RRRRVVVVVVV

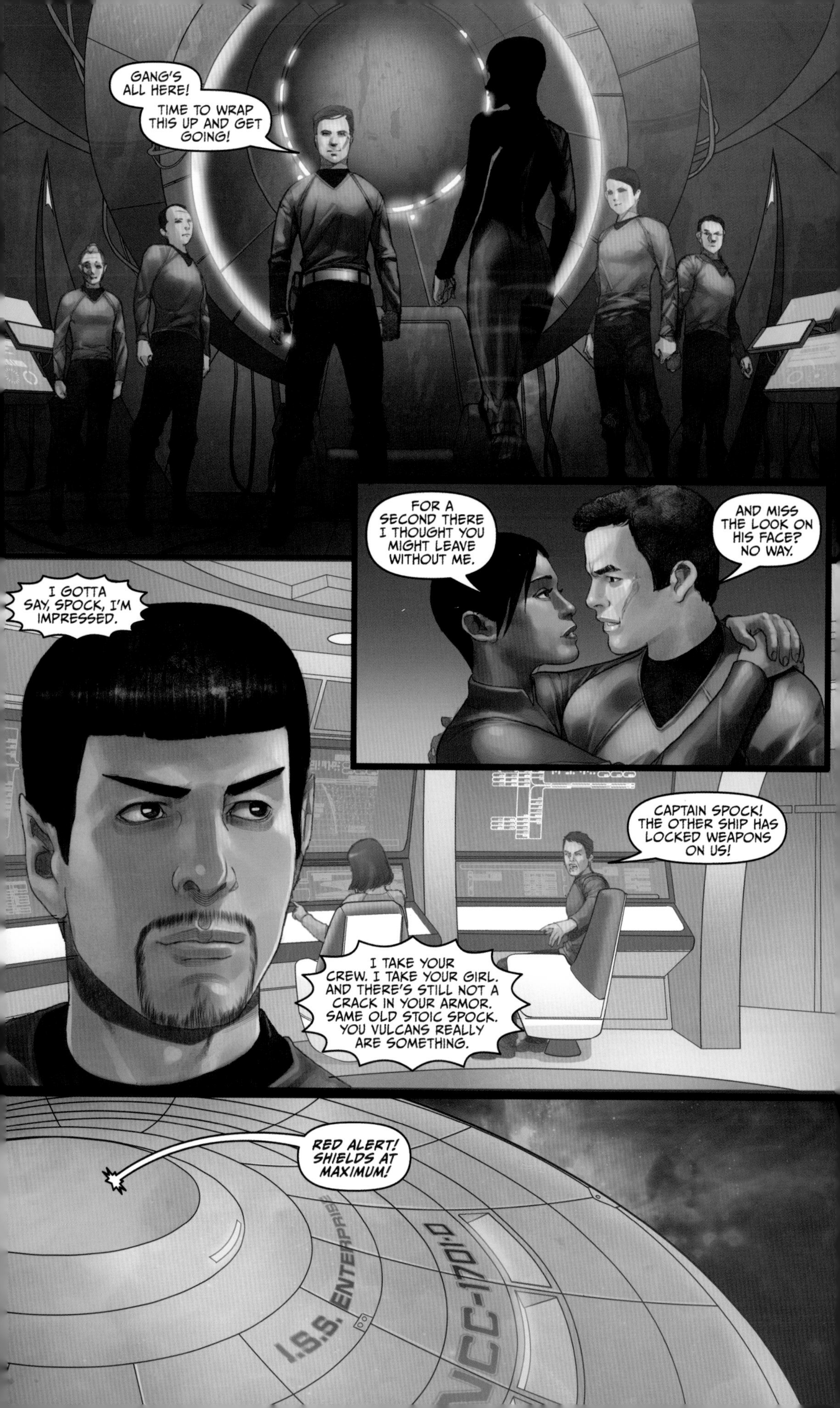
GANG'S ALL HERE!
TIME TO WRAP THIS UP AND GET GOING!
FOR A SECOND THERE I THOUGHT YOU MIGHT LEAVE WITHOUT ME.
AND MISS THE LOOK ON HIS FACE? NO WAY.
I GOTTA SAY, SPOCK, I'M IMPRESSED.
CAPTAIN SPOCK! THE OTHER SHIP HAS LOCKED WEAPONS ON US!
I TAKE YOUR CREW. I TAKE YOUR GIRL. AND THERE'S STILL NOT A CRACK IN YOUR ARMOR. SAME OLD STOIC SPOCK. YOU VULCANS REALLY ARE SOMETHING.
RED ALERT! SHIELDS AT MAXIMUM!
ENTERPRISE
I.S.S. ENTERPRISE
NCC-1701-D

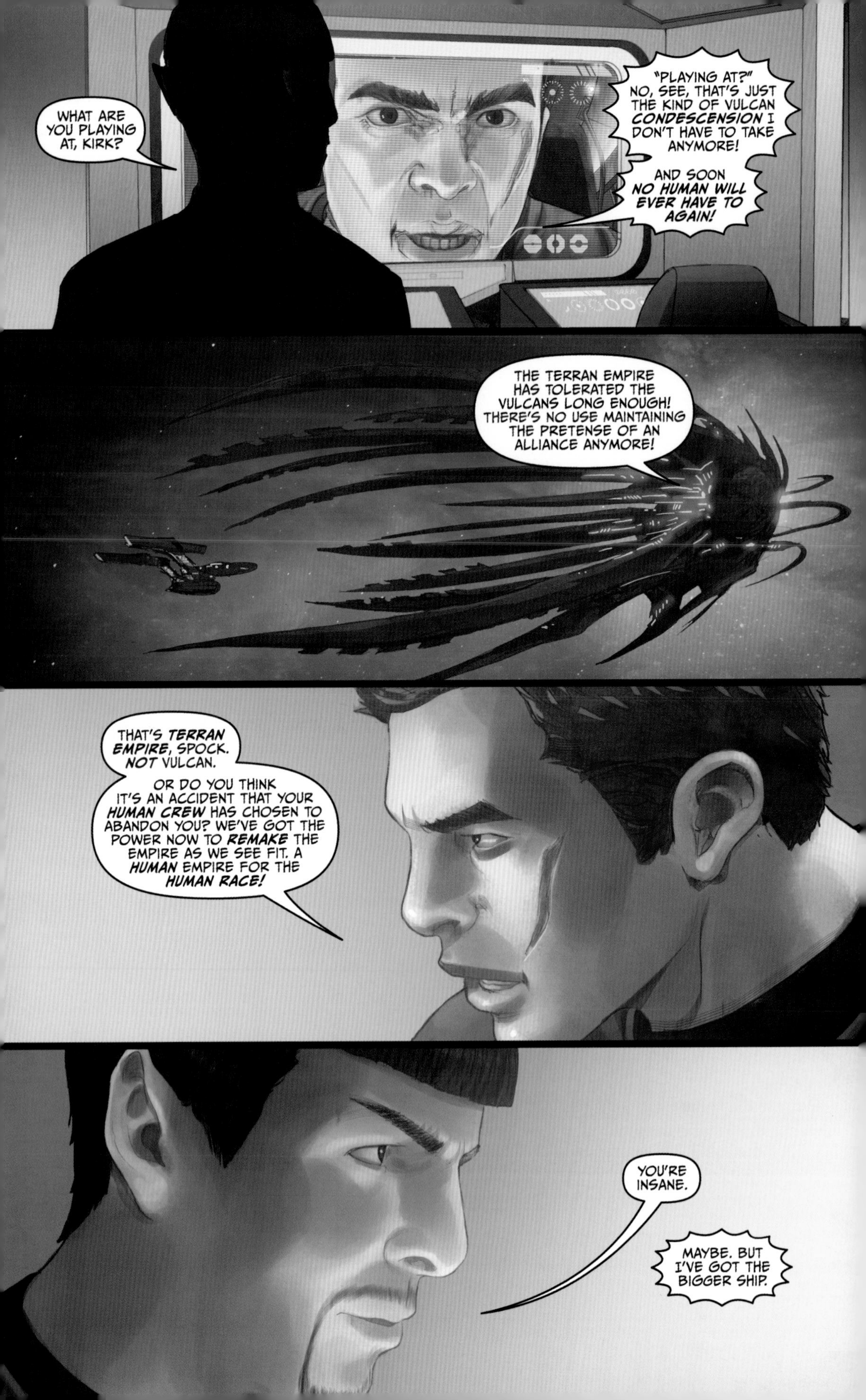
WHAT ARE YOU PLAYING AT, KIRK?
"PLAYING AT?" NO, SEE, THAT'S JUST THE KIND OF VULCAN CONDESCENSION I DON'T HAVE TO TAKE ANYMORE!
AND SOON NO HUMAN WILL EVER HAVE TO AGAIN!
THE TERRAN EMPIRE HAS TOLERATED THE VULCANS LONG ENOUGH! THERE'S NO USE MAINTAINING THE PRETENSE OF AN ALLIANCE ANYMORE!
THAT'S TERRAN EMPIRE, SPOCK. NOT VULCAN.
OR DO YOU THINK IT'S AN ACCIDENT THAT YOUR HUMAN CREW HAS CHOSEN TO ABANDON YOU? WE'VE GOT THE POWER NOW TO REMAKE THE EMPIRE AS WE SEE FIT. A HUMAN EMPIRE FOR THE HUMAN RACE!
YOU'RE INSANE.
MAYBE. BUT I'VE GOT THE BIGGER SHIP.

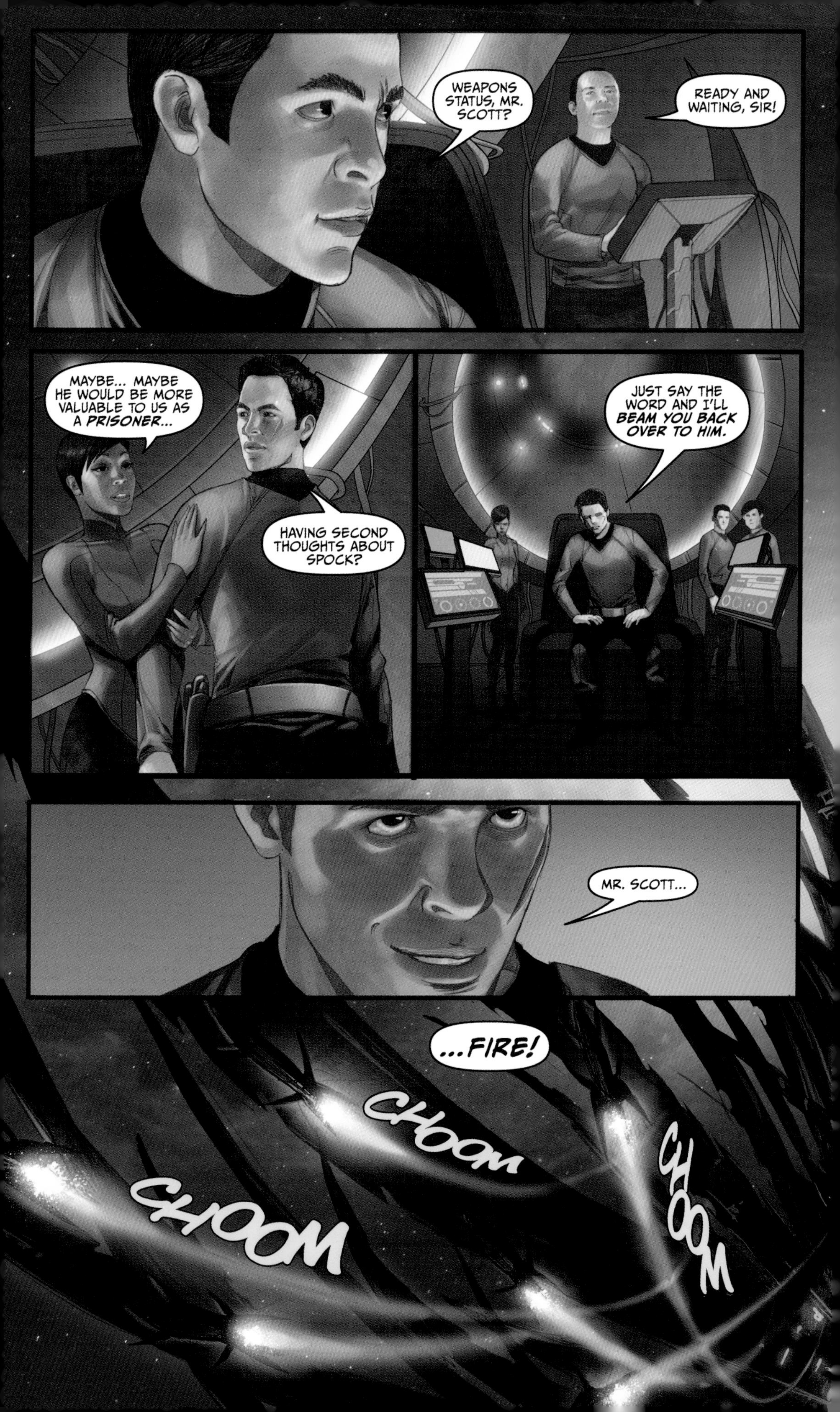
WEAPONS STATUS, MR. SCOTT?
READY AND WAITING, SIR!
MAYBE... MAYBE HE WOULD BE MORE VALUABLE TO US AS A *PRISONER*...
HAVING SECOND THOUGHTS ABOUT SPOCK?
JUST SAY THE WORD AND I'LL *BEAM YOU BACK OVER TO HIM.*
MR. SCOTT...
...FIRE!
CHOOM
CHOOM
CHOOM

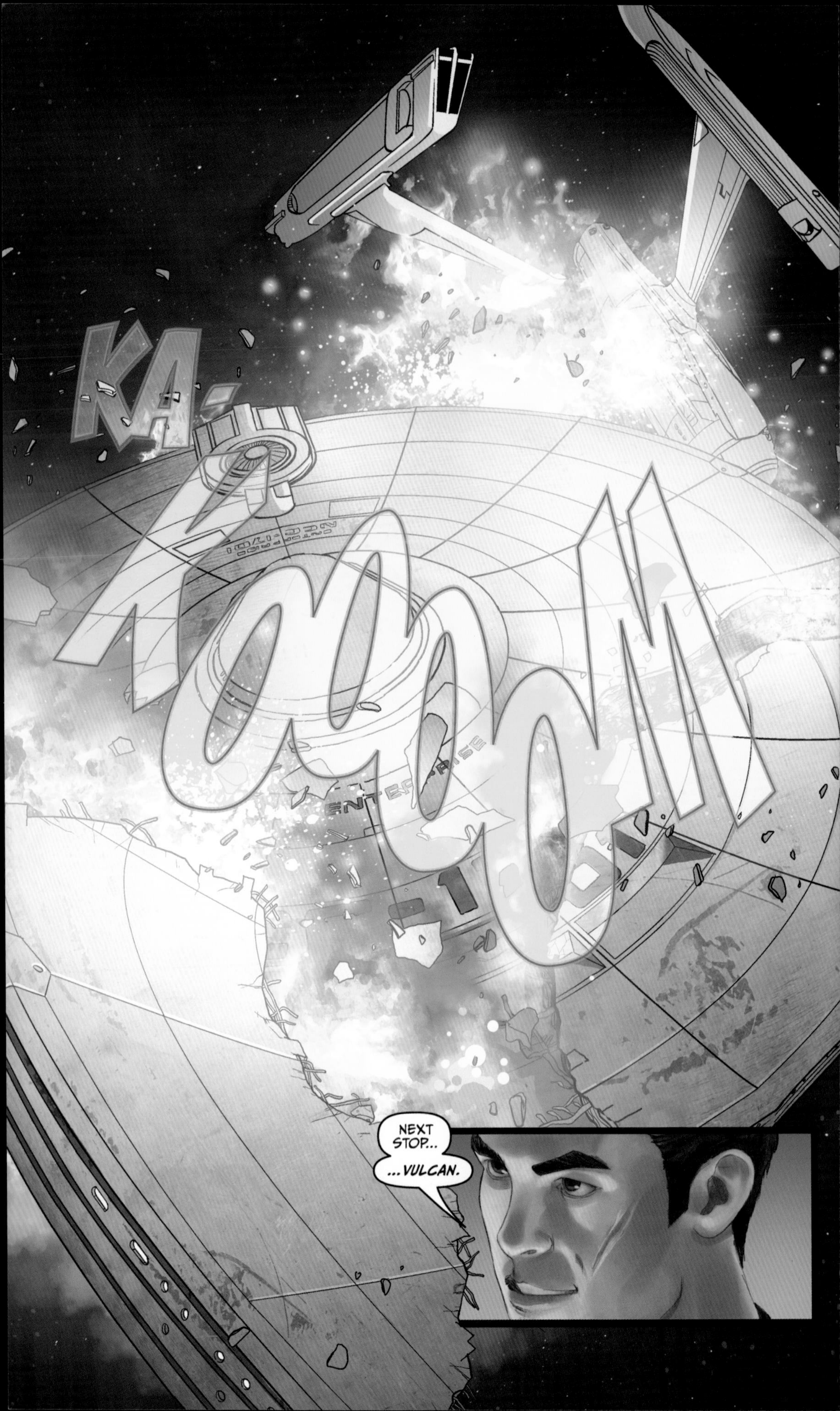
KA-BOOOM
ENTERPRISE
NEXT STOP...
...VULCAN.

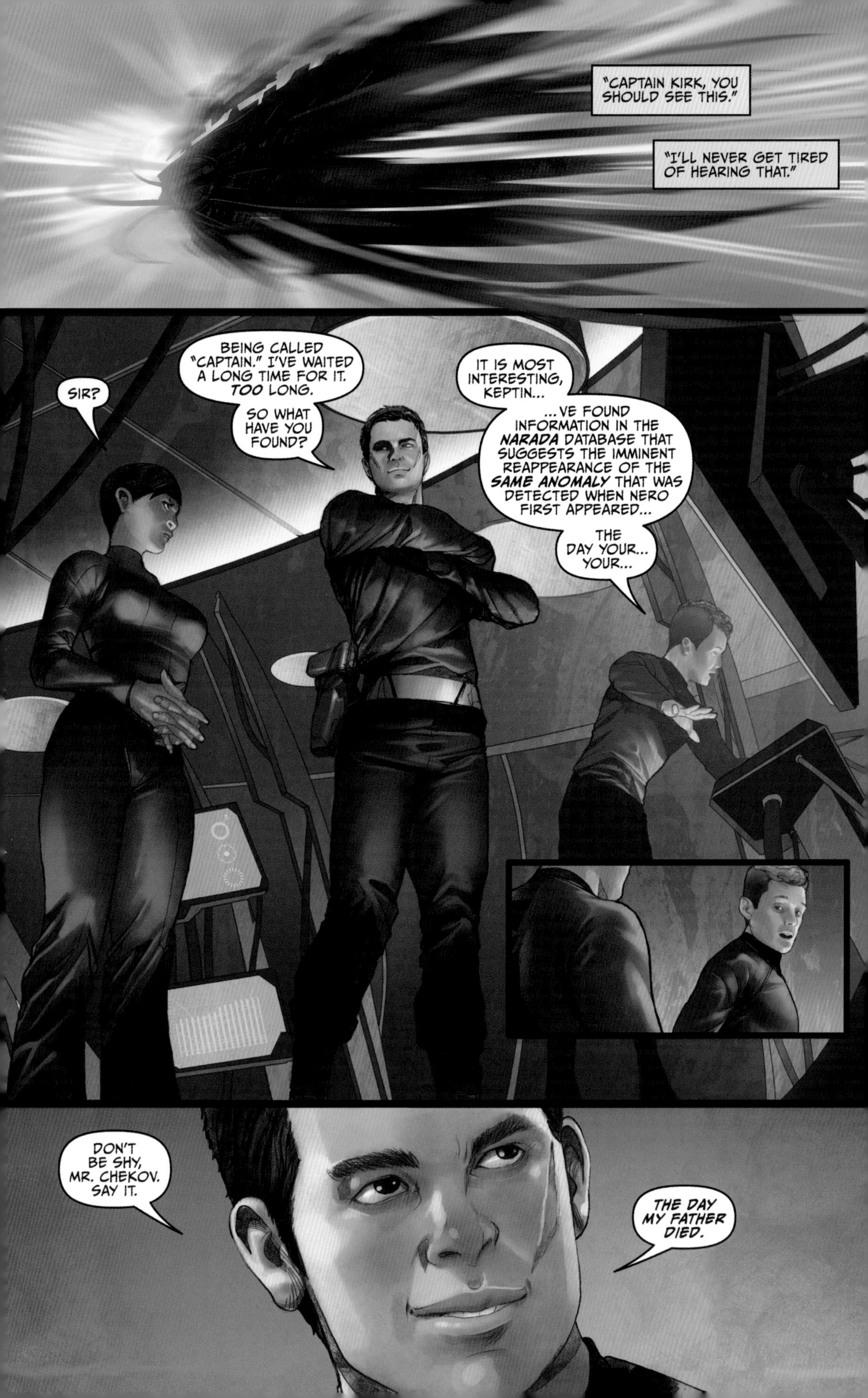
"CAPTAIN KIRK, YOU SHOULD SEE THIS."
"I'LL NEVER GET TIRED OF HEARING THAT."
SIR?
BEING CALLED "CAPTAIN." I'VE WAITED A LONG TIME FOR IT. TOO LONG.
SO WHAT HAVE YOU FOUND?
IT IS MOST INTERESTING, KEPTIN...
...VE FOUND INFORMATION IN THE NARADA DATABASE THAT SUGGESTS THE IMMINENT REAPPEARANCE OF THE SAME ANOMALY THAT WAS DETECTED WHEN NERO FIRST APPEARED...
THE DAY YOUR... YOUR...
DON'T BE SHY, MR. CHEKOV. SAY IT.
THE DAY MY FATHER DIED.

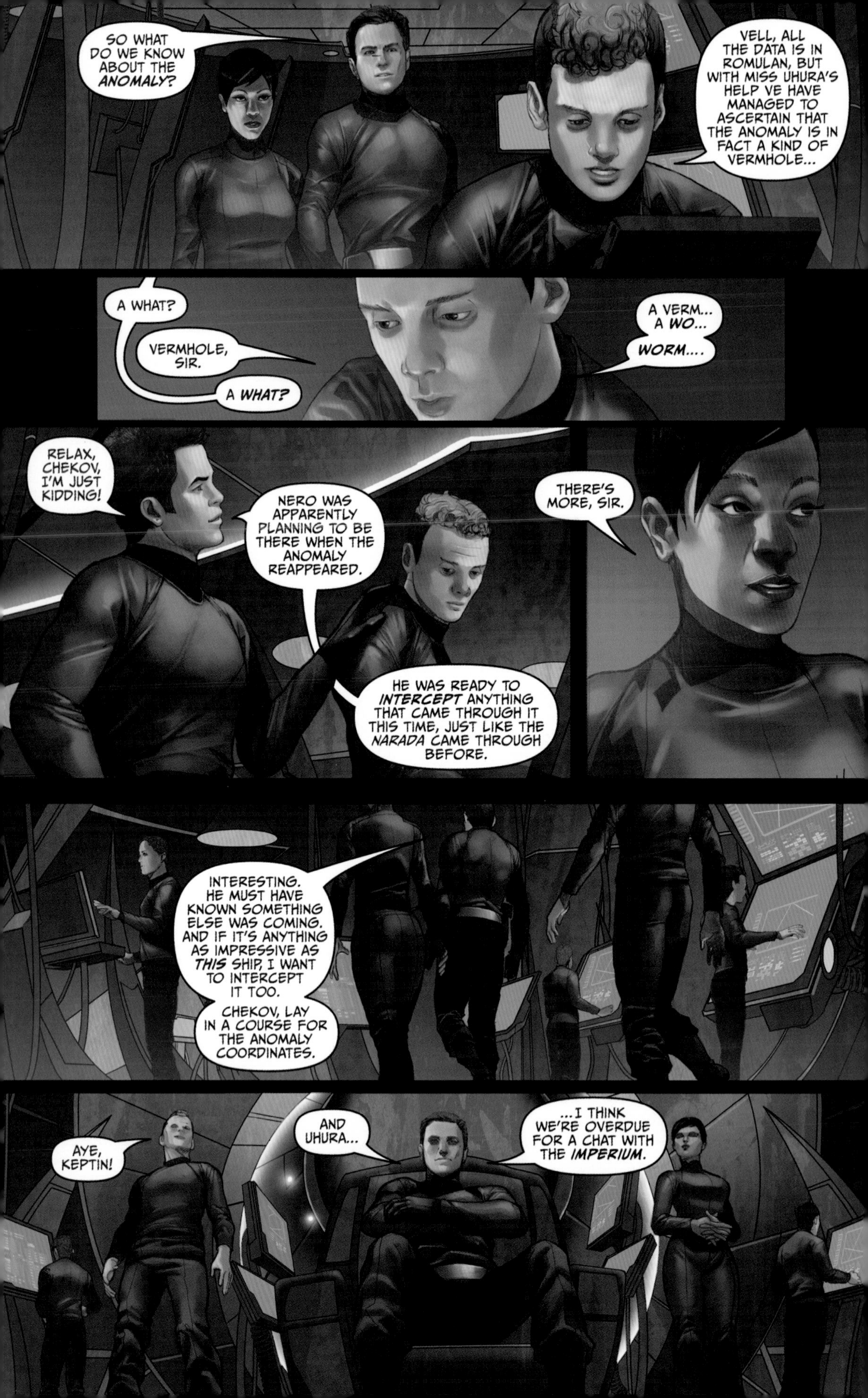

SO WHAT DO WE KNOW ABOUT THE *ANOMALY*?
VELL, ALL THE DATA IS IN ROMULAN, BUT WITH MISS UHURA'S HELP VE HAVE MANAGED TO ASCERTAIN THAT THE ANOMALY IS IN FACT A KIND OF VERMHOLE...
A WHAT?
VERMHOLE, SIR.
A *WHAT?*
A VERM... A *WO*... *WORM*....
RELAX, CHEKOV, I'M JUST KIDDING!
NERO WAS APPARENTLY PLANNING TO BE THERE WHEN THE ANOMALY REAPPEARED.
HE WAS READY TO *INTERCEPT* ANYTHING THAT CAME THROUGH IT THIS TIME, JUST LIKE THE *NARADA* CAME THROUGH BEFORE.
THERE'S MORE, SIR.
INTERESTING. HE MUST HAVE KNOWN SOMETHING ELSE WAS COMING. AND IF IT'S ANYTHING AS IMPRESSIVE AS *THIS* SHIP, I WANT TO INTERCEPT IT TOO.
CHEKOV, LAY IN A COURSE FOR THE ANOMALY COORDINATES.
AYE, KEPTIN!
AND UHURA...
...I THINK WE'RE OVERDUE FOR A CHAT WITH THE *IMPERIUM*.

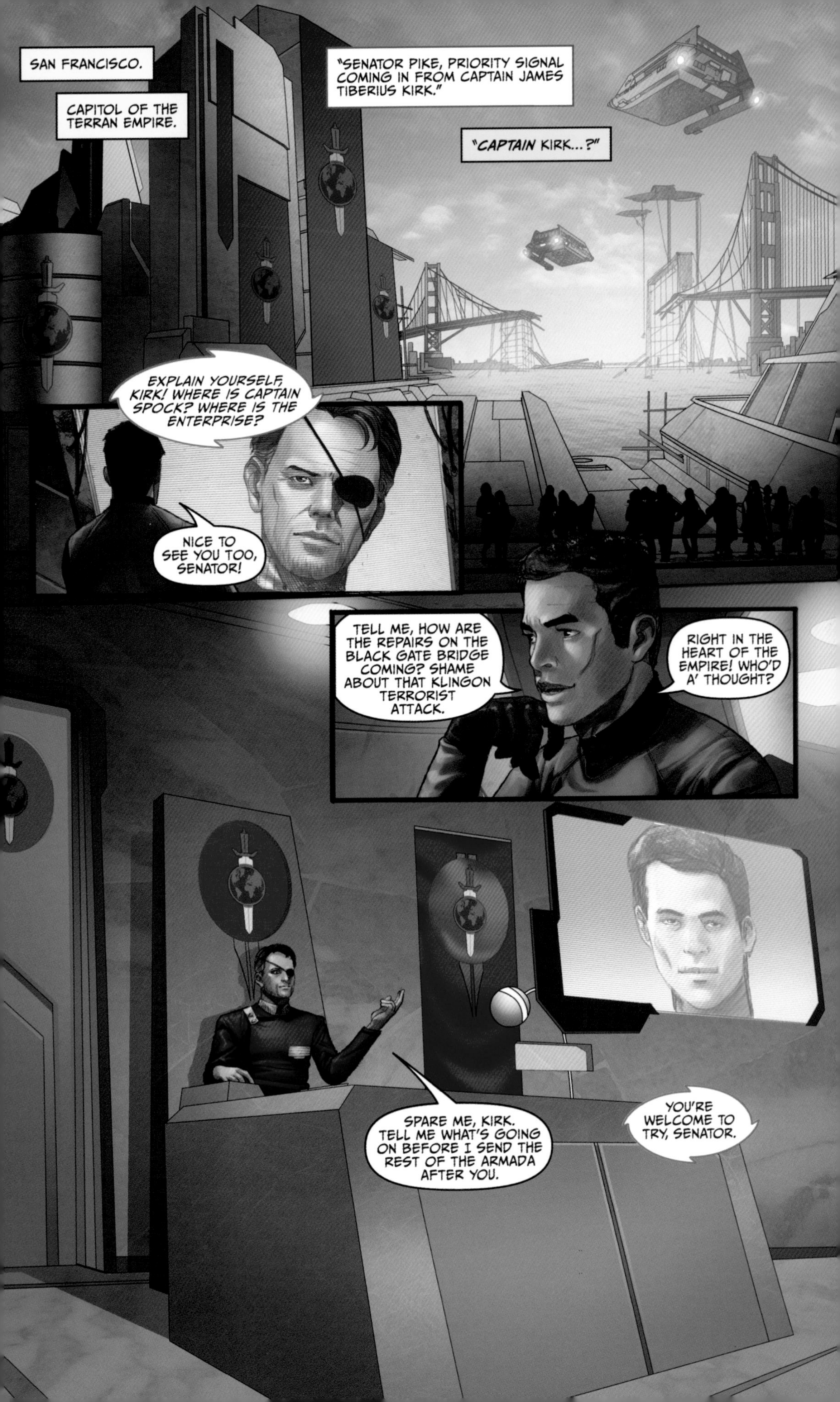
SAN FRANCISCO.
CAPITOL OF THE TERRAN EMPIRE.
"SENATOR PIKE, PRIORITY SIGNAL COMING IN FROM CAPTAIN JAMES TIBERIUS KIRK."
"CAPTAIN KIRK...?"
EXPLAIN YOURSELF, KIRK! WHERE IS CAPTAIN SPOCK? WHERE IS THE ENTERPRISE?
NICE TO SEE YOU TOO, SENATOR!
TELL ME, HOW ARE THE REPAIRS ON THE BLACK GATE BRIDGE COMING? SHAME ABOUT THAT KLINGON TERRORIST ATTACK.
RIGHT IN THE HEART OF THE EMPIRE! WHO'D A' THOUGHT?
SPARE ME, KIRK. TELL ME WHAT'S GOING ON BEFORE I SEND THE REST OF THE ARMADA AFTER YOU.
YOU'RE WELCOME TO TRY, SENATOR.

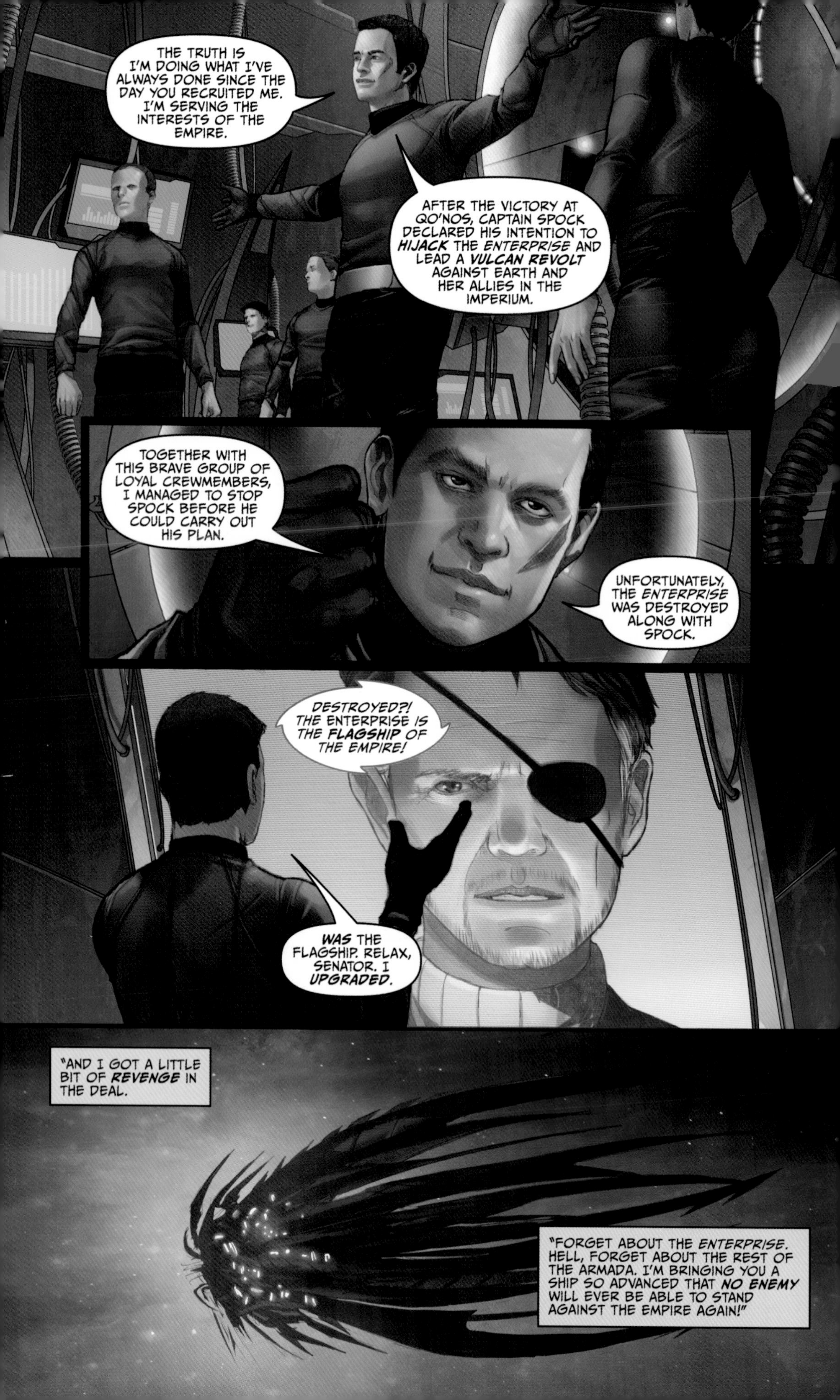
THE TRUTH IS I'M DOING WHAT I'VE ALWAYS DONE SINCE THE DAY YOU RECRUITED ME. I'M SERVING THE INTERESTS OF THE EMPIRE.
AFTER THE VICTORY AT QO'NOS, CAPTAIN SPOCK DECLARED HIS INTENTION TO ***HIJACK*** THE *ENTERPRISE* AND LEAD A ***VULCAN REVOLT*** AGAINST EARTH AND HER ALLIES IN THE IMPERIUM.
TOGETHER WITH THIS BRAVE GROUP OF LOYAL CREWMEMBERS, I MANAGED TO STOP SPOCK BEFORE HE COULD CARRY OUT HIS PLAN.
UNFORTUNATELY, THE *ENTERPRISE* WAS DESTROYED ALONG WITH SPOCK.
DESTROYED?! THE ENTERPRISE *IS* THE ***FLAGSHIP*** OF THE EMPIRE!
WAS THE FLAGSHIP. RELAX, SENATOR. I ***UPGRADED***.
"AND I GOT A LITTLE BIT OF ***REVENGE*** IN THE DEAL.
"FORGET ABOUT THE *ENTERPRISE*. HELL, FORGET ABOUT THE REST OF THE ARMADA. I'M BRINGING YOU A SHIP SO ADVANCED THAT ***NO ENEMY*** WILL EVER BE ABLE TO STAND AGAINST THE EMPIRE AGAIN!"

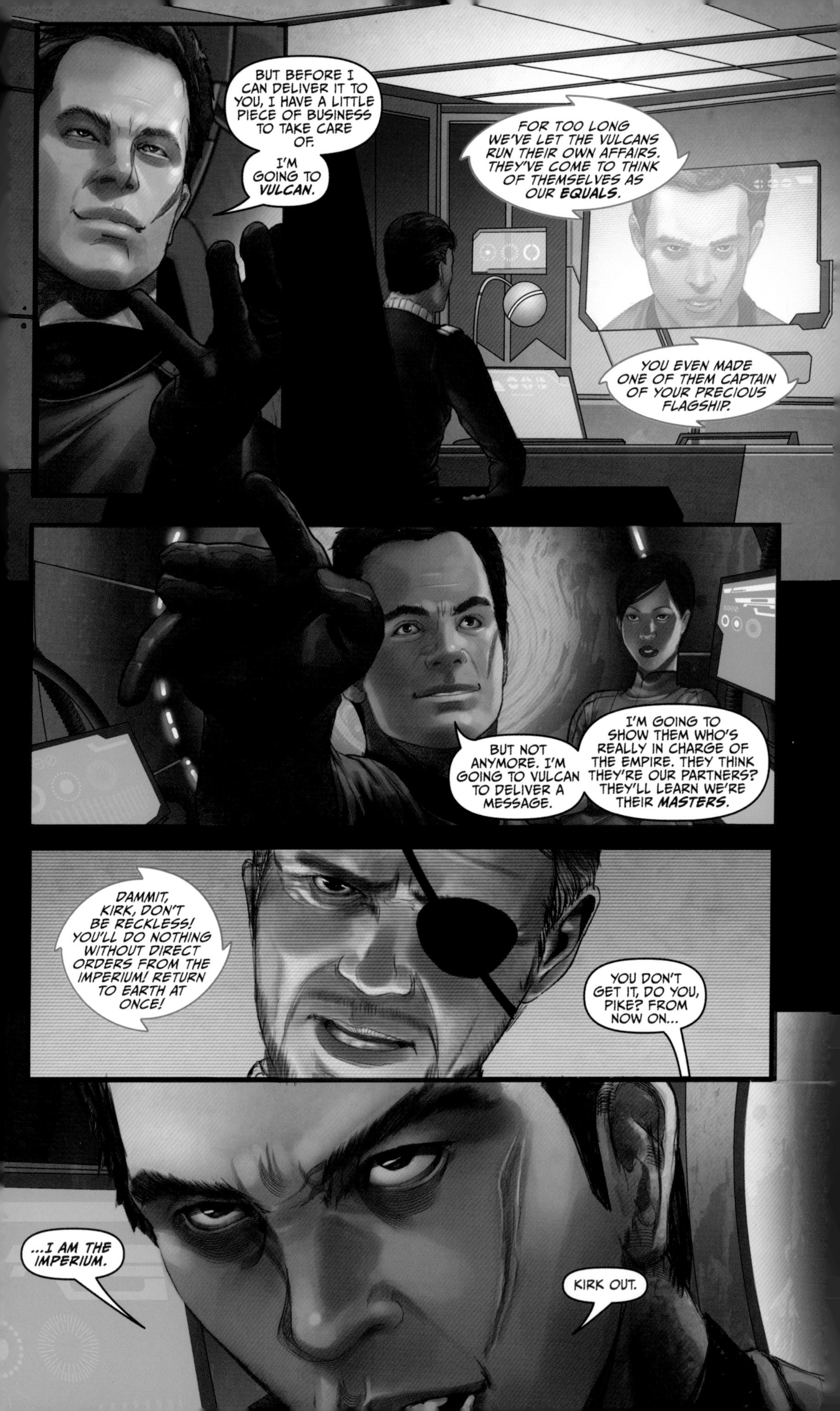
BUT BEFORE I CAN DELIVER IT TO YOU, I HAVE A LITTLE PIECE OF BUSINESS TO TAKE CARE OF.
I'M GOING TO VULCAN.
FOR TOO LONG WE'VE LET THE VULCANS RUN THEIR OWN AFFAIRS. THEY'VE COME TO THINK OF THEMSELVES AS OUR EQUALS.
YOU EVEN MADE ONE OF THEM CAPTAIN OF YOUR PRECIOUS FLAGSHIP.
BUT NOT ANYMORE. I'M GOING TO VULCAN TO DELIVER A MESSAGE.
I'M GOING TO SHOW THEM WHO'S REALLY IN CHARGE OF THE EMPIRE. THEY THINK THEY'RE OUR PARTNERS? THEY'LL LEARN WE'RE THEIR MASTERS.
DAMMIT, KIRK, DON'T BE RECKLESS! YOU'LL DO NOTHING WITHOUT DIRECT ORDERS FROM THE IMPERIUM! RETURN TO EARTH AT ONCE!
YOU DON'T GET IT, DO YOU, PIKE? FROM NOW ON...
...I AM THE IMPERIUM.
KIRK OUT.

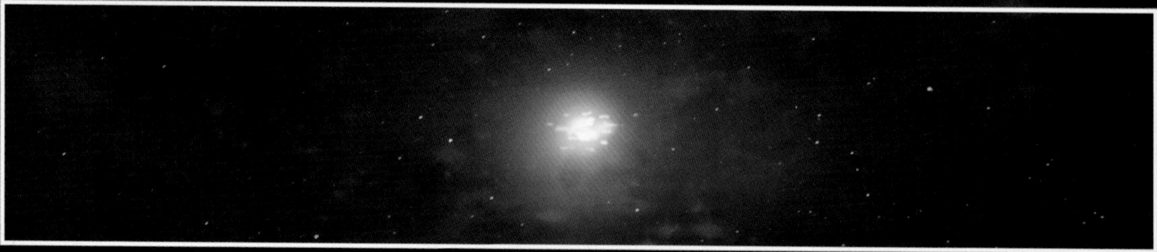

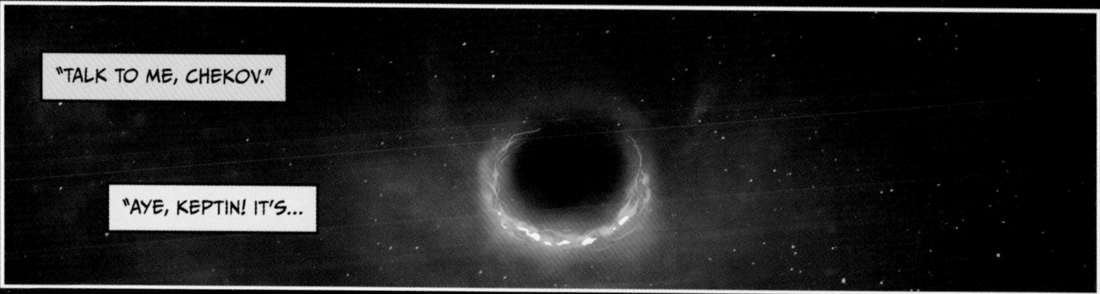
"TALK TO ME, CHEKOV."
"AYE, KEPTIN! IT'S...

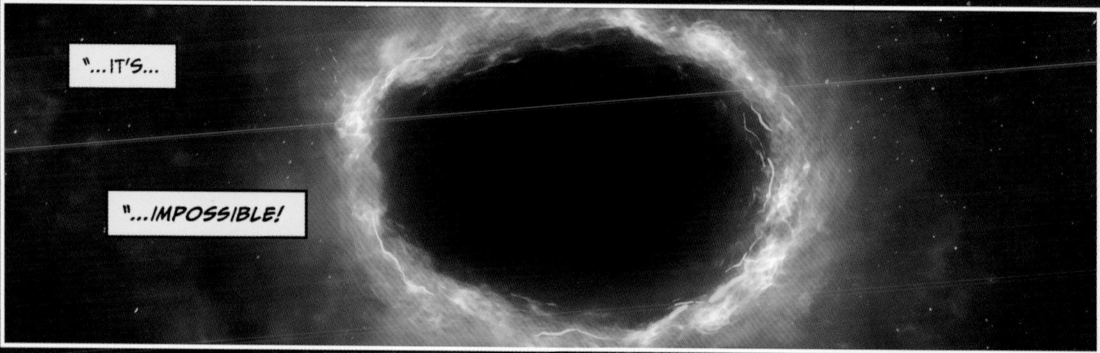
"...IT'S...
"...IMPOSSIBLE!

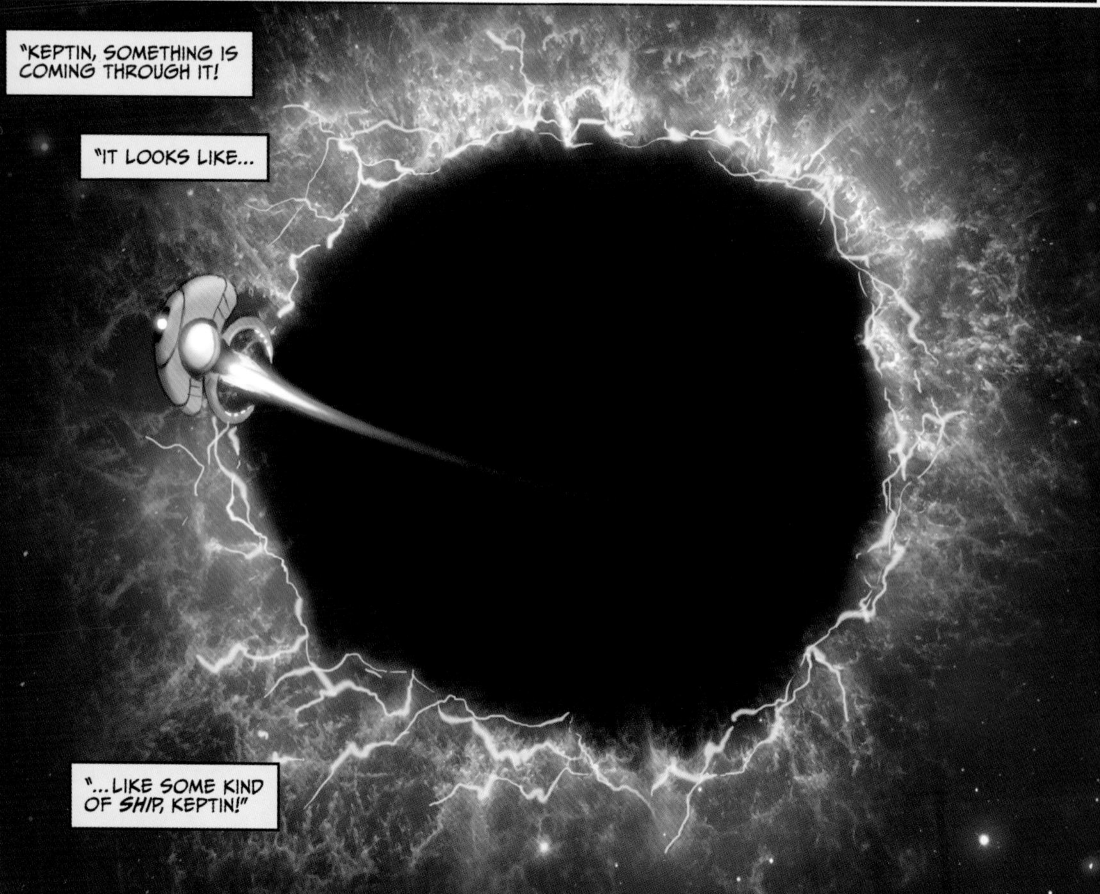
"KEPTIN, SOMETHING IS COMING THROUGH IT!
"IT LOOKS LIKE...
"...LIKE SOME KIND OF SHIP, KEPTIN!"

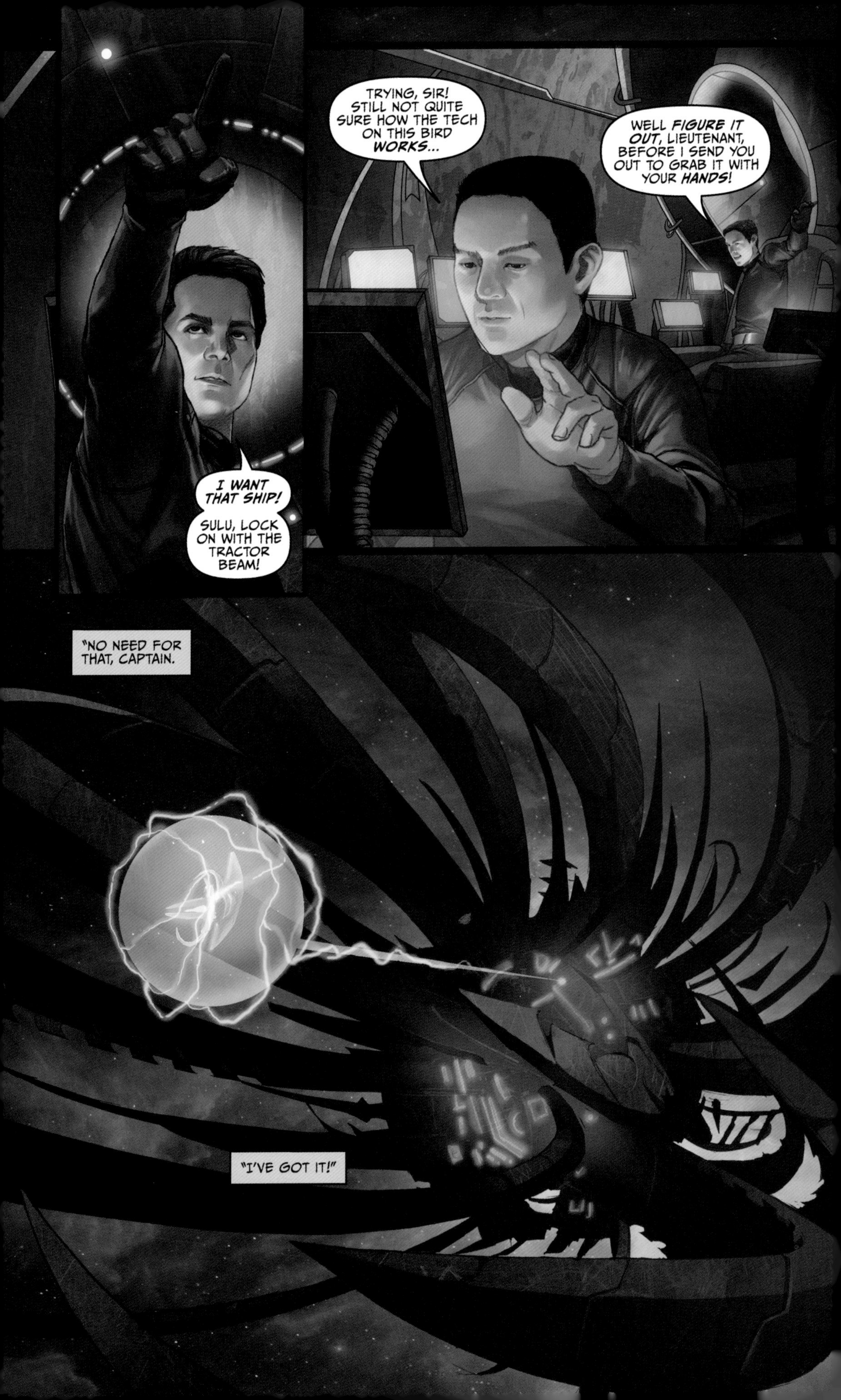
I WANT THAT SHIP!
SULU, LOCK ON WITH THE TRACTOR BEAM!
TRYING, SIR! STILL NOT QUITE SURE HOW THE TECH ON THIS BIRD WORKS...
WELL FIGURE IT OUT, LIEUTENANT, BEFORE I SEND YOU OUT TO GRAB IT WITH YOUR HANDS!
"NO NEED FOR THAT, CAPTAIN.
"I'VE GOT IT!"

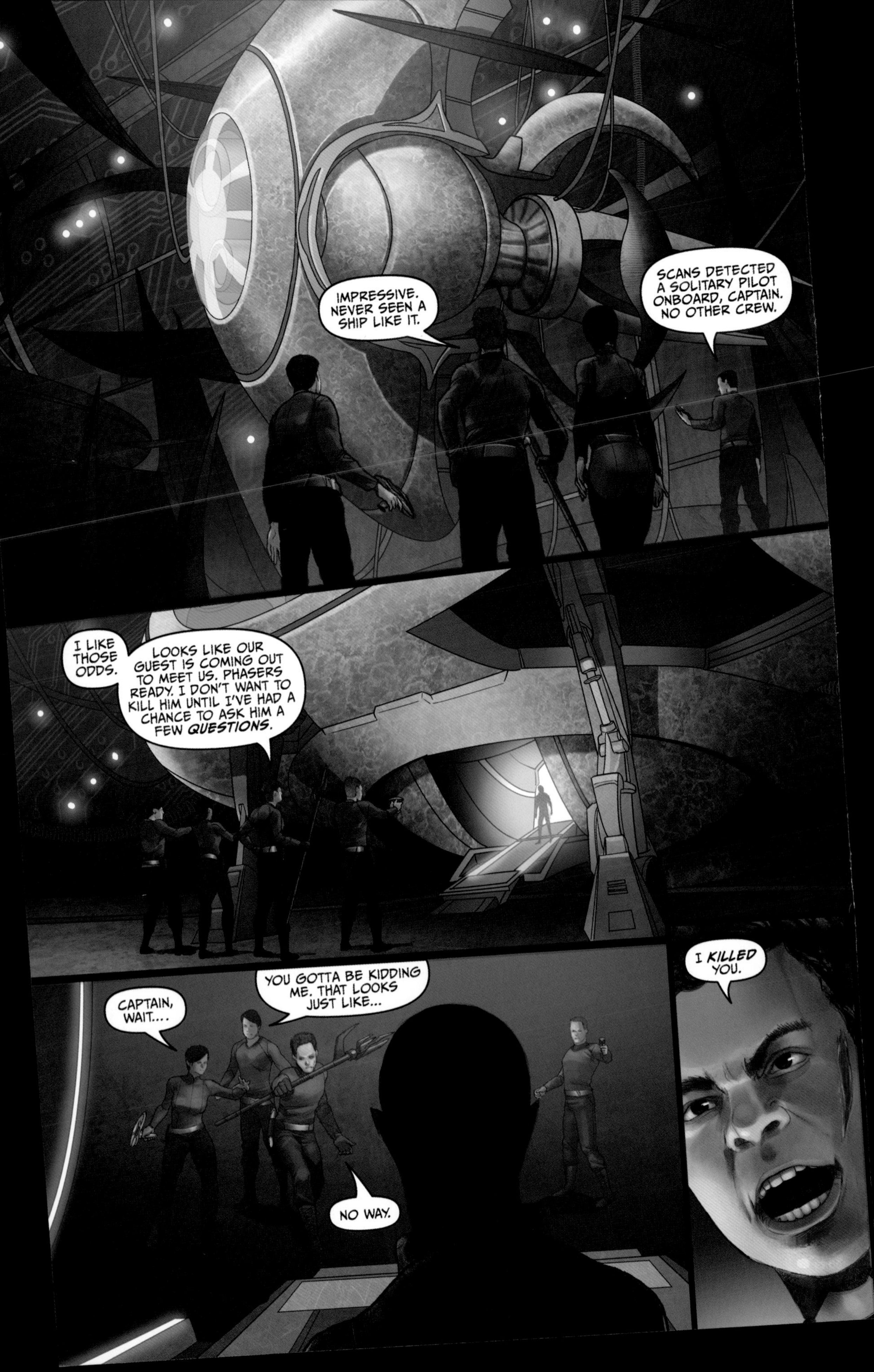
IMPRESSIVE. NEVER SEEN A SHIP LIKE IT.
SCANS DETECTED A SOLITARY PILOT ONBOARD, CAPTAIN. NO OTHER CREW.
I LIKE THOSE ODDS.
LOOKS LIKE OUR GUEST IS COMING OUT TO MEET US. PHASERS READY. I DON'T WANT TO KILL HIM UNTIL I'VE HAD A CHANCE TO ASK HIM A FEW *QUESTIONS*.
CAPTAIN, WAIT....
YOU GOTTA BE KIDDING ME. THAT LOOKS JUST LIKE...
NO WAY.
I *KILLED* YOU.

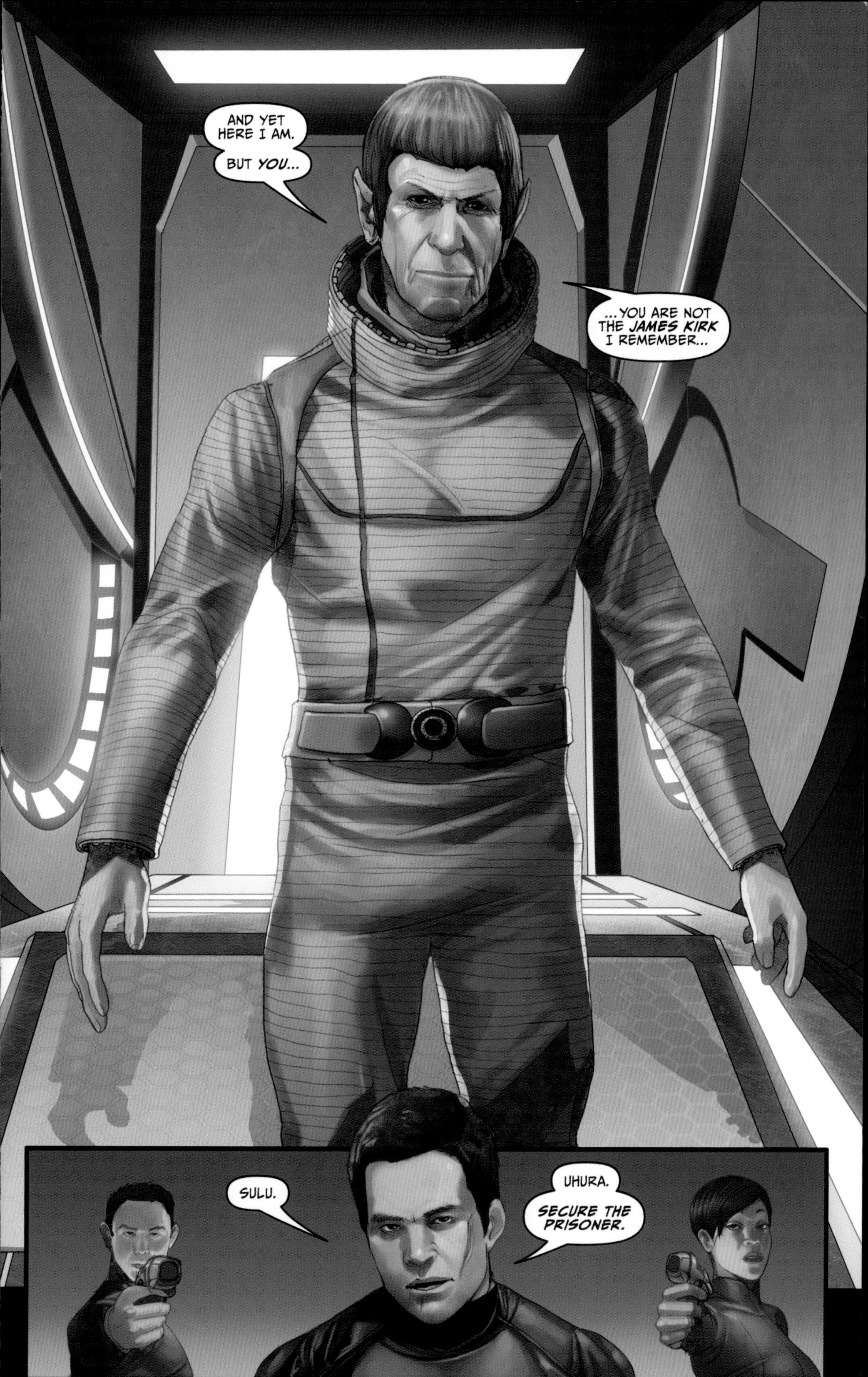
AND YET HERE I AM.
BUT *YOU*...
...YOU ARE NOT THE ***JAMES KIRK*** I REMEMBER...
SULU.
UHURA.
SECURE THE PRISONER.

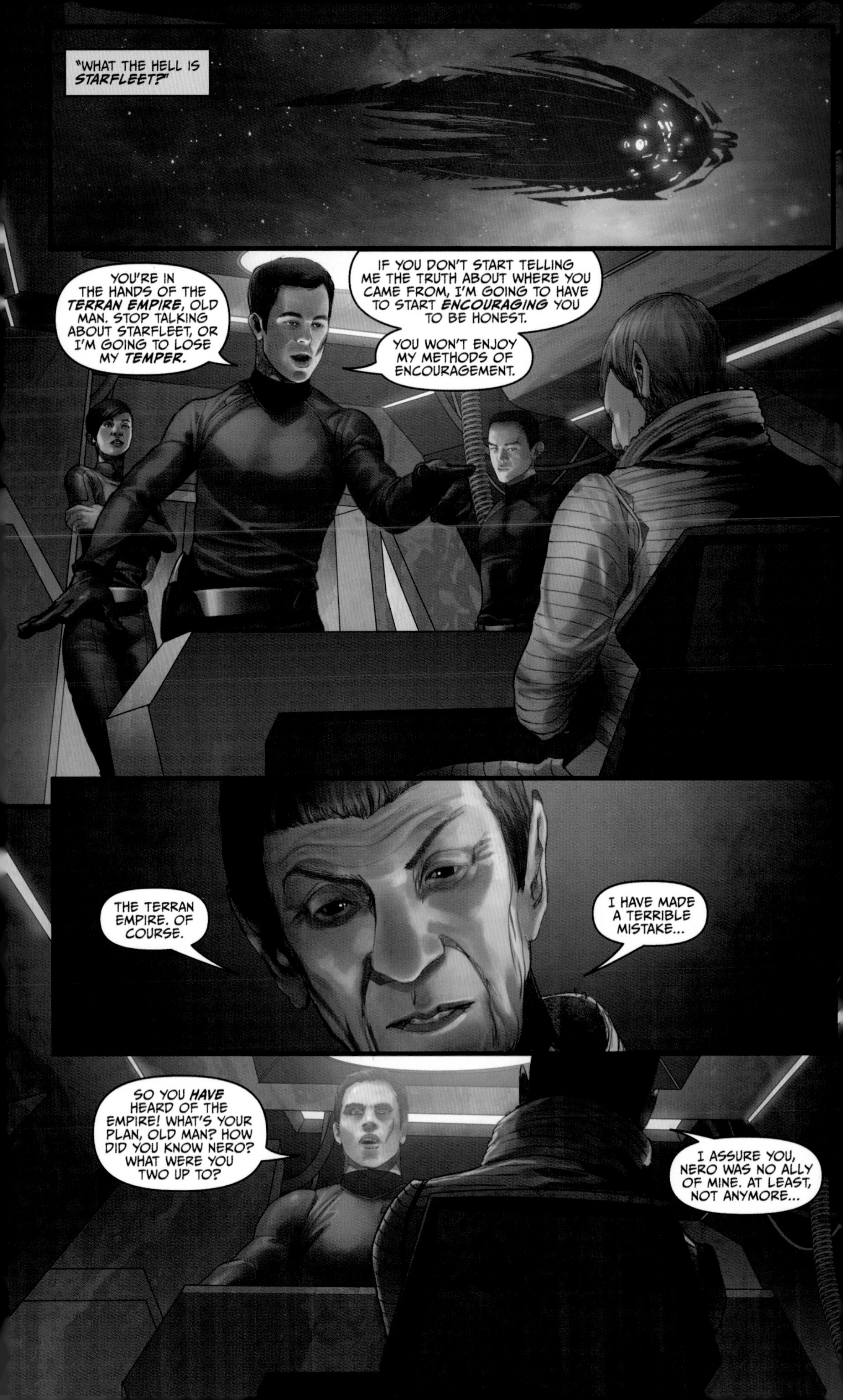
"WHAT THE HELL IS STARFLEET?"
YOU'RE IN THE HANDS OF THE TERRAN EMPIRE, OLD MAN. STOP TALKING ABOUT STARFLEET, OR I'M GOING TO LOSE MY TEMPER.
IF YOU DON'T START TELLING ME THE TRUTH ABOUT WHERE YOU CAME FROM, I'M GOING TO HAVE TO START ENCOURAGING YOU TO BE HONEST.
YOU WON'T ENJOY MY METHODS OF ENCOURAGEMENT.
THE TERRAN EMPIRE. OF COURSE.
I HAVE MADE A TERRIBLE MISTAKE...
SO YOU HAVE HEARD OF THE EMPIRE! WHAT'S YOUR PLAN, OLD MAN? HOW DID YOU KNOW NERO? WHAT WERE YOU TWO UP TO?
I ASSURE YOU, NERO WAS NO ALLY OF MINE. AT LEAST, NOT ANYMORE...

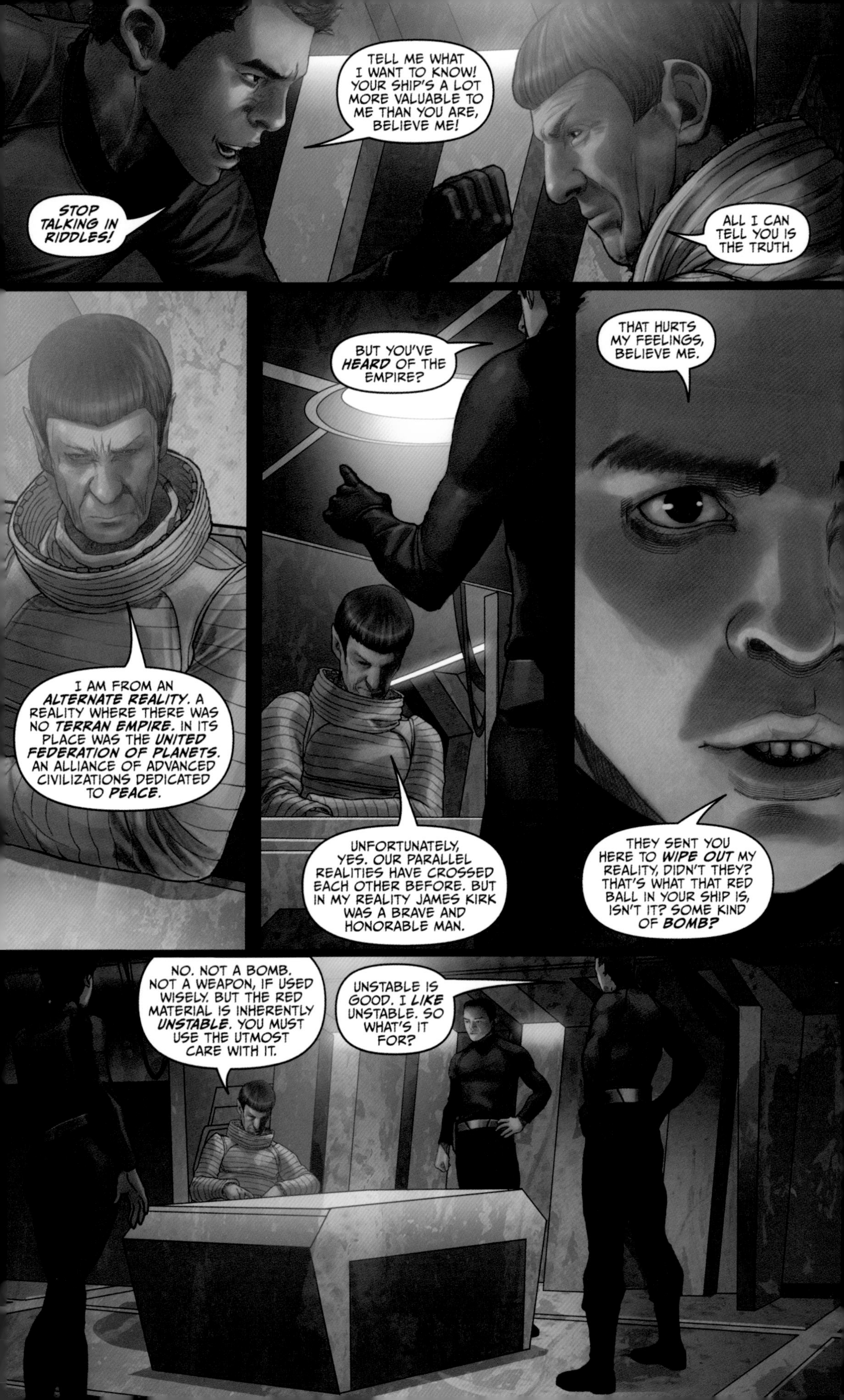

TELL ME WHAT I WANT TO KNOW! YOUR SHIP'S A LOT MORE VALUABLE TO ME THAN YOU ARE, BELIEVE ME!
STOP TALKING IN RIDDLES!
ALL I CAN TELL YOU IS THE TRUTH.
I AM FROM AN ALTERNATE REALITY. A REALITY WHERE THERE WAS NO TERRAN EMPIRE. IN ITS PLACE WAS THE UNITED FEDERATION OF PLANETS. AN ALLIANCE OF ADVANCED CIVILIZATIONS DEDICATED TO PEACE.
BUT YOU'VE HEARD OF THE EMPIRE?
UNFORTUNATELY, YES. OUR PARALLEL REALITIES HAVE CROSSED EACH OTHER BEFORE. BUT IN MY REALITY JAMES KIRK WAS A BRAVE AND HONORABLE MAN.
THAT HURTS MY FEELINGS, BELIEVE ME.
THEY SENT YOU HERE TO WIPE OUT MY REALITY, DIDN'T THEY? THAT'S WHAT THAT RED BALL IN YOUR SHIP IS, ISN'T IT? SOME KIND OF BOMB?
NO. NOT A BOMB. NOT A WEAPON, IF USED WISELY. BUT THE RED MATERIAL IS INHERENTLY UNSTABLE. YOU MUST USE THE UTMOST CARE WITH IT.
UNSTABLE IS GOOD. I LIKE UNSTABLE. SO WHAT'S IT FOR?

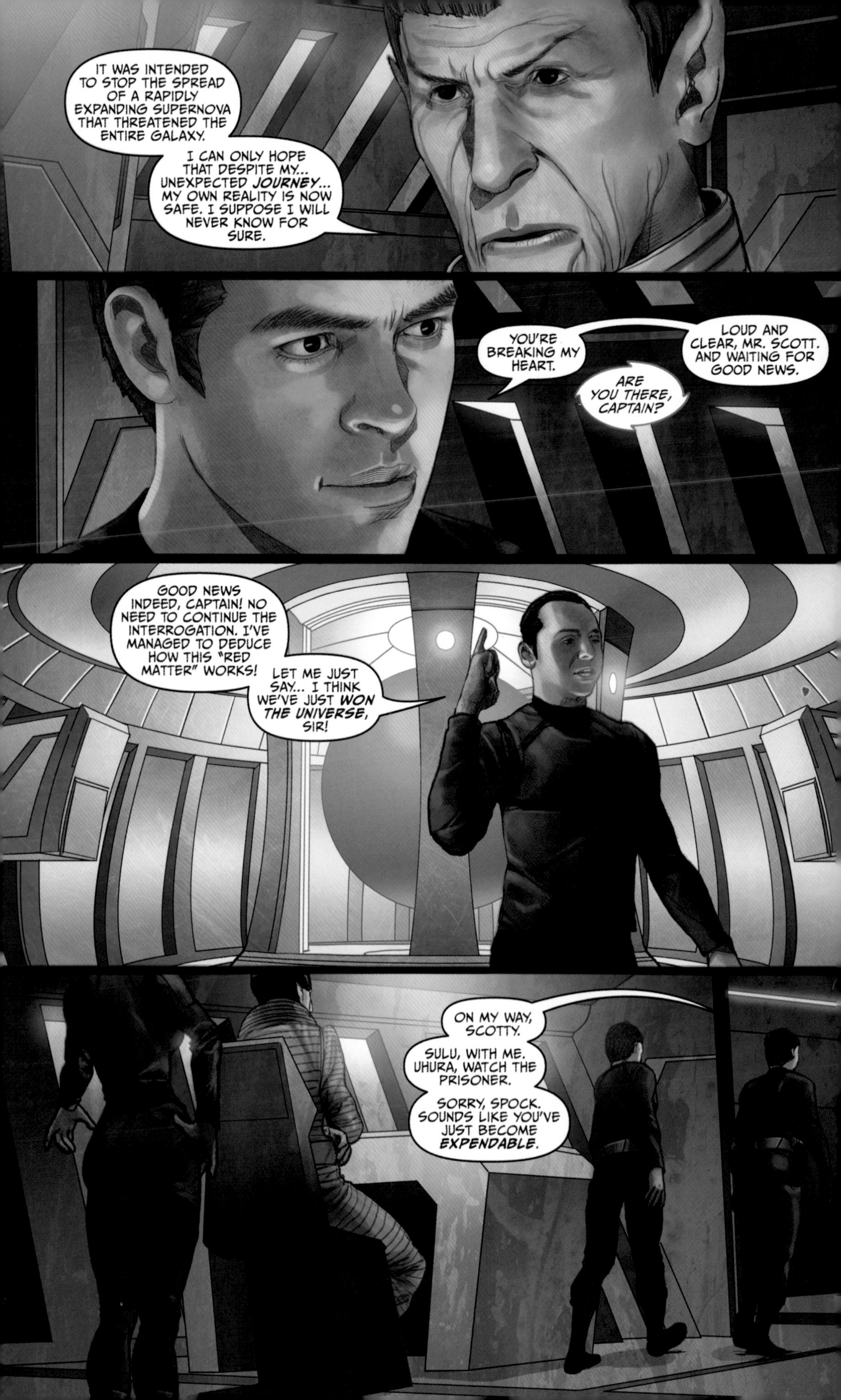

IT WAS INTENDED TO STOP THE SPREAD OF A RAPIDLY EXPANDING SUPERNOVA THAT THREATENED THE ENTIRE GALAXY.
I CAN ONLY HOPE THAT DESPITE MY... UNEXPECTED *JOURNEY*... MY OWN REALITY IS NOW SAFE. I SUPPOSE I WILL NEVER KNOW FOR SURE.
YOU'RE BREAKING MY HEART.
ARE YOU THERE, CAPTAIN?
LOUD AND CLEAR, MR. SCOTT. AND WAITING FOR GOOD NEWS.
GOOD NEWS INDEED, CAPTAIN! NO NEED TO CONTINUE THE INTERROGATION. I'VE MANAGED TO DEDUCE HOW THIS "RED MATTER" WORKS!
LET ME JUST SAY... I THINK WE'VE JUST ***WON THE UNIVERSE***, SIR!
ON MY WAY, SCOTTY.
SULU, WITH ME. UHURA, WATCH THE PRISONER.
SORRY, SPOCK. SOUNDS LIKE YOU'VE JUST BECOME ***EXPENDABLE***.

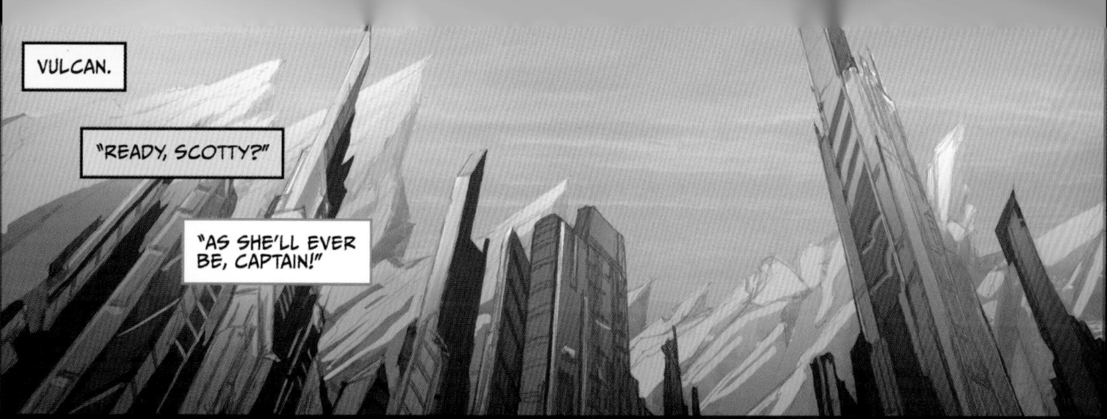
VULCAN.
"READY, SCOTTY?"
"AS SHE'LL EVER BE, CAPTAIN!"

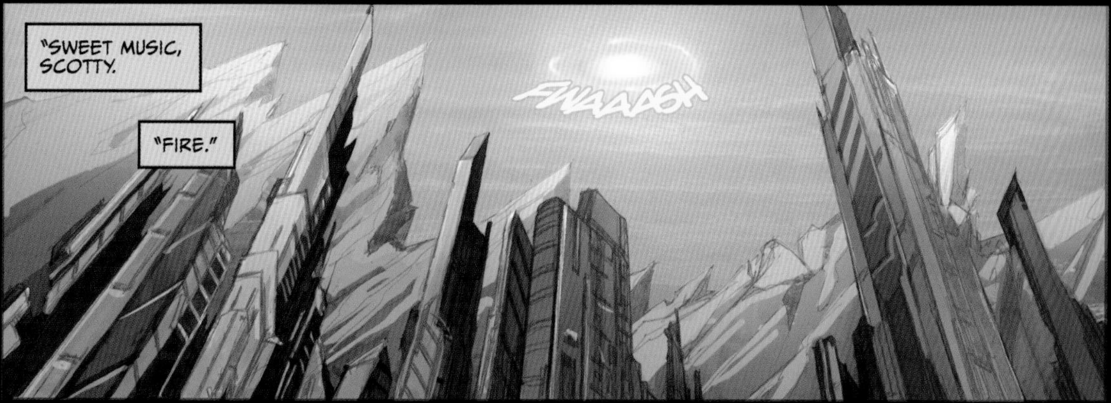
"SWEET MUSIC, SCOTTY.
FWAAAGH
"FIRE."

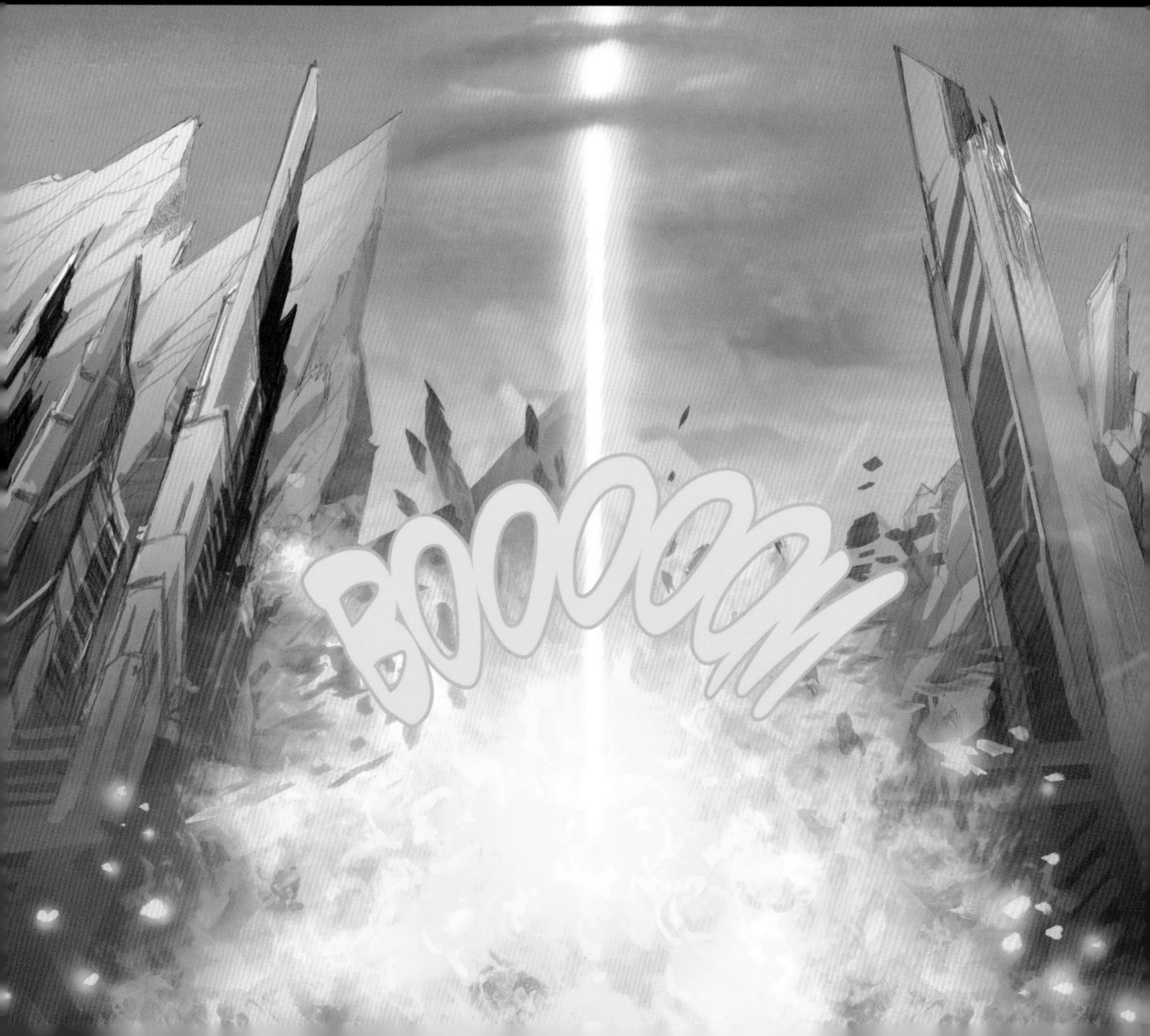
BOOOOM

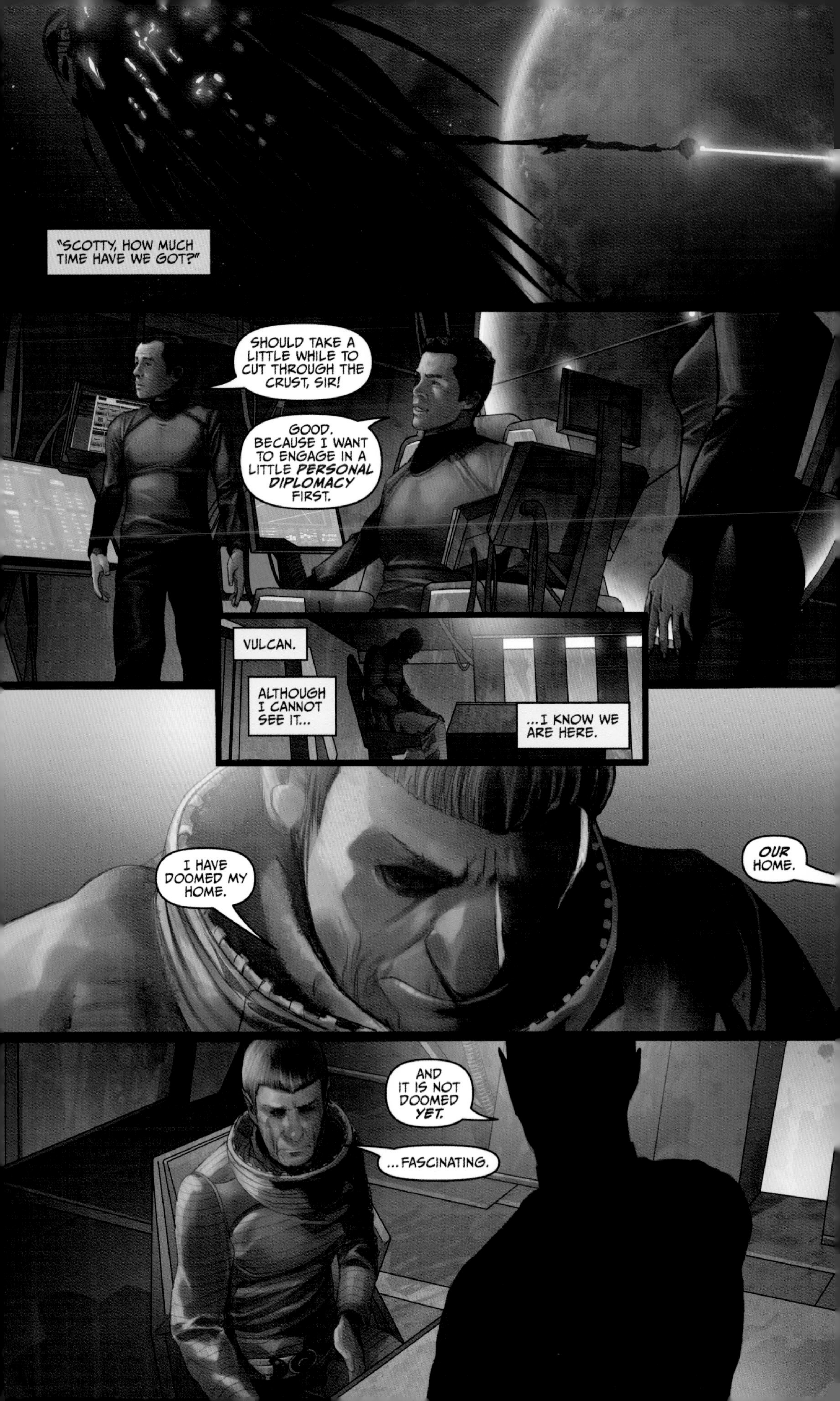
"SCOTTY, HOW MUCH TIME HAVE WE GOT?"
SHOULD TAKE A LITTLE WHILE TO CUT THROUGH THE CRUST, SIR!
GOOD. BECAUSE I WANT TO ENGAGE IN A LITTLE PERSONAL DIPLOMACY FIRST.
VULCAN.
ALTHOUGH I CANNOT SEE IT...
...I KNOW WE ARE HERE.
I HAVE DOOMED MY HOME.
OUR HOME.
AND IT IS NOT DOOMED YET.
...FASCINATING.

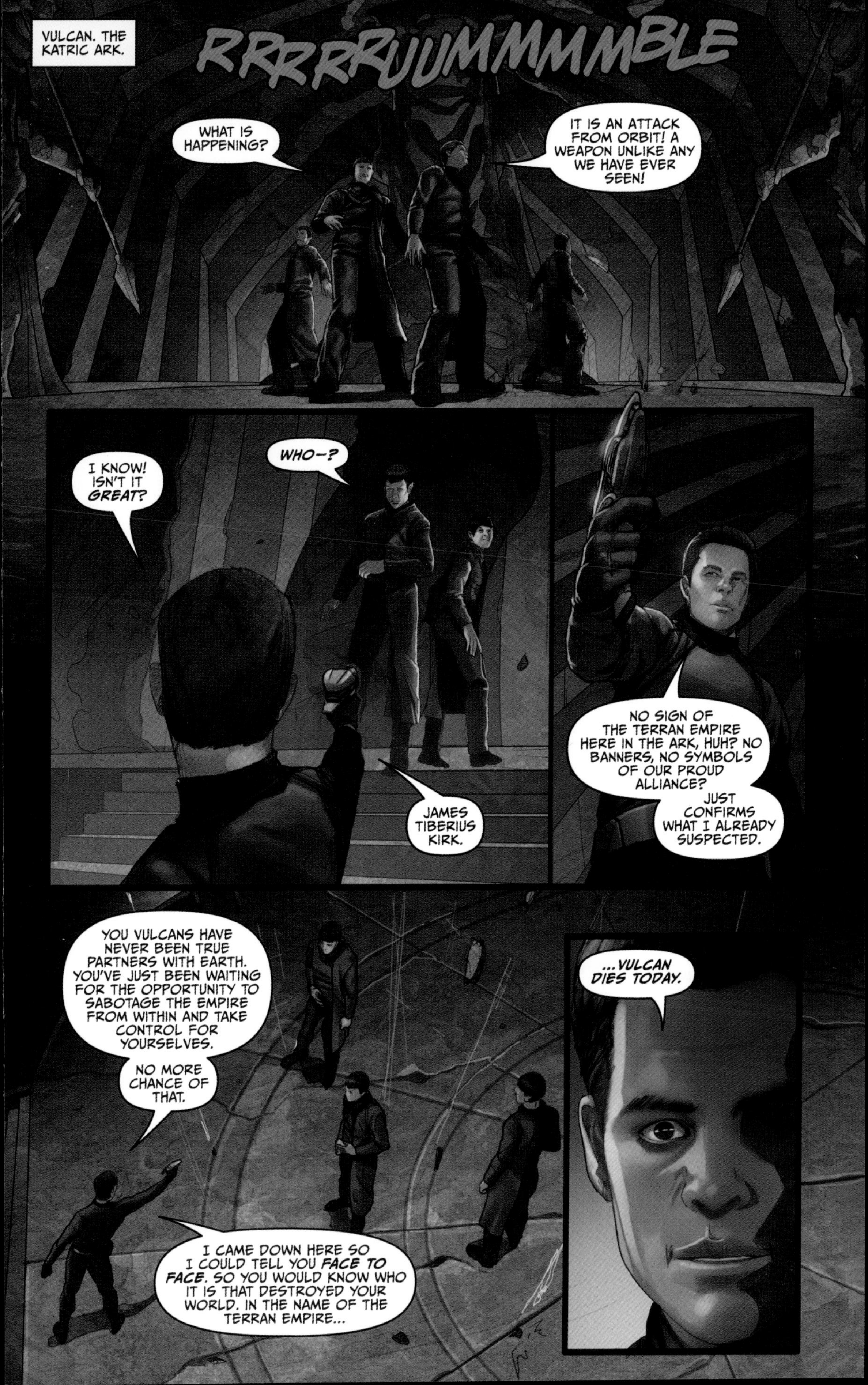
VULCAN. THE KATRIC ARK.
RRRRRRUUMMMMMBLE
WHAT IS HAPPENING?
IT IS AN ATTACK FROM ORBIT! A WEAPON UNLIKE ANY WE HAVE EVER SEEN!
I KNOW! ISN'T IT GREAT?
WHO--?
JAMES TIBERIUS KIRK.
NO SIGN OF THE TERRAN EMPIRE HERE IN THE ARK, HUH? NO BANNERS, NO SYMBOLS OF OUR PROUD ALLIANCE?
JUST CONFIRMS WHAT I ALREADY SUSPECTED.
YOU VULCANS HAVE NEVER BEEN TRUE PARTNERS WITH EARTH. YOU'VE JUST BEEN WAITING FOR THE OPPORTUNITY TO SABOTAGE THE EMPIRE FROM WITHIN AND TAKE CONTROL FOR YOURSELVES.
NO MORE CHANCE OF THAT.
I CAME DOWN HERE SO I COULD TELL YOU FACE TO FACE. SO YOU WOULD KNOW WHO IT IS THAT DESTROYED YOUR WORLD. IN THE NAME OF THE TERRAN EMPIRE...
...VULCAN DIES TODAY.

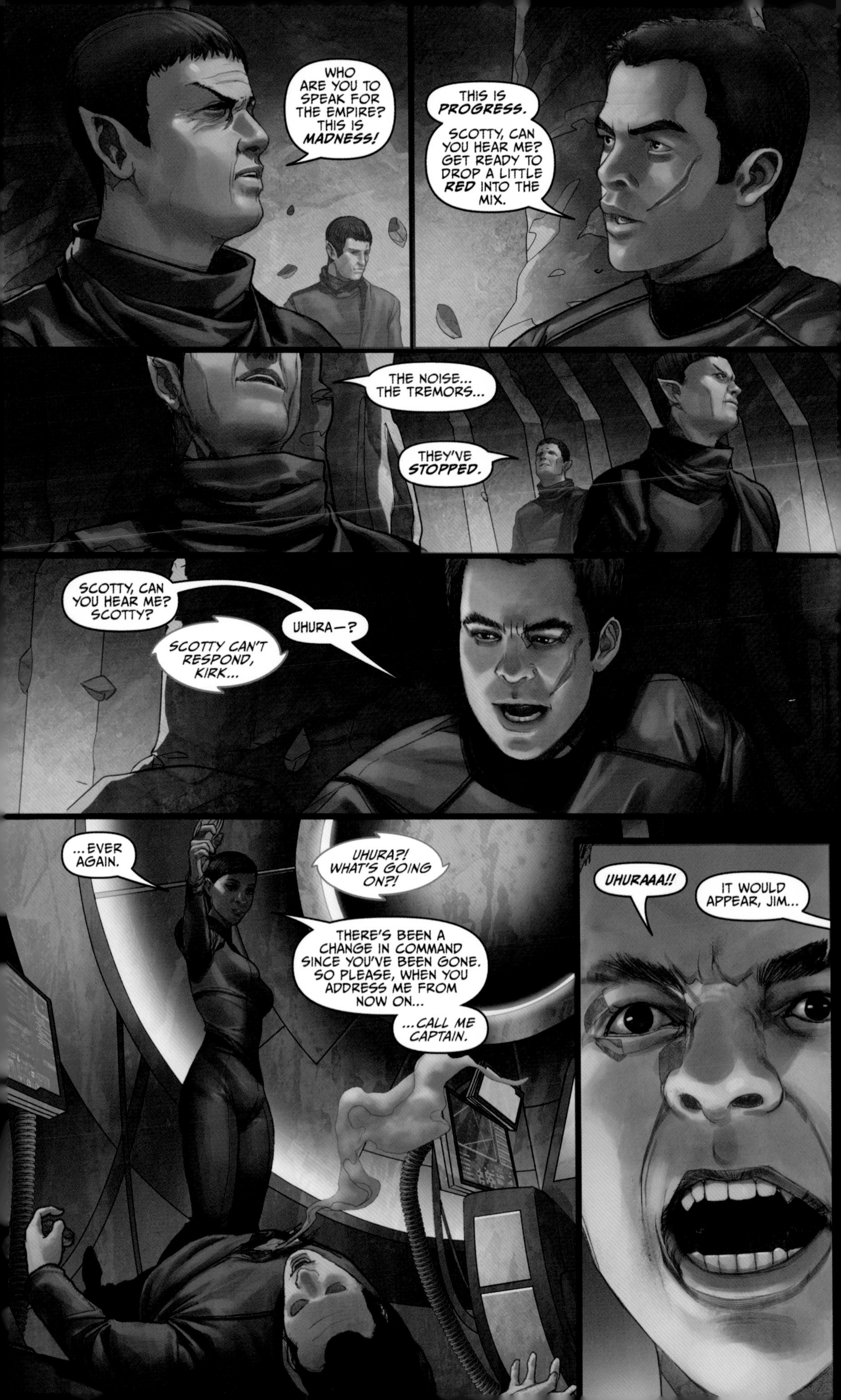
WHO ARE YOU TO SPEAK FOR THE EMPIRE? THIS IS MADNESS!
THIS IS PROGRESS.
SCOTTY, CAN YOU HEAR ME? GET READY TO DROP A LITTLE RED INTO THE MIX.
THE NOISE... THE TREMORS...
THEY'VE STOPPED.
SCOTTY, CAN YOU HEAR ME? SCOTTY?
UHURA—?
SCOTTY CAN'T RESPOND, KIRK...
...EVER AGAIN.
UHURA?! WHAT'S GOING ON?!
THERE'S BEEN A CHANGE IN COMMAND SINCE YOU'VE BEEN GONE. SO PLEASE, WHEN YOU ADDRESS ME FROM NOW ON...
...CALL ME CAPTAIN.
UHURAAA!!
IT WOULD APPEAR, JIM...

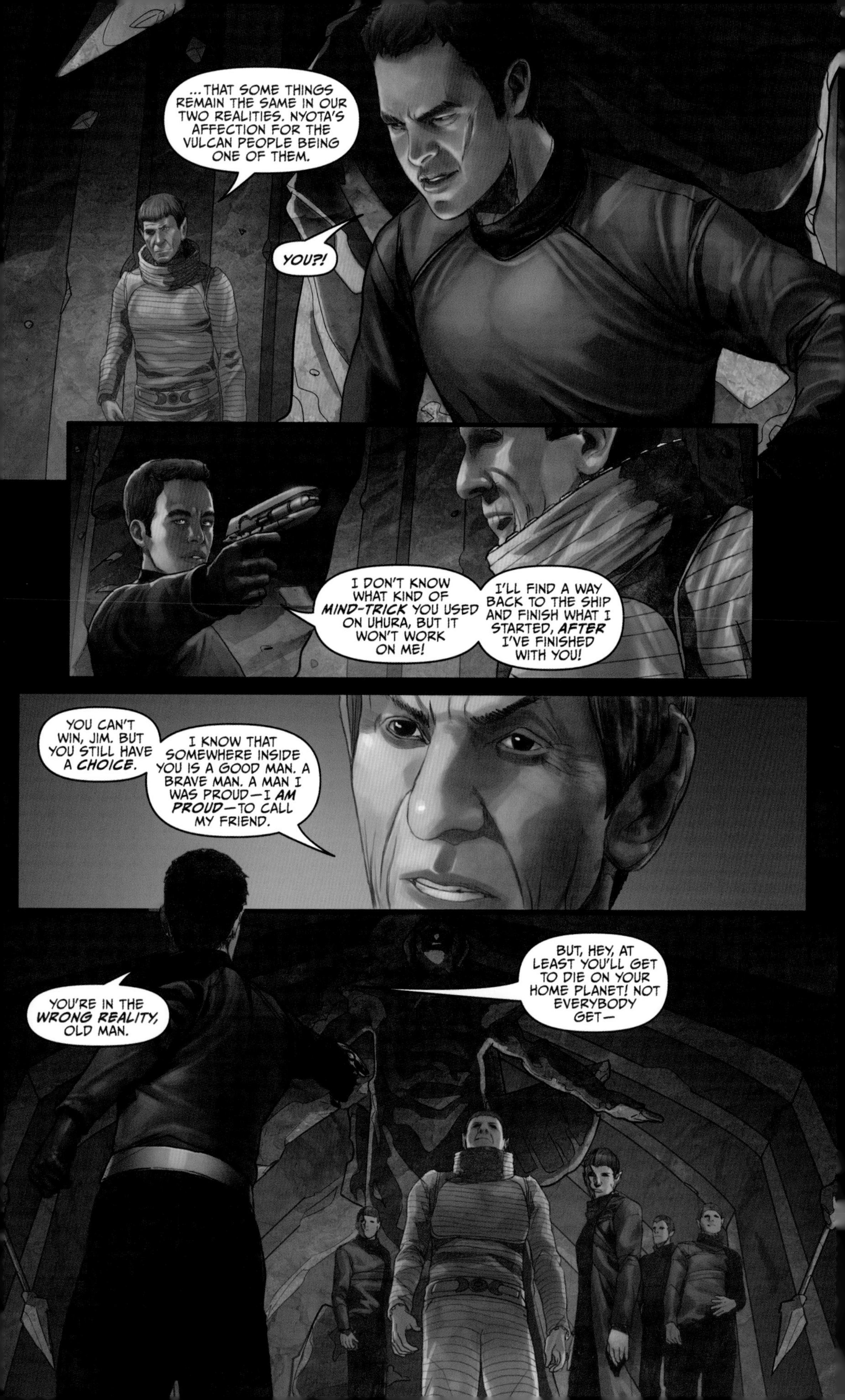
...THAT SOME THINGS REMAIN THE SAME IN OUR TWO REALITIES. NYOTA'S AFFECTION FOR THE VULCAN PEOPLE BEING ONE OF THEM.
YOU?!
I DON'T KNOW WHAT KIND OF MIND-TRICK YOU USED ON UHURA, BUT IT WON'T WORK ON ME!
I'LL FIND A WAY BACK TO THE SHIP AND FINISH WHAT I STARTED, AFTER I'VE FINISHED WITH YOU!
YOU CAN'T WIN, JIM. BUT YOU STILL HAVE A CHOICE.
I KNOW THAT SOMEWHERE INSIDE YOU IS A GOOD MAN. A BRAVE MAN. A MAN I WAS PROUD—I AM PROUD—TO CALL MY FRIEND.
YOU'RE IN THE WRONG REALITY, OLD MAN.
BUT, HEY, AT LEAST YOU'LL GET TO DIE ON YOUR HOME PLANET! NOT EVERYBODY GET—

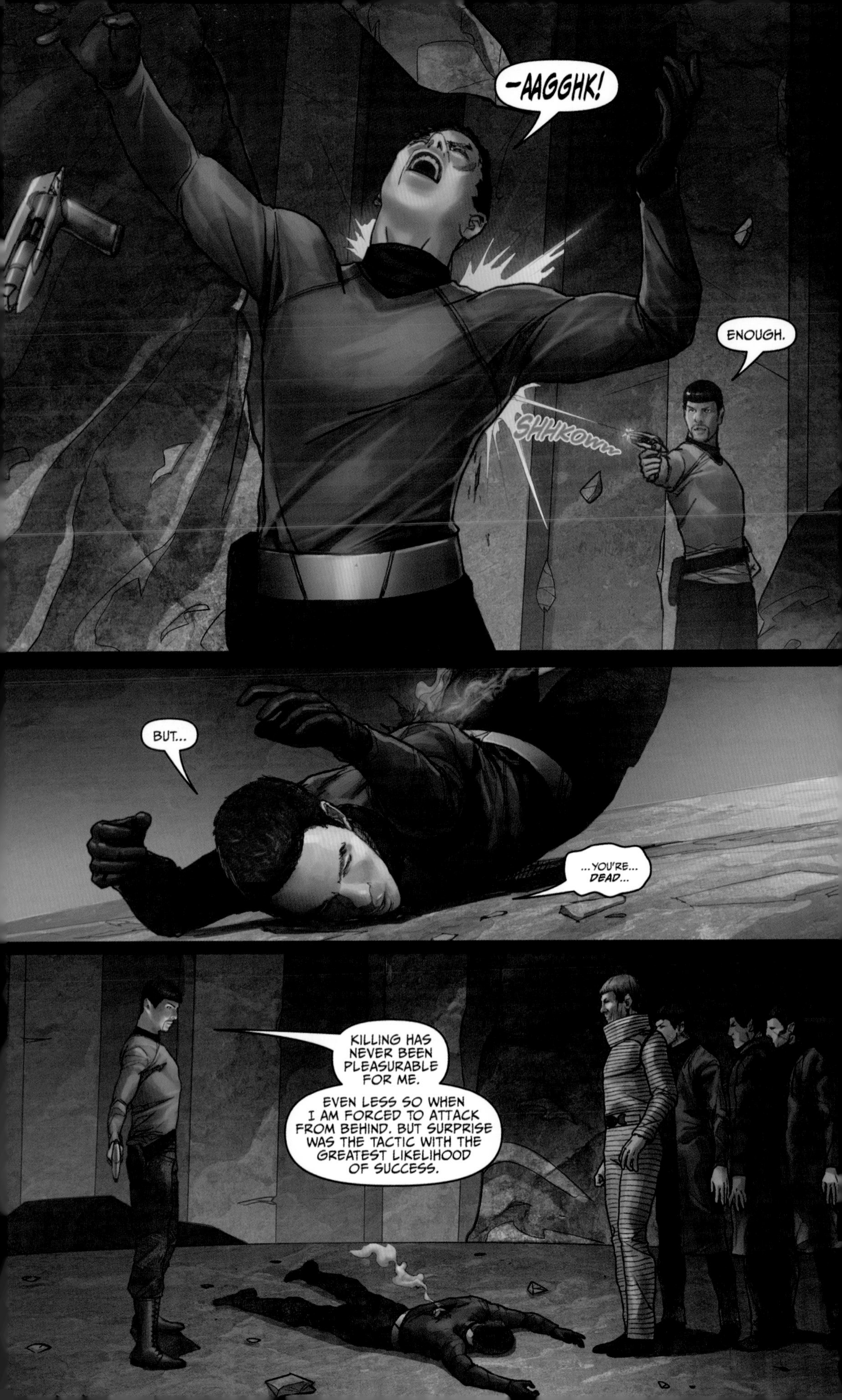
-AAGGHK!
ENOUGH.
SHHKOWW
BUT...
...YOU'RE... DEAD...
KILLING HAS NEVER BEEN PLEASURABLE FOR ME.
EVEN LESS SO WHEN I AM FORCED TO ATTACK FROM BEHIND. BUT SURPRISE WAS THE TACTIC WITH THE GREATEST LIKELIHOOD OF SUCCESS.

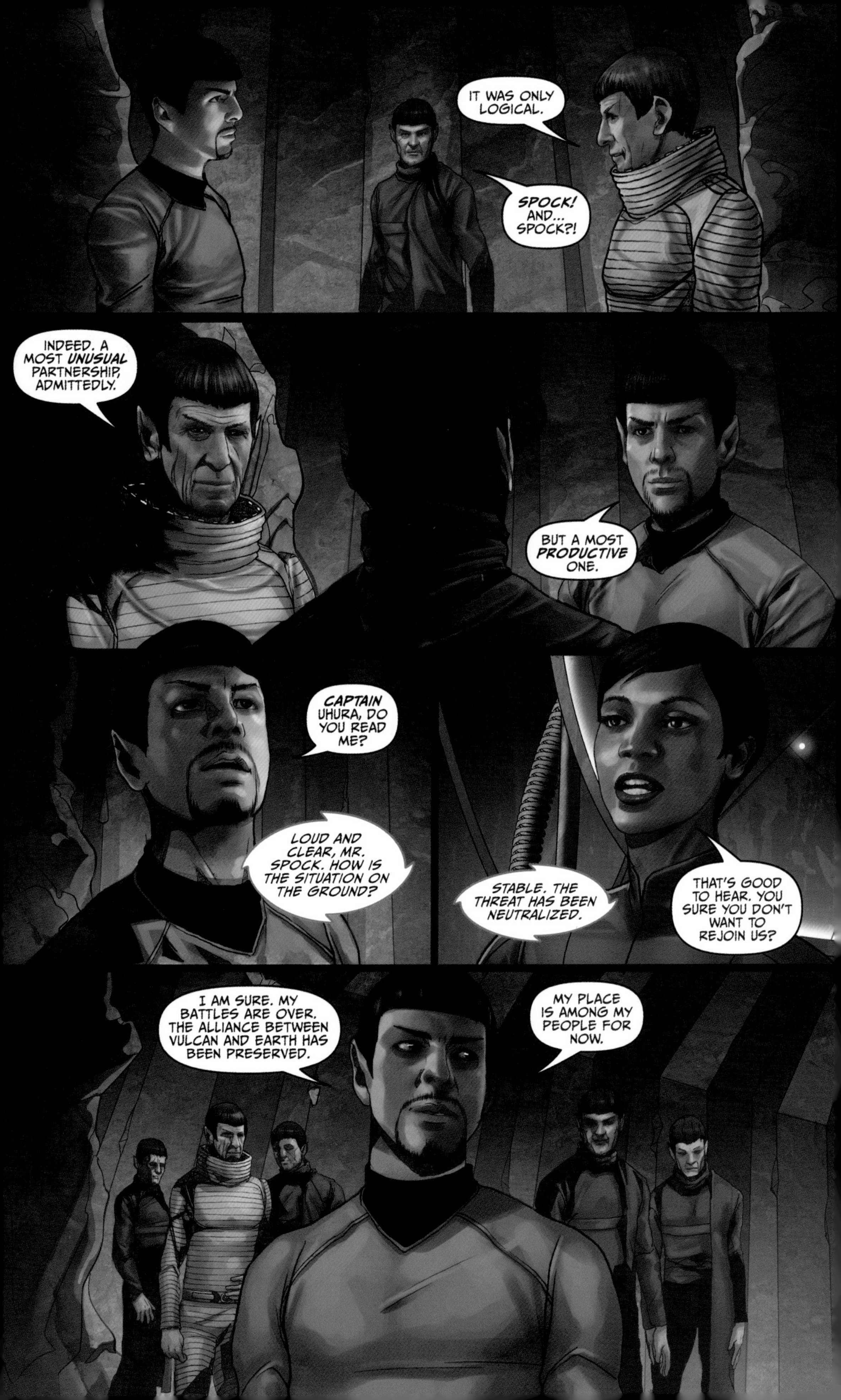
SPOCK! AND... SPOCK?!
IT WAS ONLY LOGICAL.
INDEED. A MOST UNUSUAL PARTNERSHIP, ADMITTEDLY.
BUT A MOST PRODUCTIVE ONE.
CAPTAIN UHURA, DO YOU READ ME?
LOUD AND CLEAR, MR. SPOCK. HOW IS THE SITUATION ON THE GROUND?
STABLE. THE THREAT HAS BEEN NEUTRALIZED.
THAT'S GOOD TO HEAR. YOU SURE YOU DON'T WANT TO REJOIN US?
I AM SURE. MY BATTLES ARE OVER. THE ALLIANCE BETWEEN VULCAN AND EARTH HAS BEEN PRESERVED.
MY PLACE IS AMONG MY PEOPLE FOR NOW.

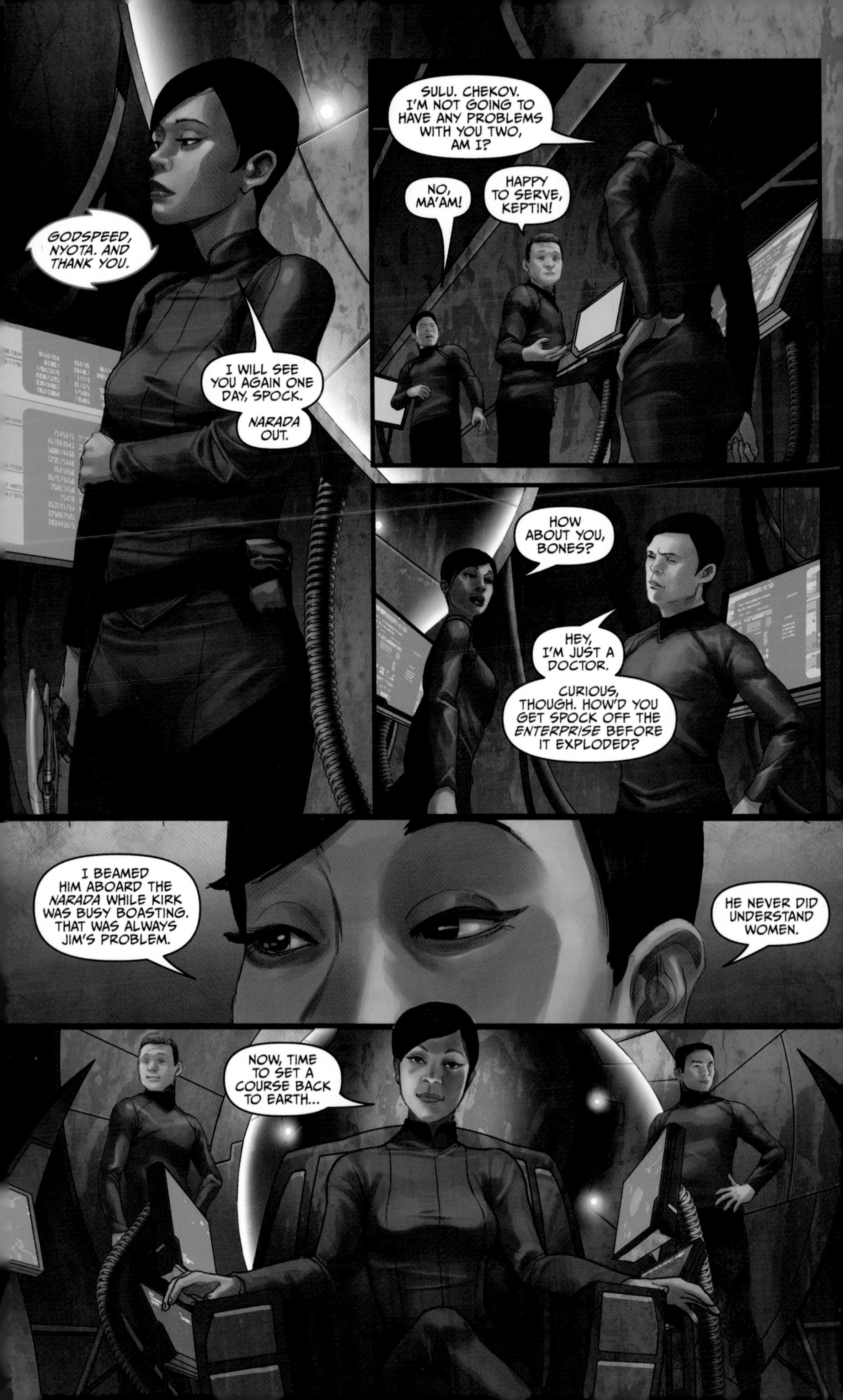
GODSPEED, NYOTA. AND THANK YOU.
I WILL SEE YOU AGAIN ONE DAY, SPOCK.
NARADA OUT.
SULU. CHEKOV. I'M NOT GOING TO HAVE ANY PROBLEMS WITH YOU TWO, AM I?
NO, MA'AM!
HAPPY TO SERVE, KEPTIN!
HOW ABOUT YOU, BONES?
HEY, I'M JUST A DOCTOR.
CURIOUS, THOUGH. HOW'D YOU GET SPOCK OFF THE ENTERPRISE BEFORE IT EXPLODED?
I BEAMED HIM ABOARD THE NARADA WHILE KIRK WAS BUSY BOASTING. THAT WAS ALWAYS JIM'S PROBLEM.
HE NEVER DID UNDERSTAND WOMEN.
NOW, TIME TO SET A COURSE BACK TO EARTH...

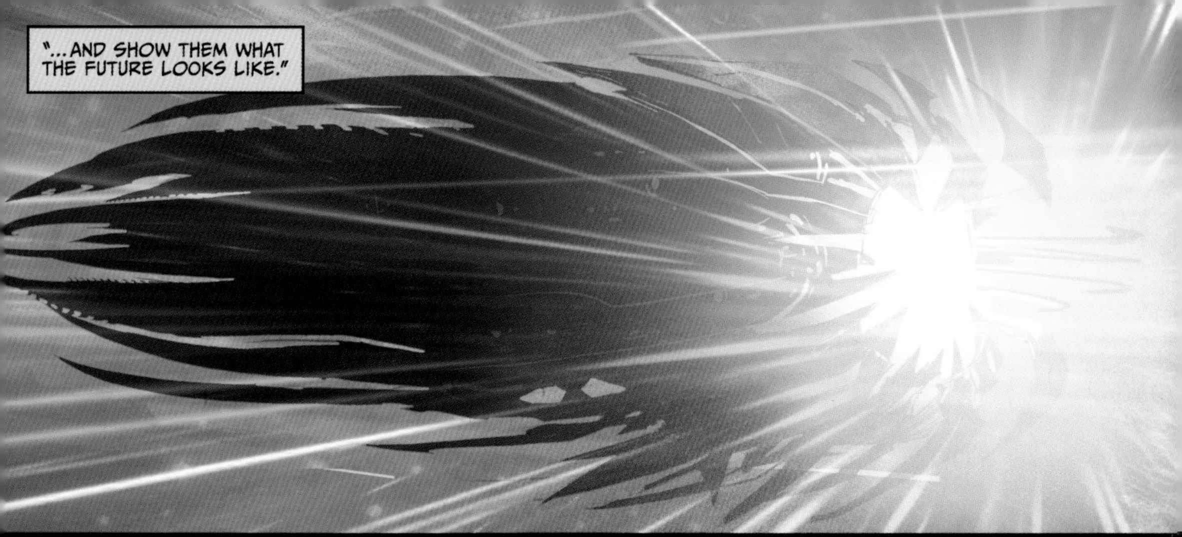
"...AND SHOW THEM WHAT THE FUTURE LOOKS LIKE."

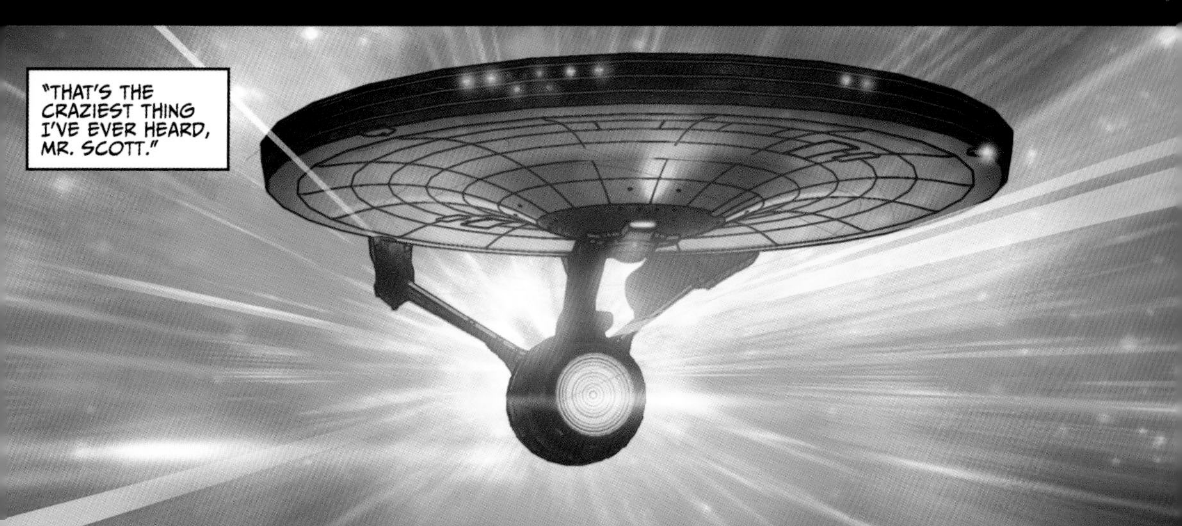
"THAT'S THE CRAZIEST THING I'VE EVER HEARD, MR. SCOTT."

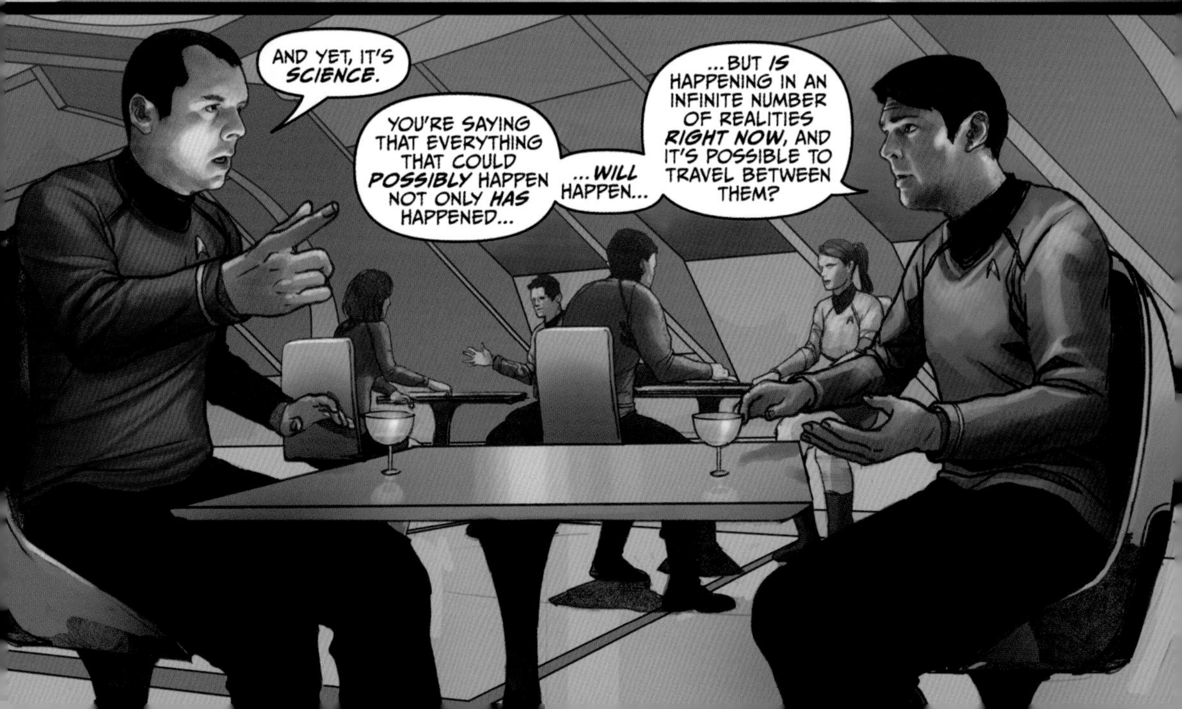
AND YET, IT'S *SCIENCE*.
YOU'RE SAYING THAT EVERYTHING THAT COULD *POSSIBLY* HAPPEN NOT ONLY *HAS* HAPPENED...
...*WILL* HAPPEN...
...BUT *IS* HAPPENING IN AN INFINITE NUMBER OF REALITIES *RIGHT NOW*, AND IT'S POSSIBLE TO TRAVEL BETWEEN THEM?

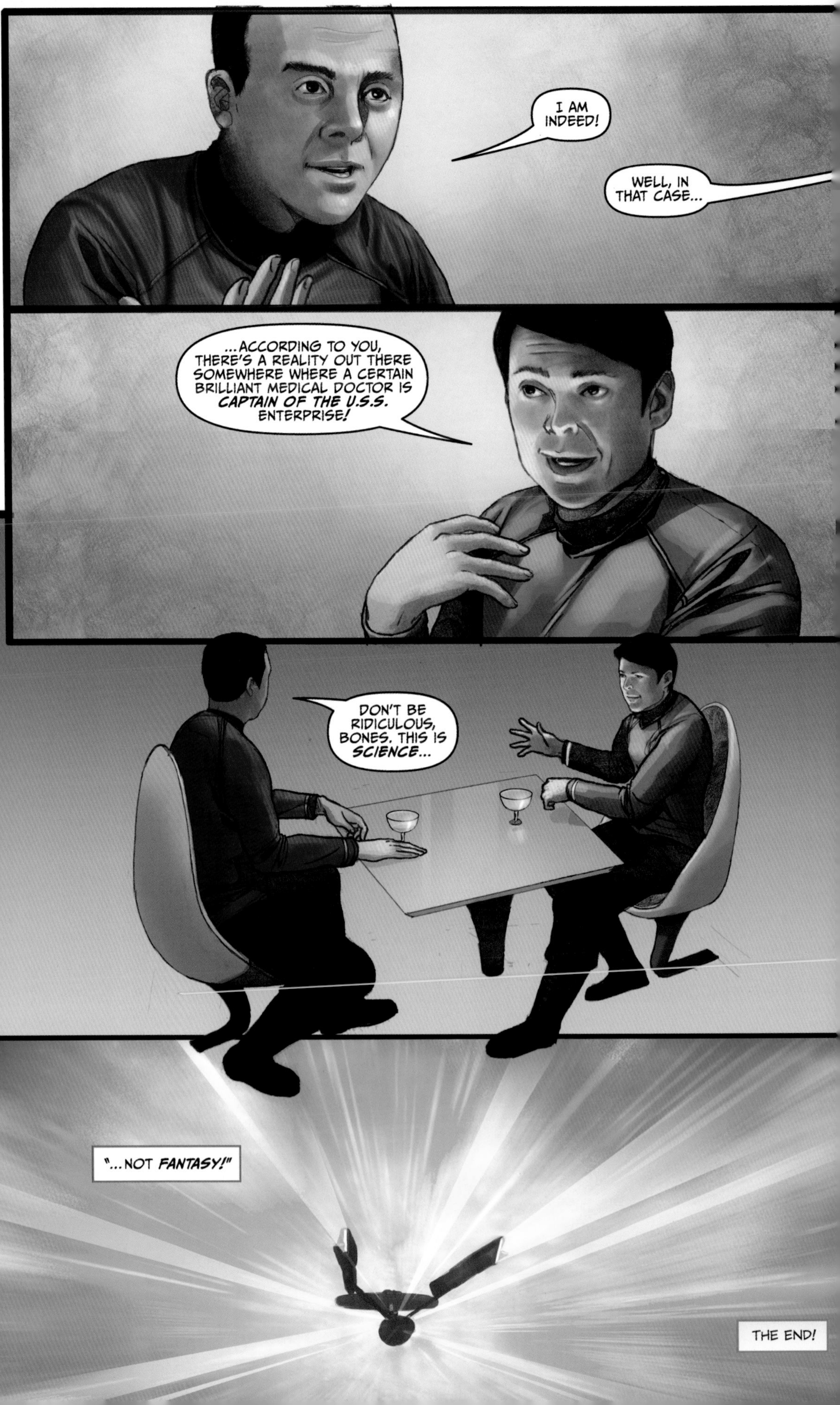
I AM INDEED!
WELL, IN THAT CASE...
...ACCORDING TO YOU, THERE'S A REALITY OUT THERE SOMEWHERE WHERE A CERTAIN BRILLIANT MEDICAL DOCTOR IS CAPTAIN OF THE U.S.S. ENTERPRISE!
DON'T BE RIDICULOUS, BONES. THIS IS SCIENCE...
"...NOT FANTASY!"
THE END!

ART GALLERY

Artwork by
Tim Bradstreet

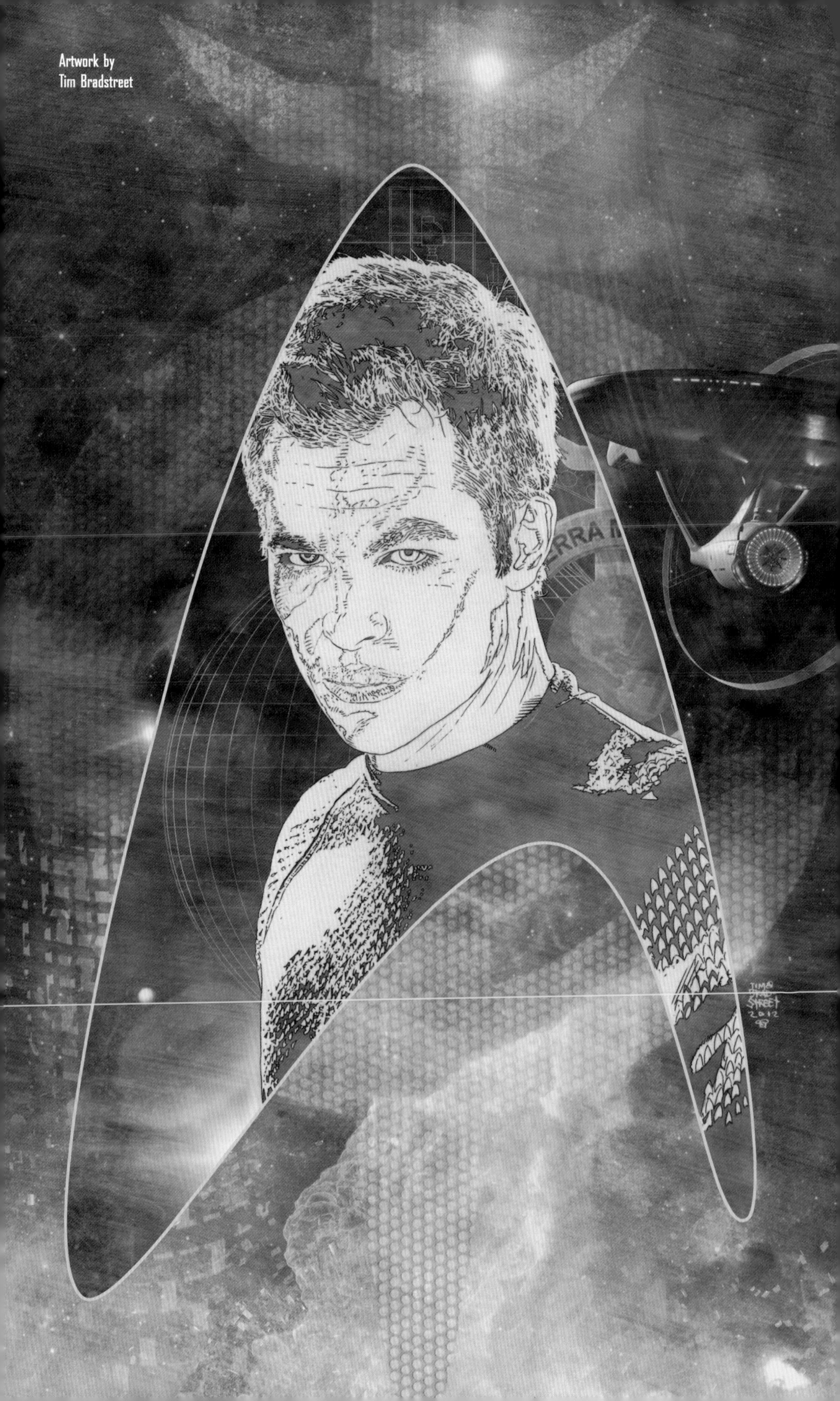

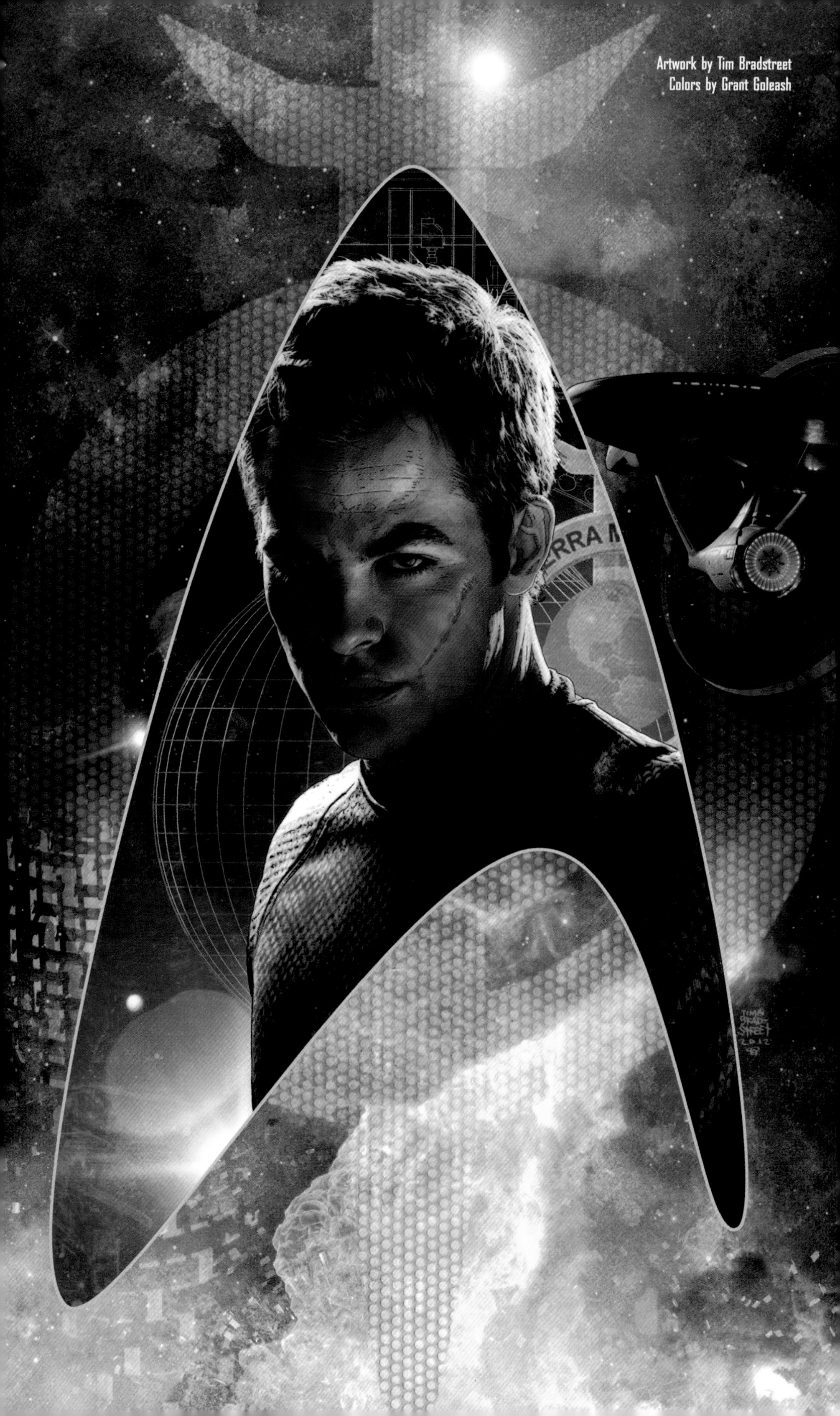

Artwork by Tim Bradstreet
Colors by Grant Goleash

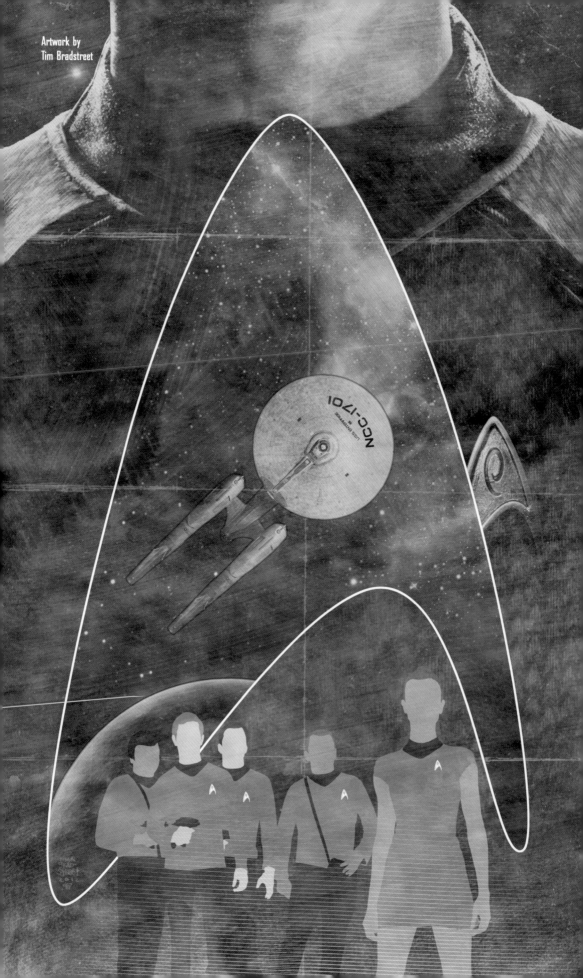

Artwork by
Tim Bradstreet

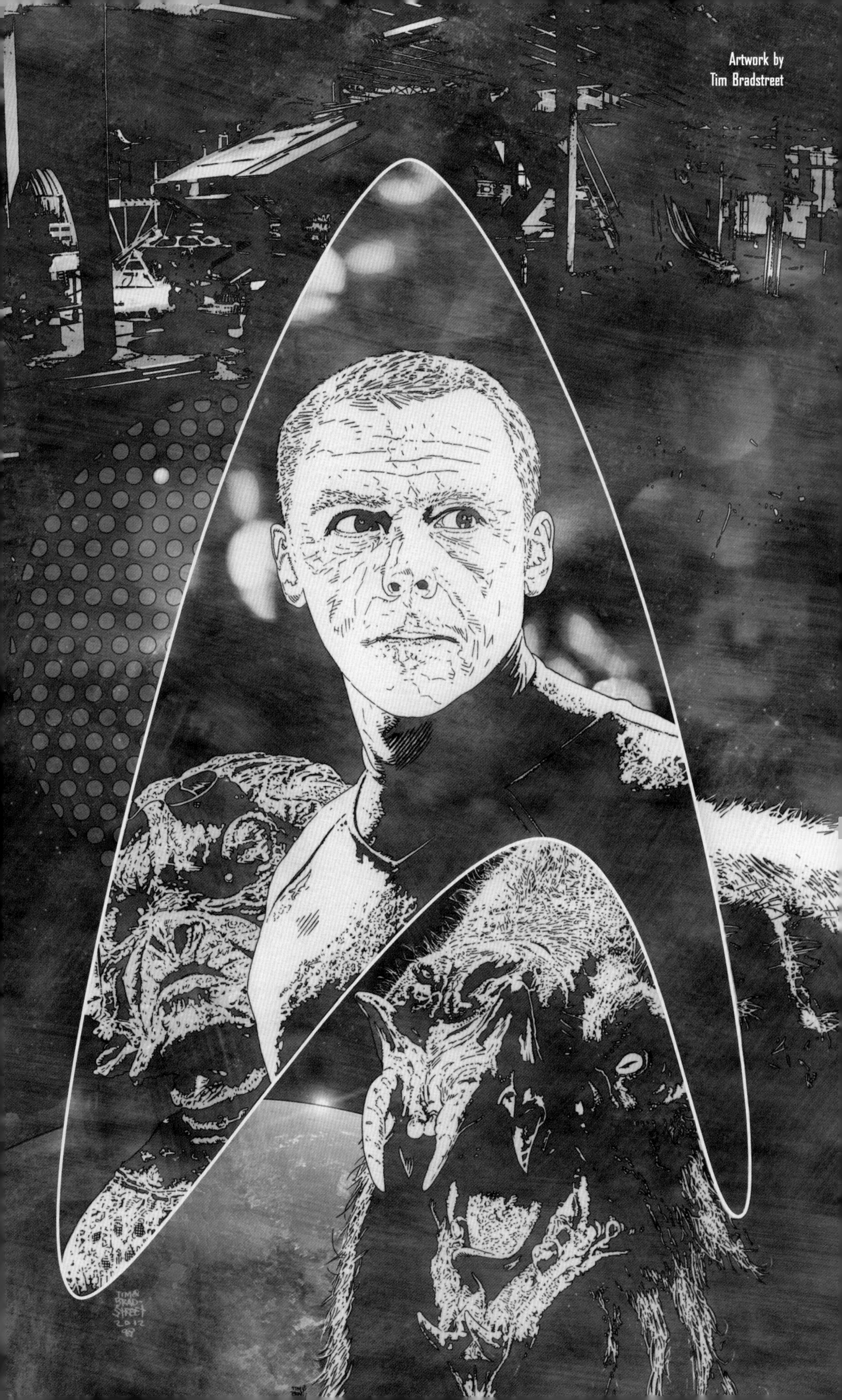

Artwork by
Tim Bradstreet

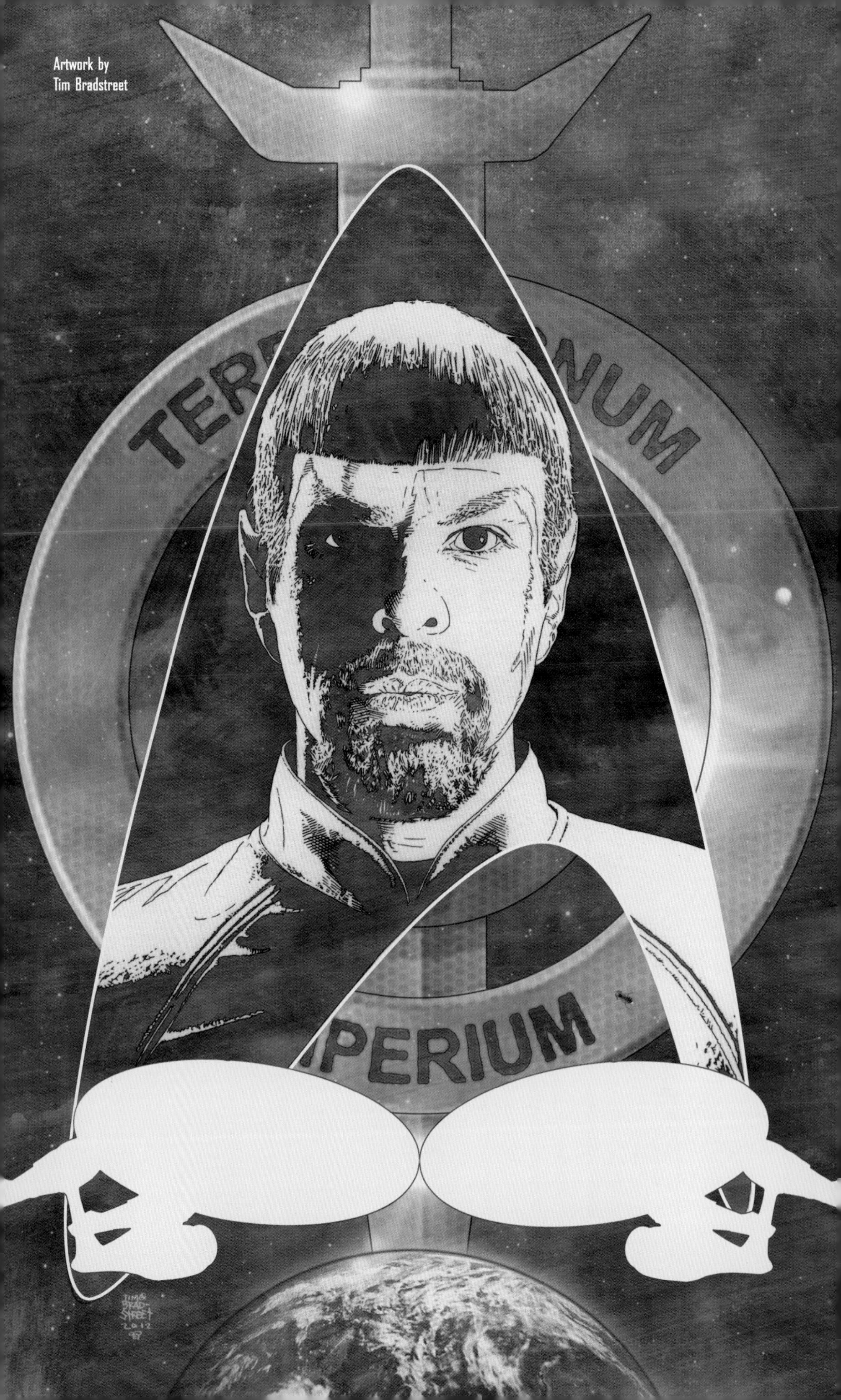
TER
NUM
PERIUM
TIM BRAD STREET 2012

Artwork by
Tim Bradstreet

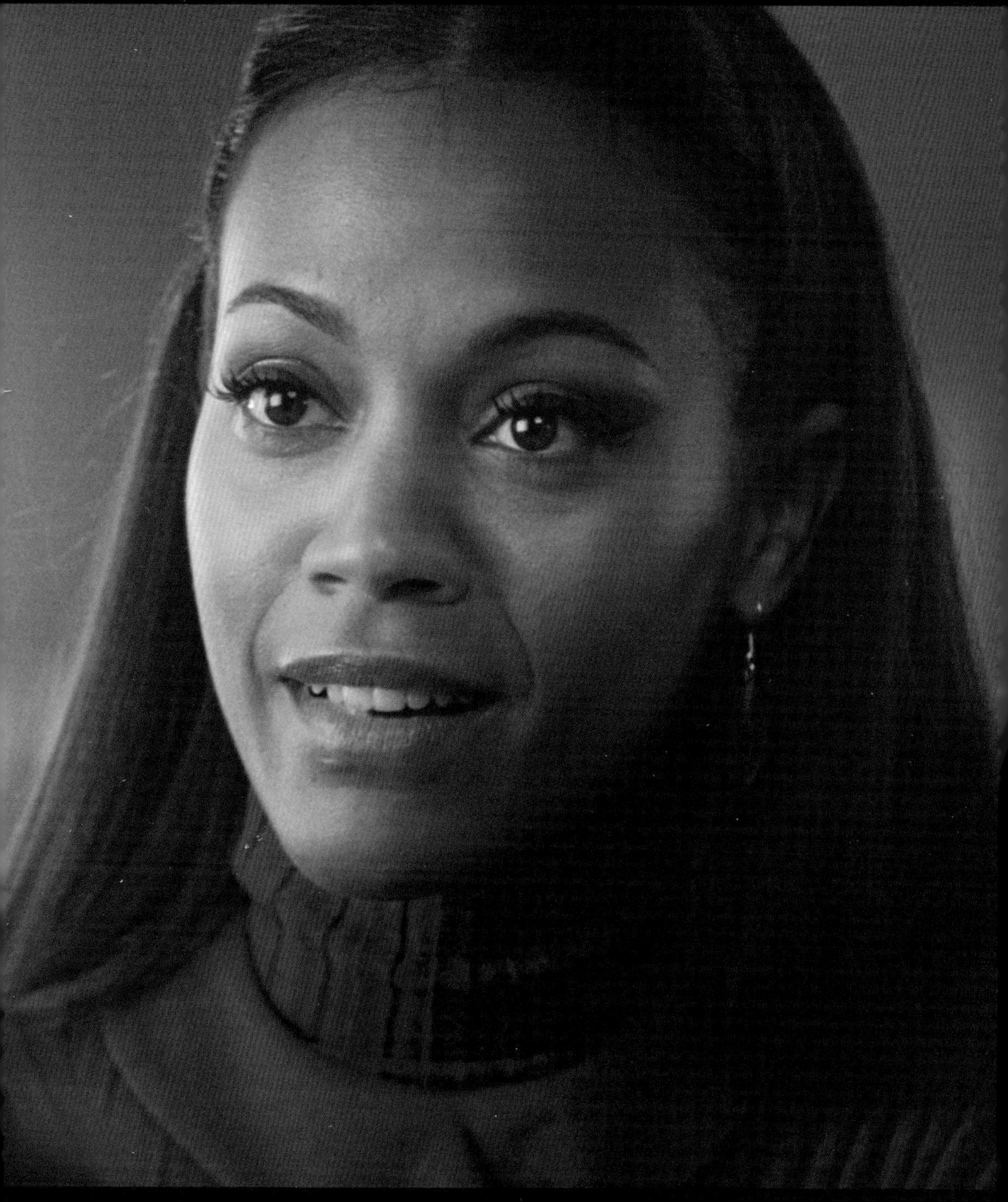